Praise for
The Battle of Milroy Station

"Fowler fills his battle scenes with credible details and tactics. . . . [This novel] compares favorably with the best of recent Civil War novels, including Charles Frazier's *Cold Mountain* and Howard Bahr's *The Year of Jubilo*."
—*Library Journal*

"This is a carefully researched and well-written historical novel that examines the horrible choices soldiers must face in the course of battle."
—*Booklist*

THE
BATTLE
OF
MILROY
STATION

• • •

A NOVEL OF THE NATURE
OF TRUE COURAGE

ROBERT H.
FOWLER

FORGE®

A TOM DOHERTY ASSOCIATES BOOK
NEW YORK

This is a work of fiction. All the characters and events portrayed in this book are either products of the author's imagination or are used fictitiously.

THE BATTLE OF MILLROY STATION: A NOVEL OF THE NATURE OF TRUE COURAGE

Copyright © 2003 by Robert H. Fowler

Map by Angela M. Cibos

A Forge Book
Published by Tom Doherty Associates, LLC
175 Fifth Avenue
New York, NY 10010

www.tor.com

Forge® is a registered trademark of Tom Doherty Associates, LLC.

ISBN: 0-765-34581-1

First edition: February 2003
First mass market edition: March 2004

Printed in the United States of America

0 9 8 7 6 5 4 3 2 1

FOR

PAT LOBRUTTO

with gratitude for reading this novel in manuscript and helping me find and express the true heart of my story

PREFACE

This is a work of fiction about an imaginary campaign conducted in an unnamed Southern state during a real war fought by our ancestors 130-odd years ago, and the political aftermath.

Some of the characters, however, are based on real persons, all dead, of course. These include U.S. President Grover Cleveland; presidential kingmaker Marcus Alonzo Hanna of Ohio; Confederate President Jefferson Davis and his wife, Varina; Confederate Secretary of War Leroy Walker; Chief Clerk of the C.S.A. Bureau of War Colonel Albert T. Bledsoe; C.S.A. Secretary of State Judah P. Benjamin; General Robert E. Lee; and Charles Dickens, the English novelist. I apologize for the liberties I have taken with these historical personages.

The other, more numerous fictional characters are based on no particular persons. And I make no apologies for the many liberties I have taken with them.

Unlike the other six historical novels I have written during the past quarter century, this one required little research or travel. I did have to "read up" on Richmond, Virginia, as the capital of the Confederacy and some details on the use of field artillery in the Civil War, however. For their help, I thank William C. Davis, program director of the Virginia Center for Civil War Studies at Virginia Technical University; and John Stanchak, former editor of *Civil War Times Illustrated* magazine.

I also had to educate myself about the state of the nation and its presidential politics during 1896. There I received some valuable guidance from Dr. Charles Glatfelter, professor emeritus of history, Gettysburg College.

—ROBERT H. FOWLER
Camp Hill, Pennsylvania

For of all sad words of tongue and pen,
The saddest are these: "It might have been."

JOHN GREENLEAF WHITTIER

Now therefore keep thy sorrow to thyself,
and bear with good courage that which hath
befallen thee.

BOOK OF ESDRAS, THE APOCRYPHA

CAST OF CHARACTERS

(in order of appearance)

ANDREW JACKSON MUNDY, newspaper editor and ex–U.S. Senator

MARTHA JANE, his wife

DR. CHARLES FITZWATER, state university president

MARC HANNA, Ohio millionaire, political kingmaker

AUNT MATTIE, Mundy's cook and former slave

MUNDY'S FATHER and **MOTHER**

MUNDY'S TWO SISTERS, Emmaline and Mary Bell

BEN, Mattie's husband, the plantation blacksmith

SLOCUM, plantation foreman

AUNT TIBBIE, African-born slave

HORACE MUNDY, a cousin

LUCINDA, Horace's daughter

ABERNATHY and **RANKIN,** slave traders

EDITH SELBY, Richmond boarding house proprietor

EVAN JENKINS MARTIN, Philadelphia-born Confederate

LEROY WALKER, Confederate secretary of war

COLONEL ALBERT T. BLEDSOE, Walker's Bureau of War chief

JUDAH P. BENJAMIN, Confederate secretary of state

JEFFERSON DAVIS, president, C.S.A.

VARINA DAVIS, his wife

ROBERT E. LEE, Confederate general

MIRIAM MARTIN, wife of Evan Martin

SARAH MARTIN, their daughter

CHARLES DICKENS, the English novelist

MOSE, livery stable owner's slave

BRIGADIER GENERALS WIGGINS and **BRISTOE,** Confederate officers

COLONEL TURNBULL, militia officer

MAJOR CALKINS, Confederate supply officer

GOVERNOR TIMMONS, state governor

GENERAL EPHRAIM POSTLE-THWAITE, state adjutant general

CYRUS HOOKER, Confederate spy

MAJOR BOLICK and **CAPTAIN DILSON,** Confederate artillerymen

BRIGADIER GENERAL MONROE WALTHER, Confederate cavalry commander

GENERAL ALEXANDER MCINTYRE, Union corps commander

COLONEL JONATHAN KANE, Union division commander

MR. FRANKLIN, operator of river ferry

MAJOR FEREBEE, brigade surgeon

COLONEL TRASKER, commander of Texas regiment

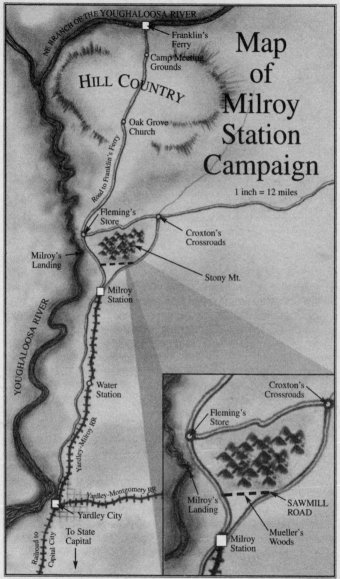

ILLUSTRATED BY ANGELA M. CIBOS

● ● ●   *Sunday A.M., September 22, 1901*

Dear Fitz:

    Thank you for your letter about my tribute to President McKinley. Glad you liked it so much. Praise from a distinguished university president such as you is praise indeed.

    Although he died in Buffalo on Saturday a week ago, I did not learn of his death until last Monday morning when I arrived for work at The Leader *office. Thus I had little time to compose my thoughts before our deadline for Tuesday's press time.*

    Yes, it is a tragic end for a man just getting into his second term as our chief executive to die as he did from bullets fired by a madman. Republican and Yankee that McKinley was, I—like you—regard his death as a loss for the entire nation, including our own long-suffering native Southland.

    You expressed disappointment that my tribute did not draw more deeply on the experiences of my six years in Washington as a Senator. Since the last four of those years did coincide with McKinley's first term, it is true I could have written much more about our late president, and in a more personal vein, had there been more time and had I been inclined to do so, which, frankly, I was not.

    My true opinion of McKinley and the connection between us, (or what could have been our connection), these are not related in my editorial tribute. Even Martha Jane does not know the full story, and I am determined that she never shall learn of what could have been for us both now in 1901 had I seized a certain curious opportunity offered me back in '96.

Sorry, old friend, to write in riddles but, you see, I am far more upset by McKinley's death than I care to reveal even (perhaps especially) to Martha Jane privately, not so much out of affection for the man but for the realization that an undeserving blowhard like Theodore Roosevelt has now become president. God knows what Martha Jane's reaction would be if she knew all that bubbles and boils in my heart and mind on that score this Sunday morning.

You well remember the circumstances into which I was thrust in '94 when you used your considerable influence with members of our state legislature to see me of all people, a so-called reconstructed newspaper editor-publisher, sent up to Washington to represent our fair state in the U.S. Senate.

You also will recall my letters to you during my hectic first two years in Washington in which I complained of my frustration in dealing with Grover Cleveland as President. (I shall never forgive that self-righteous son-of-a-bitch, a fellow Democrat, for refusing to accept my choice to fill the postmastership here in Yardley City. What an ingrate!)

Martha Jane preferred Cleveland to McKinley, not on political grounds, but because the young Mrs. Cleveland was a more gracious, outgoing White House hostess than the drab, sickly Mrs. McKinley. Some have noted that Martha Jane made a better senator's wife than I a senator. She does set a large store on social affairs. That was the reason she enjoyed our six years in Washington so much and why she was so disappointed when the Legislature chose not to return me to my seat last year, despite your efforts to persuade them otherwise.

At any rate, I did find it more satisfactory dealing with the Republican McKinley—despite some serious differences with his tariff policy—than with Cleveland, the putative Democrat. McKinley showed me more consideration than would have been expected for a junior, first-term senator from a poor Southern state which gave its electoral college votes in '96 to Bryan.

What gnaws at my psyche today are thoughts of the far

closer, more important association with McKinley I could have enjoyed.

I have toyed with the notion of writing an account of the incident and leaving it sealed in a bank vault to be opened only after Martha Jane and I have gone to our rewards (or in my case, punishment) in the hereafter. Historians might well find the story of at least passing interest.

No time to go into that now, Fitz; I do thank you for your complimentary remarks as well as your staunch friendship over the years.

Your devoted friend,
Jackson Mundy

P.S. I came down to the office early this morning, expressly to write this answer to your letter. Martha Jane is expecting me to join her at church for the 11 o'clock service, On my way to church, I will drop this letter off at the train depot.

Sunday, September 29, 1901

Dear Fitz:

I am sorry that you found my letter of the 22nd "puzzling" and that you suspect me of "cruel teasing," if not deliberate leg-pulling, with my allusions to that unspecified incident that occurred back in '96.

Truly, Fitz, I was not trying to be coy. I really am wrestling with rueful thoughts of what might have been for Martha Jane and me had I reacted differently to the opportunity to which I referred.

First let me clear up what may be a misapprehension of my regard for McKinley. He was a superb, if stodgy, politician. His policies did pull most of the country out of the depression to which Cleveland had turned a blind eye in his second term. He did improve relations between labor interests and those of industry whereas Cleveland had exacerbated them. And he did lead the nation into and out of a successful war with Spain. Furthermore, with two pistol shots, Czolgosz bestowed the mantle of martyrdom on him just as did John Wilkes Booth on Abraham Lincoln in 1865.

Despite the adulation being expressed by many Northern papers, I do not regard McKinley as a hero, however. I got painfully and thoroughly cured of hero worship back during the War Between the States, in 1864, for reasons I have never discussed with you or anyone else. No longer do I place anyone on a pedestal. We all have feet of clay. None of us is perfect. None of us, in our inner, true selves, is exactly what he appears to be.

You have called me a natural born poker player because I keep so much of myself to myself. Martha Jane makes the same complaint. I have "kept to myself" much more than the events of '96, things in which I was personally involved during the war and which, if fully revealed, would explain certain actions I have or have not taken in the past 37 years.

There I go again, Fitz, talking in riddles. You and I have been friends since our days at boarding school and the university. Each of us was the other's best man at our weddings. And, although you had the grace not to remind me, it was you who created Andrew Jackson Mundy, the reluctant politician, from the common clay of a country newspaper publisher.

So when you say that you think it important for me to leave a record of my experiences in Washington—a full record, that is—and you urge me to entrust it to your library archives there at the university on your solemn promise as president of the institution, that my account would be sealed and left unopened for at least 100 years, I say: Let me give it some thought. Meanwhile, as ever, I remain your devoted friend,

Jackson Mundy

Saturday, October 5, 1901

Dear Fitz:

Boy, give you an inch and you demand a mile. You want the whole story, a full account of what I did in the War Between the States as well as what happened in '96? That is a tall order.

I do have a lot to get off my chest about my part in the War, and, to tell the truth, there is not all that much for me to do anymore here at The Leader *most days. The staff learned how to run the paper on their own while I was in Washington.*

As for the personal feelings generated by McKinley's death, it might help my state of mind to write them out of my system rather than allow them to stew on in my bosom.

As you note, I have always been "close-mouthed" about what I did during the War. You urge me to include a full account of that part of my life, as well. Bear in mind that while you were serving as a colonel of a regiment in the vaunted Army of North Virginia, I was nothing more than a Confederate War Department clerk in Richmond, then a diplomatic amanuensis and, finally, a captain in the home guard. While you were fighting great battles such as Chancellorsville and the Wilderness under the generalship of the noble Robert E. Lee in the East, I merely served briefly as an aide-de-camp in the campaign that culminated at Milroy Station and which is little known outside of our state. As for the general under whom I served, well, the less said about him at this stage, the better.

Fortunately, my parents never discarded anything I wrote to them during the war. Although some of that material will be helpful, mostly I will be depending on my memory.

So, now let's be clear about this, Fitz. You give me your word as a Southern Christian gentleman that whatever I might write shall be seen by no eyes other than yours until a century has passed. By that time, we who served the Confederacy and the next generation as well will be no more. Surely the scars of that tragic conflict will have disappeared by the twenty-first century.

I must plan how to go about this project so that Martha Jane will not know what I am up to. She would die if she learned at this stage what I will be telling you. Already she has grown suspicious about my uncharacteristic visits to the office on Sunday morning. Must join her at church now.

Your devoted friend, Jackson Mundy.

PART ONE

ONE

• • • In the early days of 1896, both the United States and my own Democratic Party had fallen into great difficulties. The second administration of Grover Cleveland, nearing its end, had become a disaster. We had been in the worst depression of our history for three years and our bull-headed president persisted in treating the crisis as a business, not a governmental, problem. He had come back into office in '92 preaching against what he called raids on the treasury by President Harrison. Yet our gold reserves had dipped dangerously low. He had antagonized the laboring man. His (and my) party was being taken over by silverites and wild-eyed populists, yet he refused to organize his own political resources to halt them. Worse, he refused to say whether he intended to seek a third term, which left our more level-headed Democrats unprepared for the coming fall presidential election.

I had served only the first two years of my six-year term as junior senator, and so comforted myself that I had four more years for the situation to resolve itself. My wife, the former Martha Jane Pettis, and I occupied a handsome, comfortable house on Massachusetts Avenue. Thanks to her skill as a hostess, not to mention an inheritance from her father, we enjoyed a full and pleasant social life in Washington.

My standing in the Senate hardly compared with that of titans such as Rhode Island's Aldrich, Connecticut's Platt, or Ohio's Sherman, but the national press had taken favorable note of some of my speeches, which called for reconciliation between North and South, improved education for Negroes, removal of protectionist tariffs, and maintaining the gold standard.

Imagine my amazement one Friday morning when I arrived at my Senate office to find a messenger with a letter he said required an immediate response. I bristled at what seemed the fellow's effrontery until he confided in a low tone, "It's from Mr. Hanna. Mr. Marc Hanna."

I entered my inner office to read the note, which went something like this:

Dear Senator Mundy:

I invite you to dine with me this evening in my room at the Willard to discuss a matter of great import for our nation in these troubled political and economic times and, I trust, for yourself.

Knowing how busy you are kept these days with your Senatorial duties, I leave it to you to choose the exact time of our dinner.

Please forgive my boldness in asking you to keep this letter and our meeting in confidence. I have instructed my messenger to await your written reply.

I am your respectful servant,
Marcus A. Hanna

I had never met Hanna, but it was well known how this millionaire industrialist was busy raising money and pulling strings to get William McKinley, former Congressman and ex-governor of Ohio, named as the Republican candidate for the presidency in the fall.

Martha Jane and I had a standing arrangement whereby we reserved Friday nights for dining alone at home. This gave us an opportunity to compare notes, she from her many social functions and I from my political activities. I dashed off a reply explaining that while dinner was out of the question, I was willing to drop by the Willard at five o'clock to talk and trusted that this would be a satisfactory compromise. Although mistrustful of Hanna, I was curious to hear what he had up his sleeve.

I arrived at the Willard at five to find the same messenger

in the lobby waiting to escort me up to Hanna's commodious suite on the second floor and into a room rank with stale cigar smoke.

Hanna was nothing like what I expected. An auburn-haired, roly-poly fellow, he carried more flesh on his small-boned frame than was called for. Wearing a checkered vest, rumpled coat and a bow tie, he put me in mind of an unmade bed.

His face was undistinguished except for its rather rubbery appearance. But it quickly became apparent that behind his unkempt surface, there lay a lively, sharp mind.

His deep brown eyes shone with shrewdness (or guile?) as he shook my hand and thanked me for coming to him. He had me sit facing him under a window while his messenger friend brought us our bourbon and water. After dismissing the flunkey, he said in a conspiratorial tone that he wished everything he had to say to remain "within this room" and added that he likewise would not disclose anything I said to him.

I saw no reason not to agree to his terms, whereupon he launched into a rambling monologue.

First he expressed his dismay at the inroads the free silver men and populists were making "in both our parties." This was true. I could not argue with his assertion that a majority of Congress was at least leaning toward the free coinage of silver.

"But you, I understand, still favor the gold standard."

I acknowledged that this was the case.

"And, although the populists and silverites pose the greater threat to the Democratic Party, there is a growing faction among Republicans of those who also want to abandon the gold standard."

Then he asked me if I would not regard it as dangerous if "these fanatical anarchists were to seize control of either party and, worse still, if they were to elect our next president."

Not yet getting his drift, I agreed that this was a worrisome prospect.

He then turned his remarks toward President Cleveland.

"I have heard it whispered that although you made a seconding speech for him at your '92 convention in Chicago, your attitude is no longer so warm."

"Actually, I only made a seconding speech for Stevenson for vice president."

"All the same, your relations with President Cleveland have not been all that . . . how shall I put it—"

Growing irritated by his indirections and mindful of the time, I broke in with "Like many in my party, I find some of his behavior, how shall I put it? . . . Baffling."

He snorted with laughter and tried to continue by saying, "Such as his refusal to say whether—"

"Whether he will seek a third term? Yes, that does leave us up in the air. But does not that play into your Republican hands?"

"To be truthful, for the good of the country, I would prefer a third term for Cleveland over a first term for an idiot like William Jennings Bryan. But my goal, you might say my mission, is to see my friend and fellow Ohioan, William McKinley, become our next president."

"I have heard reports to that effect."

Ignoring my sarcasm, he drew his chair closer and lowered his voice.

"I am going to confide in you, Senator Mundy. It is my intention to move my headquarters to Georgia this spring and there maintain an open house to entertain both white and black southern delegates to the Republican convention. I want to show up in St. Louis in June with a solid block of support from Dixie to make Governor McKinley our nominee for president. That, I feel confident, can be accomplished. The trick will be to move him beyond the nomination to the presidency."

"Your dedication to Governor McKinley is impressive," I replied, thinking as I did of his hero's congressional role some years earlier in erecting artificially high tariffs that harmed the South as much as they protected the industrial North.

"I supported him for Congress and I backed him for the governorship. I regard him as the one man capable of ending the days of bloody shirt politics, North and South, capable of leading our grand nation into the twentieth century with prosperity for the laboring man as well as men of means such as you and I."

"Mister Hanna, my means can hardly be compared with yours."

"Yes, but you have much in common with both Governor McKinley and me."

"How is that?"

"You and I both own newspapers. Oh yes, the *Cleveland Ledger* is one of my enterprises. And both you and McKinley served in the late unpleasantness between North and South, he as a major, and you, as I understand it, as a captain."

I smiled at his comparison, but before I could point out that we served opposing causes, he pressed on with, "Oh yes, I have made inquiries in your state. You have a reputation as a hero. Lost your foot in a campaign I had never heard of."

"It was the Milroy Station campaign. It occurred in October of 1864. My foot had to be amputated. Somehow my part in that brief period of active service got blown out of proportion after the war."

"Nevertheless, your white constitutents perceive you as a wounded hero, whereas your colored fellow citizens regard you as a champion for sticking up for their basic rights."

Interpreting my frown as disagreement, I suppose, he said, "Oh yes, I was told that the Klan burned your newspaper building in the late sixties but that you did not back down. You just rebuilt your office of brick, put bars in the windows, strapped a revolver to your waist and went back to editorializing for better schools for both races and for fair play in general. Now in my book that would be regarded as real heroism."

"I hardly regarded my actions as heroic. A measure of self-interest was involved."

"And one of my colored delegates told me that you stood in the jailhouse door with the county sheriff to save two members of his race from a lynch mob. Said that you, leaning on a crutch, shamed them into backing off."

By now I had become embarrassed by his knowledge of my background and impatient to learn where all this was leading.

"Mister Hanna, excuse me for interrupting but, as I explained in my note, I am expected at home for dinner."

"And you would like me to get to the point. Have you any notion as to my real purpose in inviting you here?"

"It sounds very much like you want me to jump party lines and support McKinley in the fall election, something I have no intention of doing. That would be political suicide."

"Ah, Senator Mundy, be not so hasty. I am inviting you to take a far bolder step . . . bolder for you and for me and Governor McKinley."

"I don't know what you are getting at."

"You may recall that back in the spring of 1864 it seemed to many in the North that Abraham Lincoln might well lose the upcoming fall presidential election. The country was weary of war. The Army of the Potomac was suffering enormous casualties in Grant's drive on Richmond. And Sherman's advance on Atlanta was being skillfully delayed by General Johnston. Things looked very bleak indeed. And Lincoln's likely Democratic opponent, McClellan, enjoyed considerable popularity, especially among Federal soldiers. So what did Lincoln do?"

"He held his course. And the war wore on to its bloody end."

"No, while the military issue was still in doubt, he got Andrew Johnson, a War Democrat, the Federal governor of Tennessee and a Southerner, to run with him for the vice presidency on a Union-Republican ticket. Yes, yes, I know, Johnson turned out to be a disaster as president after Lincoln's assassination, but my point is that the election strategy paid off at the polls."

"Actually, Mr. Hanna, I would rather think that the fall of Atlanta and Sheridan's rape of the Shenandoah Valley would have insured Mr. Lincoln's election success, no matter whom he had chosen as his running mate. At any rate, I doubt that you would get many men in my party to join a crusade for McKinley. The times are not analogous. This is 1896, not 1864."

Then he said something that stunned me. In a low, calm voice he said, "I am not looking for what you call 'many men.' I only want one. And that one is you, Andrew Jackson Mundy."

TWO

• • • To say that I was flabbergasted both by what Hanna was suggesting and by the audacity of his manner would be to understate my reaction. It took me a moment to find my voice.

"Surely you are not suggesting me as a candidate for the vice presidency to run with McKinley? Me, a Democrat and a Southerner?"

"That is exactly what I am not just suggesting, but urging. Please, Senator Mundy, hear me out. Governor McKinley, with his record as a Union officer in the Civil War, his support of a protective tariff, and his record of speaking out for labor unions, can carry our major cities in the East. Now if we can make some inroads in the South, that could spell the difference for us. If a nationally respected, moderate Southerner like you would cross party lines and run as his vice president, well you see my point. And the fact that you support the gold standard appeals very much to my own tastes and the governor's. I like the fact that you own a newspaper, too. Your profession would go down well with the press North and South. And then there is the powerful symbolic message of sectional peace with a Union major running for the presidency on the same ticket with a Confederate captain."

He held up his hand to stifle my protests.

"Again, I must confide in you. Mrs. McKinley is something of an invalid. The governor is devoted to her, so devoted that he declines to travel from their home in Lisbon to campaign. It is my plan, following the convention, to encourage those interested in seeing him and hearing him speak on the many issues of the day, to come to his home where he will hold court on his front porch. I will have my men on duty to keep anyone from monopolizing his time, of course. To keep the line moving, so to speak."

I shook my head. "Mr. Hanna, you are a piece of work, you really are."

"I take that as a compliment. And speaking of compliments, I hear from many persons here in Washington concerning your good wife, Mary Ann."

"Mary Jane," I corrected him.

"Yes. She seems to have established quite a following, socially, that is. Her skills as a hostess would be useful to you in a national campaign, I should think."

"They certainly have not hurt my modest career in the Senate."

"Beyond that, you would not be tied down by an ailing wife. You would be free to travel about the country speaking to crowds and helping me beat the drum for the governor. Really, Senator, you would be a wonderful asset."

"You realize, Mr. Hanna, that while I see eye-to-eye with McKinley on the gold standard and fair play for the laboring man, I ardently oppose his policy of high protective tariffs. You would have to be from a state not yet recovered from a ruinous war, that depends on cotton cultivation, to understand my point of view. Our farmers get only nine cents a pound for their cotton and then must pay exorbitant prices for items manufactured overseas. We feel that we are subsidizing Northern industries."

"The governor would not expect you to speak out on his behalf on any such point of difference. Really, Senator, I need you. McKinley needs you. But most important, our nation needs you. Come take my hand and tell me that you will join our crusade."

"No, I cannot."

"Then will you at least consider the possibility?"

He seized my hand and held on to it, as those shrewd eyes searched my face.

Pulling my hand free from his grasp, I said, "I will give it some thought, but don't get your hopes up—but wait, let me ask you this: Are you here as McKinley's envoy on this matter? Is this your idea or his?"

His face assumed a hurt look.

"True, he is considering several possible running mates. When I mentioned your name, however, he did not reject you. It would be up to me to push him off the fence. With an enthusiastic yes from you, the thing could be done. It would be the boldest political stroke this country has seen in many a year. Please say yes."

"How long would I have to consider the idea?"

"I am to take a Monday afternoon train for Lisbon to confer with the governor."

"Only two days hence."

"Time is of the essence, Senator. Of the essence."

I drew out my watch. Seeing that it was already seven o'clock, I arose.

"What you propose is an intriguing idea. I will give it careful consideration over the weekend but don't count on an acceptance. At any rate, you shall have your answer before you leave for Lisbon. Say by noon Monday." I paused, then added, "Normally, I discuss all matters with my wife. She has excellent political instincts."

"In this case, with all due respect, I request that nothing I have said to you, indeed that this meeting itself occurred, absolutely nothing should be revealed to anyone. Not even your wife, not just yet."

"That leaves me with the decision to be made entirely on my own."

From the satisfied look on his face, I gathered that Hanna mistakenly felt that he had made his sale. He took command of my hand again and made his final pitch regarding the historical significance my acceptance of his offer would represent.

He apologized for not seeing me to the door of the hotel, saying "We wouldn't want one of our brethren of the press to see us together in public, not yet."

So, we said our good-byes in the hallway. My head spinning with the effect of our conversation, I walked down to the lobby, where Hanna's messenger remained on station. He led me to a waiting hack.

During my fifty-five years, I had experienced many emotional episodes, but never one anything like this. Still trying to sort out what Hanna had said to me, trying to distinguish what was puffery and what had real substance, I alit from the hack at the doorway of my home and asked the driver the fare.

"The gentleman back at the Willard instructed me to put it on Mr. Hanna's account. Evening, sir."

As I entered my front door to begin the longest weekend of my life, Martha Jane was waiting in the hall, puzzled by my uncharacteristic lateness. I hated having to lie to her, but when she demanded the reason for my tardiness, I told her merely that "Something came up at the last minute. No, no, nothing special. Just routine."

"Aunt Mattie has held dinner for nearly an hour. Here, give me your cane and coat. Go warm your backside in front of the fire and I will tell her the master finally has seen fit to arrive."

I should explain that the seventy-year-old Mattie had been one my father's slaves. She liked to remind me that, as our family cook, she had helped raise me, she and her husband, Ben, the plantation blacksmith. I will have much more to say about Mattie and Ben later in my story. They had a very real bearing on what happened during the war and on my decision regarding Marc Hanna's offer to put me forward as McKinley's vice-presidential running mate.

The chain of events that led to that offer began with the War Between the States . . . the Civil War . . . the War of Northern Aggression . . . whatever you want to call it. Except for my experiences in that war, I never would have become either a newspaper editor and publisher or senator. Certainly, I would not have been given the choice of running for vice president. Nor would I have developed the character and moral courage to do some risky things in which I take a quiet pride.

Nor would I be stewing over the knowledge that at this very moment I, Andrew Jackson Mundy—not Theodore

Roosevelt—might now be the new president of the United States or that the former Martha Jane Pettis—not Edith Carow Roosevelt—would be our nation's new first lady.

It all began, for me, with the so-called Civil War. So let me open with an account of the curious part I played in that ghastly conflict which cost the North and South so very much and which had such a profound, unexpected effect on my life's course and that of many others.

PART TWO

ONE

• • • At the outbreak of the war in April 1861, having graduated from the state university the previous year, I was at home reluctantly learning how to run our family's plantation by day and straining my eyes at night reading the novels of Sir Walter Scott, Charles Dickens and Victor Hugo. I spent much time also in mooning over my second cousin, Lucinda, but that is another story.

Unbeknownst to Father, I had determined that managing a cotton plantation was not my forte. No, literature was my grand passion (followed closely by my infatuation for Lucinda) but, realizing that it—literature, that is—would be impossible as a profession, I was getting up my nerve to inform the family that I wanted to try for the next best thing, i.e., to read for the bar.

There was a place for literary skills in the law, I reckoned. And, although I was tongue-tied in the presence of Lucinda, I had excelled as a member of the university debating society.

I never had to tell Father of my decision for, when news of Fort Sumter and Lincoln's call for 75,000 troops to put down the "Rebellion" reached Yardley County, the thoughts of every young man—even those of a clubfoot with weak lungs—turned to war. I set aside my novels and took up the works of Jomini and Clausewitz on the art of war and, also, began reading a biography of Napoleon.

And I joined the ranks of the Yardley Invincibles, a local militia company. The newly elected captain, my longtime friend and college roommate, Charles Fitzwater, disregarding my infirmity, accepted me as company clerk with the rank of corporal. The other fellows did not resent my quick rise in rank. After all, I rode a horse as well as any normal person and, setting modesty aside, played poker better than most. Besides, keeping records was a chore no able-bodied young blood wanted.

Perhaps I deceived myself, but it seemed that Lucinda treated me with a little less disdain after I appeared in my new gray-blue uniform at our one-and-only company dance, held in the ballroom of the Yardley City Hotel. It was out of the question for me to ask her to dance, but we had a nice heart-to-heart talk in which she assured me that she would be happy to correspond with me when our company went off to teach the hateful Yankees a lesson. I cheered myself with the thought that I might win her heart with my pen while also wearing a sword for my country.

Alas, when the call came a few weeks later for the Invincibles to present themselves at the state capital for induction into the Confederate forces, Fitz, with much embarrassment, informed me that the regimental doctor had decreed that company clerk or not, he would not accept a lame man for active duty.

This was a cruel blow to my feelings, but of course the doctor was right. There was no place in the active ranks for a fellow who wore a great backward-turned boot on one foot.

Father tried to console me by observing that my energies would be better spent at Glenwood, helping him oversee our twenty slaves in the production of food and fiber for the troops in the field. This was not my notion of serving my native land, however. So, without informing him, I wrote a letter to the Confederate secretary of war, Leroy Walker, and mailed it to the new capital in Montgomery. In it I set forth my qualifications and offered my services to the government.

To my amazement, late in May, I received a reply from Mr. Walker himself, offering me a post as an assistant bureau clerk at a salary of $50 per month.

Father was loath to see me go, but when he realized how determined I was to serve the war effort, he came around and gave me his blessings and a cache of $300 in U.S. gold coins.

"The war will be short," he said. "You'll be home soon. Walker impressed me at the last Democratic Convention. The experience you gain under him could be useful here at Glenwood."

The evening before my departure, my family gave a dinner in my honor, which Lucinda attended with her parents and other neighbors. The conversation around the table centered on the war. Lucinda's father was the only guest who thought the conflict would last more than a year. This first cousin of my father also was the only person present who had ever been north of the Mason-Dixon Line.

"They are a perfidious breed, those Yankees," he said in his pompous way. "But they are a stubborn lot, and they have considerable resources, financial and industrial. Why I remember when I was in Pittsburgh—"

"Yes, but Cousin Horace," my father said, "they would rather make money than fight. My friends who were in the Mexican War say it was the Southerners who did most of the hard fighting."

"Be that as it may, we must be careful we don't bite off more than we can chew. Don't forget how they outnumber us."

"We have other strengths than mere numbers or manufactures," Father replied. "A vast expanse of territory, plenty of fertile soil, an extensive coastline, and then . . ." He lowered his voice and glanced over his shoulder toward the kitchen before continuing, ". . . and then we have a great resource in our slave population. Our Negroes will continue our agricultural production while the bulk of our young white men take the field."

While all this pontifical talk flowed back and forth, I sat across the table from Lucinda, admiring the way her light brown hair shone in the candlelight and trying to catch her eye.

It took a moment for me to realize that Cousin Horace had spoken to me and that everyone was waiting for me to respond.

"Cousin Horace was asking your views on the war," Father said.

"Yes, Jackson. You have always struck me as a bright young fellow. College educated. And now you are going off to serve our new government. What do you think of our prospects?"

"The South doesn't have to conquer the North to win," I answered. "Clauswitz calls warfare an extension of politics. All we have to do is convince Lincoln and other northern politicians that the best course for both sections is to separate. It may take a couple of defeats on the battlefield to make them see this, but I reckon we can manage that."

I glanced at Lucinda to see her reaction to my contribution. She was whispering something to my sister Mary Bell. Only after the dinner, as her family was leaving, was I able to speak to her alone.

"I won't forget my promise." I ventured.

"What promise, Cousin Jackson?"

"To write to you. I promised, remember?"

"Did you? It would be nice to hear from you . . . sometime."

"And you will answer my letters?"

"If I have time. Several of the Invincibles said they wanted to write to me. It will keep me busy if I answer all those letters." Then, seeing the hurt look on my face, she added, "But of course I will be glad to hear from you, Cousin Jackson."

The next morning, the first Sunday in June of 1861, to be specific, while Mother packed my bags for the journey, I hobbled down to the slave quarters to say good-bye to our Negroes. Beginning with Old Slocum, the plantation foreman, I shook hands with each, and each wished me well.

"Now don't forget old Aunt Tibbie. Her feelings be hurt if you don't tell her good-bye," Slocum said.

"I was saving her for last," I said and made for the hut in which lived Glenwood's oldest slave.

No one was certain of Tibbie's age. She had been born in Africa and clearly remembered being marched from her village by Arab slave traders down to the coast and being put

aboard a ship for New Orleans, where she had been purchased by my great-grandfather, himself newly arrived from
North Carolina.

Now shrivelled with age and nearly blind, Tibbie was regarded with awe by some of the slaves for what they regarded as her "second sight."

Sitting on a stool in front of her hut, she clung to my hand.
When I tried to withdraw it, she put her other hand on top
of it.

"You got no business to be leaving, young Massa."

"I don't expect I will be gone very long, Aunt Tibbie. And
I am not going all that far from home anyway."

"Naw, naw, that ain't right. You goan be away for a long,
long time. And you goan go far, far away, across the water."

"Why do you say that, Aunt Tibbie?"

"I just sees it in my mind."

"Aunt Tibbie, this war will be over before we know it."

"No, it ain't goan be. It goan be a long time. There goan
be a whole lot of trouble. You got no business goan. You
better stay here where you belongs."

The other Negroes stood about in a semicircle listening to
the old woman.

"Well, I really am going, Aunt Tibbie. You take care of
yourself, and don't worry about me."

"I don't 'spect I will be here when you gets back cause it
goan be a long time. There goan be lots of folks dead, white
and black. Ain't nothing goan be the same. I be gone by then
cause I old. You goan see lots blood."

Ben, our blacksmith and husband of Mattie, our cook, res-
cued me from her clutch. "Your daddy say for me to fetch
you. They ready to go now."

"Who was dat?" Tibbie asked, as she finally released my
hand.

"Ben. He says my family is ready to take me to Yardley
City to catch the train. So I will say good-bye now."

"Ben, yeah, the blacksmith man," she said. "He better be
careful too. Stay where he is. They goan be trouble for ev-
erbody if they don't stay here. Big trouble coming, I tell you.
I done seen it in my mind."

On the way to Yardley City in our carriage, I told my parents and sisters what Tibbie had said. They all laughed at the old woman's remarks.

"She has been a little off in the head ever since she reached the change of life," Father said. "Some folks would have sold her off, but that is not my policy."

"Well, she warned me and Ben to be careful, didn't she, Ben?"

"Old Tibbie?" Ben said, as though he had not been listening. "She always talking kind of crazy talk. I don't pay her no attention."

Six hours after bidding my family and Ben farewell and boarding the train, I arrived in Montgomery and asked the stationmaster the way to the Secretary of War's office.

"Ain't you heard? They have moved the whole Goddamned Confederate Government lock, stock and barrel to Richmond, Virginia. Done it without hardly any warning. Folks around here ain't too happy about it."

"I am not exactly overjoyed myself," I replied. "Can you direct me to a good hotel?"

"If you had of come two weeks ago, there wouldn't have been a bed available for love nor money. Now you can have your pick of the best for fifty cents a night."

I lay awake during a long night in the Exchange Hotel, debating just what to do. The prospects of returning to Glenwood and sitting out the war appalled me. The next morning, after writing letters to my family and to Lucinda, I brushed my clothes, partook of a hearty breakfast, persuaded the hotel cook to pack me a basket of victuals, and boarded a train for the first leg of a three-day journey to Richmond.

It was a daunting trip, on crowded trains, with changes at Atlanta, Columbia and Raleigh, but each mile that carried me farther north strengthened my resolve to serve my native Southland and see it through its birth pangs as a new nation. Then I would return to read for the law and conjure up the courage to ask for Cousin Lucinda's hand in marriage.

On the train from Atlanta to Columbia, I sat facing a short, portly man wearing a goatee, and his big, flaccid-looking companion. They were slave traders returning from a trip to the Deep South.

As the train rattled along, the short man pointed at a gang of Negroes chopping weeds in a cotton field. "Look there, Rankin, you know how much money is represented in that one lot of nigras?"

"Why, Mr. Abernathy, I did not bother to count them."

"Well, I did. There was four males, six grown females, and three younguns. I would offer their owner seven thousand dollars just from what I could see out the window."

"Well, Mr. Abernathy, you do have a shrewd, quick eye. Do you reckon they would take it?"

"Probably not, but if I really wanted them nigras and seen a chance of getting them, I would raise my price to seventy-five hundred, with a show of reluctance, of course."

"What if they wouldn't take that?"

"Then, I would have to ask what was their price. Now they would probably say ten thousand dollars because that is a big round figure and I would have to say that much as I would like to accommodate them, I would be stretching myself to go even as high as eight thousand."

"What if they wouldn't take eight?"

"Then I would express my regrets, give them my card, and leave them to think about how much money eight thousand dollars really is."

"What do you think would happen then?"

"It would depend on their circumstances. If they returned to talk things over again, with a little more give and take, I might let them squeeze me up to eighty-five hundred, or maybe nine thousand, and then you know what I would do?"

"Not exactly."

"I would employ you to help me haul them off down to the sugarcane country in Louisiana and sell them nigras one by one for a total of at least twelve thousand, maybe more."

The man folded his hands across his pot belly as though satisfied with actually having completed a profitable transaction. I made the mistake of glancing at him just then.

"What is your line of work, young man?"

I explained that I was on my way to take a job with the Confederate War Department.

"Well, I hope that your department will make quick work of this war. We need to get the Yankee abolitionists off our backs and the only way to do that is to go it on our own. I am most sanguine about the future of our fair Confederacy. With our salubrious climate, our fertile plantations, and our wealth of slave labor, we shall take our place among the richest nations in the history of this world. That is my fervant belief."

I shared my father's aversion to professional slave traders, but replied that I, too, felt optimistic about the future for a strong, independent South.

"But you know what this war is really about, young man?"

"States' rights. Freedom to go our own way, just as the American colonies broke away from England, I reckon."

"Not states' rights, no. The abolitionists are correct. The issue really is slavery. That is our source of wealth and that is what Lincoln and the abolitionists hate. They want the South to be poor. They want to take away the millions upon millions of dollars represented by our nigra slaves. We must fight to preserve our property rights. And I feel that we will prevail."

"I am sure that we will," I said.

"Then here, I happen to have a small supply of brandy. Perhaps you will join me and Mr. Rankin in a toast to the Confederate States of America."

"I am sorry, but I don't drink hard liquor."

"Now that is a pity. Here, Mr. Rankin. We will drink alone."

I was glad to say good-bye to the odious pair in Columbia.

So, on to Richmond I rode. Bless my mother's heart for keeping all my letters from that period. To avoid dragging out the story of my early days in that city I attach what I wrote back home about three weeks later.

TWO

Richmond, Virginia
Sunday, June 30, 1861

Dear Father, Mother, Sisters Mary Bell and Emmaline, and
Mattie:

I hope that my hasty letter from Montgomery did not upset
you. I would have written again sooner, but the past few
weeks have been the most hectic in my life.

Anyway, I am now safe and sound here in Richmond. This
is a wonderful city but it is fast filling up with a great hurly
burly of humanity. It seems as though every favor-seeker and
profit-minded tradesman in the South has taken it into his
head to descend upon the banks of the mighty James River
now that Richmond has become the permanent seat of our
new government.

As for myself, I got here three weeks ago on a steamy hot
day with my coat riddled by cinder burns and my body ach-
ing from the long ride on wooden seats. I have taken up
residence at a boarding house within walking distance of the
War Department, which is temporarily housed in the new
Customs House on Main Street. The establishment is owned
and presided over by a middle-aged amazon, by name Mrs.
Edith Selby. The widow of a Virginia state legislator, this
formidable female tries (in vain) to conceal a coarse streak
of cupidity under a veneer of gentility. You all would have
been mightily amused by the interview that took place be-
tween Mrs. Selby and yours truly.

"You say you have a job with the government, Mr. Mundy?" she asked as she looked me up and down with a critical eye.

"With the War Department, yes ma'am. As a bureau clerk."

She demanded to know whether I smoked or chewed.

After I assured her that I had never taken up either of those loathsome habits, she wanted to know how *"you might be paying for a room, if I was to have one, that is."*

Her face took on a kindlier aspect when I told her that the payment could be in gold coins, if she preferred, but then her countenance hardened as she said, *"You understand that I won't tolerate women in the rooms of my men boarders."*

In my most pious manner, I replied *"I would have been very much surprised and disappointed if that were not a rule"* and decided to press the advantage I saw that paying in gold gave me by saying, *"I hope you understand, Mrs. Selby, that I require a private room. I do not wish to share my quarters with anyone else. And I shall need a good reading lamp."*

She pondered that point a bit before replying, *"I just happen to have a small room on the third floor that should meet your requirements, but I expect to be paid on the first of each month, in advance."*

I pursed my mouth in imitation of her expression and replied, *"Naturally I would like to inspect the quarters before we settle on the terms and I would like to see your kitchen and inquire about your meal services."*

So now, dear family, I am happily ensconced in Madame Selby's boarding house. The meals fall far short of those you prepare, Mattie, but they are adequate. As for the room, I am kept too busy by my job to enjoy its comfort and privacy.

The day after settling in at Mrs. Selby's, I presented my letter from Mr. Walker at the War Department and was promptly ushered into the presence of the author himself, who, incidentally, Father, sends you his best regards, and who apologized for his failure to notify me of the move from Montgomery.

As Father knows, Mr. Walker is a thin, stooped gentleman

with a high forehead and intelligent, gray eyes. His long nose and full beard, sans moustache, give him a mournful appearance. Everyone in the Confederacy seems to be importuning him for favors. He turned me over to his new head of the Bureau of War, a portly and—in my opinion—lazy so-called colonel named Albert T. Bledsoe. My duties, along with three other clerks, are to help with the composing of letters to contractors, governors of the states, and persons lobbying to gain commissions in the army.

Colonel Bledsoe was much fretted by the news that his and certain other bureaus of the department shortly were to be moved to permanent quarters on the second floor of the Old Mechanics Building at 9th and Bank Streets. That is why I have been so lax in writing to you. My fellow clerks and I have been engrossed in organizing and effecting this move, which Colonel Bledsoe, out of lethargy, so much dreaded.

My job is far more demanding than I expected. On many nights, I find it necessary to return to the office, after partaking of Mrs. Selby's suppers, to labor by candlelight until midnight. Secretary Walker seems to appreciate my work, for he rarely rejects the letters I prepare for his signature. My fellow clerks—as irreverant a lot as you would ever want to meet, but good fellows in the main—make light of him, calling him "Slow Coach" Walker, but I have no criticism of the gentleman beyond noting that he might have an easier time of it if he were to make his decisions with less procrastination.

As for Colonel Bledsoe, he might be a more effective head of our bureau if he did more work himself and less complaining about his burdens of office. . . . That is the view I and my colleagues have of our immediate superior.

Speaking of my fellow clerks, they all lay claim to being young men of education and good family backgrounds. Like myself, each is in one way or another physically unacceptable for active military service, but we flatter ourselves that we are accomplishing far more for the cause of Southern Independence here in the War Department than if we were carrying muskets in the ranks.

I am running out of paper, which, incidentally, is in short

supply here, so I had better close. Please give my best regards to Ben, Slocum and all the other darkies. Tell old Aunt
Tibbie that she need fear no more for my safety. I am in no
danger.

Love, Jackson

THREE

• • • I spent the next fifteen months in that War Department office, first under Mr. Walker and, after his health broke later in the year from the strain of overwork and conflicts with President Davis, under his successor, the celebrated Judah P. Benjamin, and, later, under George W. Randolph.

I often reflect on how lessons in punctuality and attention to detail I learned while working under these men stood me in good stead in managing and editing *The Leader*, and, later, in carrying out my duties in the U.S. Senate. I was sorry when Walker resigned his post in September of 1861, following a difference of opinion with President Davis, to be replaced by Judah P. Benjamin.

The war went well for the South that first year. The Confederates won a brilliant victory in July at Manassas Junction, but failed to seize the opportunity to take Washington. As for Richmond, by the end of 1861, it had doubled in population. Mrs. Selby's establishment became more and more crowded, so that she began providing two settings at each meal time and started placing two, three and more persons in her rented rooms. She honored her promise to protect my privacy until one morning in January of 1862, when she drew me aside after breakfast to say that she had a request for lodging from "a most unusual gentleman."

"He is a Northern-born gentleman but a true Southerner at heart. He has been living for some years in England. Married to an English woman, he is. And he has made his way across the ocean to offer his services to the Confederate government."

Then she got to her point, which was to inquire whether I might be willing to share my room with this gentleman.

I would have turned her down flatly had she not added that "they do say he attended the military academy at West Point and he was a great hero in the war with Mexico."

"Mrs. Selby, you did assure me when I rented my room—"

"Indeed, but you see how crowded we have become. And you know how fearfully the cost of every necessity has risen. I hate to say so, sir, but I've been meaning to discuss whether we might consider an increase in your rent. In fact, the only way around our problem would be for you to share your room, with a person agreeable to yourself, it goes without saying."

Mrs. Selby was right. I was the only clerk in the War Department who enjoyed the luxury of a private room. So, grudgingly, I agreed to be introduced to the man.

He was sitting before a meager fire in Mrs. Selby's living room upon my return from the office that evening. Evidently the landlady had described me to him, for he arose and greeted me by name.

Aside from Robert E. Lee himself, I have never met a more handsome, better set-up man, nor one better dressed. He stood just over average height, but his shoulders were so square and his posture so erect that he appeared at least six feet tall. He wore his chestnut-colored hair in long waves. His strong, full jaw was clean shaven. Dark eyes sparkled under shaggy eyebrows. His clothes, cut in the English style, would have done credit to a dandy.

He stood with outstretched hand, saying in a mixed Yankee-English accent, "So you are Jackson Mundy? My name is Evan Martin, and I am delighted to make your acquaintance. Mrs. Selby tells me you are an official in the Confederate government."

He made me feel as if I were the secretary of war himself rather than a mere clerk in the War Department. At the supper table, he held the assembled diners entranced with his story of crossing the Atlantic from Liverpool to Philadelphia and then of passing through the lines of both armies, disguised as an intinerant preacher, to "offer my services to the Confederate government."

I expressed surprise that one northern-born should do such a thing.

He explained that he had been born in Philadelphia and had spent his early years in that city. Following the death of his parents in a fever epidemic when he was fifteen, he had been sent south to Mobile to live with an uncle who had taken up residence there as a cotton factor.

"I lived with that good man and his family until I was eighteen and they were the best years of my life. You might say that the South is in my blood, anyway, for my grandfather came from Virginia. He served the American cause in the Revolutionary War on land and sea and then settled in Philadelphia."

"And you are a graduate of West Point?" I asked.

"Not actually a graduate. I left the academy in '46 when the Mexican War began. My uncle wrote that a company was being raised in Mobile to serve. I had the honor to be elected captain. Later, my uncle, who has since died, prevailed upon me to go to England to set up a cotton importing office there. The rest is history. . . ."

"And you married in England and have a family there?" Mrs. Selby inquired from the kitchen doorway.

"My wife is English. At the outbreak of this war, I assumed it would end quickly but when I realized it would be a protracted conflict, I put my affairs in order, and did what it seemed my duty to do. So here I am, and that is enough talk about myself." Then, turning to me, he said, "I should like the opportunity of speaking to you in private later."

After supper, he said, "Mr. Mundy, you have heard my story and know my wish to serve. What advice can you offer?"

"What sort of advice?"

"As to how to gain the ear of President Davis. You know of my experience. I seek a commission."

"I do not enjoy the confidence of President Davis," I replied. Then, seeing his face fall, added, "I could ask my bureau chief to mention your case to Mr. Benjamin, who is our secretary of war."

"Excellent," he said as he drew an envelope from his coat pocket. "Here is a resume setting forth my qualifications."

That night I informed Mrs. Selby than I had no objection to sharing my room with Captain Martin. She had a day bed moved into my quarters. And the next day Colonel Bledsoe accepted the resume to show to Mr. Benjamin.

Judah P. Benjamin, often called "the brains of the Confederacy," would soon be moved from the War Department to become the secretary of state, which was a good move, for he was the soul of diplomacy.

Benjamin summoned Captain Martin to meet with him that very afternoon. I heard all about it that night after supper.

"He could not have been more accommodating. I could see that he was quite busy, but he kept a room full of people waiting while we discussed the progress of the war. Mr. Benjamin was especially interested in my views of the public reaction in England to the Battle of Manassas. I must say that he is a most gracious man, especially so for a Jew. He assures me that a commission will be forthcoming. . . ."

That night, as we prepared for bed, Captain Martin examined the books on my writing table.

"It is good to be billeted with someone who shares my interest in the military arts."

After we had extinguished our lamp and retired, he talked about the war and his theories of how it should be fought.

"All of the great military thinkers advocate carrying the war to the enemy," he said. "To sit and wait for your adversary to strike is to abdicate the initiative. That can be fatal."

I countered with, "But the South has no wish to conquer the North. We want only to be left alone to forge our own destiny."

"Ah, but the North will never allow that. The thing will have to be settled on the battlefield, and that battlefield should be on northern, not southern soil. Had Johnston and Beauregard moved quickly after winning at Manassas Station, they could have captured Washington. The war would have been won at one bold stroke. Well, I mustn't tax you with my opinions. Good night."

We had several such conversations during the next week. I learned much about Captain Martin in that time. The progenitor of his family in America was an English Quaker who, after a sojourn in Barbados in the late 1600s, settled in Virginia and married a half-Indian girl of the Powhatan tribe. He was particularly proud of his paternal grandfather, who had fought with Washington against the British and also had owned and commanded several privateering vessels in the West Indies, thereby creating a fortune which had dissipated following the death of his—Captain Martin's—own father who, likewise, was something of a hero in the War of 1812. He said little about his life in England, and modestly declined to talk about his experiences in the Mexican War. Beyond saying that he had a daughter, he was close-mouthed about his family. Still, he was fascinating company. I did not regret my decision to share my room with him.

One evening toward the end of the first week of our acquaintanceship, he was waiting with glittering eyes when I returned from my day's labors.

"We did it, Mundy, by God we did it."

"Did what, Captain Martin?"

"I hold in my hand a commission as a colonel in the Confederate Army. They are sending me down to North Carolina to assume command of a green regiment that did badly in its first battle. They want me to whip it into shape."

He stamped his feet and smote his hands together. "I have lived my entire life for this opportunity. And I have you to thank for it. I shall always be grateful to you, Mundy."

I was pleased for his sake, naturally, but in truth had come to enjoy his company so that the news saddened me.

"Look here, my good fellow, I shall be leaving tomorrow, but I intend to pay Mrs. Selby to keep my bed and my belongings here. It would be a comfort to know that I have a home away from home and access to your ear in the War Department. Would you object to that?"

The thought pleased me. I was further pleased by his invitation to accompany him to the Spotswood Hotel for dinner with wine to celebrate his commission. I had been living the life of a recluse shuttling between the War Department office and Mrs. Selby's boarding house, with the routine broken only by an occasional game of whist or chess with the other boarders, or weekly poker with my fellow clerks. I was most impressed by the savoir faire with which my new friend conducted himself. He seemed to me, in my youthful innocence, to be a sort of wise and courtly knight.

The next morning, Captain Martin shook my hand warmly, thanked me again for helping him at the War Department, and left. I really did not expect to see him again for many months.

FOUR

• • • With Captain Martin no longer around to stimulate me, I began to feel the strain of nine months of night-and-day labors at the War Department. My salary could not keep up with the inflation that continued apace throughout the Confederacy, especially there in Richmond. Father's going-away purse was nearing exhaustion and, for that matter, so were my nerves.

All around me was gaiety and adventure, but the social life of wartime Richmond had no place for a civilian with a deformed foot. The belles of the city had eyes only for strapping young men in uniform. Even my hopes for winning Lucinda's heart were fading, for, despite my writing long and increasingly bolder letters to her, I had received only three replies, none of which included anything more personal than poorly spelled accounts of local news and complaints about the dullness of her life with all the young men gone off to war. My own existence suddenly seemed so useless and without hope that I began to consider asking for a leave of absence to return to Glenwood and my family for a long rest. While at home, with the field cleared of competition, perhaps I could put myself on a stronger footing with Lucinda. The more I thought about this idea, the better I liked it.

I was sitting at my desk writing a trial draft of a request to Colonel Bledsoe for a leave when a fellow clerk, a cocky little South Carolinian with a withered arm named Cogburn, interrupted with, "Hey, Jackie, Richards and Aikens and me are going over to the Ballard House for dinner tonight. You look down at the mouth. Why not come along and enjoy a decent meal instead of that boarding house slop you eat?"

I hated being called Jackie but replied with civil gloom, "I can't afford it, Cogburn. My money is running low."

"I just got a bank draft from home this morning. I'll foot the bill. With the army out of town, the hotel will be glad to have our business. Come on, it's time you had a little fun."

I can't recall at what time my friends returned me to Mrs. Selby's establishment. Indeed the next morning, with an aching head from the unaccustomed wine I had drunk, I barely remembered the circumstances of my arrival. Mrs. Selby had to hammer at the door to awaken me for breakfast. She treated me with disdain as I sat choking down her hot mush and ersatz coffee.

When I had finished breakfast, she followed me to the door and said archly, "When you took lodgings here, Mister Mundy, I assumed you would be a quiet gentleman who would not disturb me or my lodgers."

"Why, Mrs. Selby, what are you getting at?"

"I am getting at the disturbance you and your friends created in front of my house in the wee hours of this morning."

"I did not realize that we were making so much noise."

"Well, you were. Singing rude songs at the top of your voices. It is a wonder the provost guards did not arrest you. I run a respectable boarding house here and I don't propose to stand by quietly and have my reputation ruined by you and your drunkard friends."

"I am sorry about that. Some of my comrades did drink more than they are used to, it is true. We all have been under a great deal of strain at the War Department. The work is very demanding."

"That is no excuse. What would Captain Martin think if he knew of your behavior? He held you in such high regard."

"I hope that he will never hear of it and that you will never have reason again to complain of my deportment."

"Then we shall speak no more of it."

"I certainly shall not," I said with a bow.

With relief I realized Mrs. Selby had not divined the cause

for all the hilarity in front of her boarding house the night before. My colleagues and I had engaged in a manly contest to determine which of us, to use the parlance of firemen, could throw the longest and strongest stream into the cobbled street. If I were more modest, I would not reveal our game, nor would I mention that I had been declared the clear winner of the contest.

Back at the office, I tore up the letter I had written requesting a leave of absence. Life in Richmond was not so bad that I could not bear it for a while longer, at least until my money ran out.

Besides, the war suddenly entered a new and critical phase. It would have been cowardly and selfish for me to have deserted my post.

Rather than rely on my memory, let me turn to two letters from me which my family preserved. They tell the story better than I could now from memory nearly forty years later.

FIVE

May 28, 1862

Dear Father:

Your man-to-man letter arrived. I hasten to reply in the entre nous spirit in which you wrote. You are uneasy regarding my moral behavior away from the influence of my family? Be assured that I am aware of the pitfalls of strong drink and loose women. Sadly, the reports you have heard about Richmond are correct, however. The city has attracted many persons of low repute. The government hires some pretty tough provost marshals called 'plug uglies'—many of them pro-Confederate former Baltimore policemen. They keep the worst of the loose women off the streets.

I would have written to you and the family weeks ago, but my duties at the War Department have been so demanding that I have lacked the energy or time to take up the pen in my few hours away from the office. I don't want to upset Mother or the girls, and please don't repeat this to your friends, but we are in a crisis here, and I am not sure we will survive it.

As you know, the war has gone badly in recent months. Forts Henry and Donelson have fallen in Tennessee, then Nashville soon after. Roanoke Island in North Carolina is now in enemy hands, followed by a humiliating defeat at New Berne. As if these debacles were not enough, New Orleans fell to a Federal fleet in April and we lost many men at Pittsburgh Landing in Tennessee.

But those reverses pale in comparison to the threat posed by McClellan's advance up the Peninsula between the James and York Rivers with an army of more than 100,000. Our General Joseph E. Johnston has skillfully delayed McClellan for several weeks, but the enemy's superior numbers have forced him to withdraw to the outskirts of Richmond. McClellan has thrown one wing of his army across the Chickahominy River, to within sight of the spires of fair Richmond. He has an observation balloon which can be seen bobbing on the eastern horizon. He also has hauled a huge train of artillery whose blasts echo through the city streets, rattling windows and frightening the womenfolk of the capital.

The situation is so desperate that I and my fellow War Department clerks have spent the past few days crating up all of our records and hauling them down to be loaded on trains for transport out of Richmond, if the city should be abandoned.

The War Department has received much criticism for our reverses this year. That is what lay behind Mr. Benjamin's recent resignation as secretary of war to become secretary of state. My fellow clerks and I wonder at President Davis's choice of a replacement. He is George W. Randolph, grandson of Thomas Jefferson, who was a lawyer before the war. He has served briefly as an artillery officer, but he is a sickly man, perhaps not equal to the demands of his office. Give him credit for some good ideas, however. He is lobbying Congress to pass a conscription law and extend the term of enlistments to three years, both badly needed.

Richmond has become even more of a madhouse in recent days, with troops pouring in from the west and south and then out again to swell Johnston's force. Matters have been made even worse by an influx of civilian refugees from Norfolk and the Peninsula. I shudder to think what their fate may be if Richmond should fall to McClellan; indeed what the fate of the Confederacy would be.

Robert E. Lee, a former superintendent of the U.S. Military Academy at West Point, as chief military adviser to President Davis, now occupies a front office on the second floor of our building. I wish you could meet him, Father. A hero of the Mexican War, he is the most impressive-looking man I ever met. He exudes calm and intelligence and efficiency. I feel less apprehensive for our cause when I gaze upon his noble countenance. You have always preached the virtue of self control, Father. General Lee is a paragon of that virtue. It is his sure hand, rather than Secretary Randolph's, that is coordinating the amassing of troops to keep the Yankee hordes at bay.

President Davis comes often to consult with General Lee. Gaunt and care-worn, he is like a violin too tightly strung.

By the way, I wrote about the gentleman from England who briefly shared my quarters here at Mrs. Selby's. The other night, returning from the office, I found the door to my little room unlocked. There, at my writing table, dressed in a resplendent gray uniform, sat Captain, or rather, Colonel Martin, himself.

My weariness erased in a moment by the sight of my friend, I sat up until nearly 1 o'clock listening to his stories of how he has whipped his regiment into fighting shape. They were an unruly mob when he took command, but he now claims there is not a better drilled or more ready regiment in the Confederate army. He left his regiment bivouacked at Petersburg and took the train to Richmond to await their arrival. He was eager to hear the gossip from the War Department, what promotions had been handed out, and whether Secretary Randolph is up to his task.

He expressed dismay at the position the Confederacy finds itself in. In his words, "We should be advancing on Washington, not being pressed back on our own capital."

I praised General Johnston, pointing out how he saved the day for us at Manassas last year.

Colonel Martin replied "Yes, but the man lacks the offensive spirit. What will it profit us to beat off McClellan? He has the resources behind him to try again and again until he has worn us out. No, we should carry the war to the North." And then he pressed me for my opinion of General Lee.

I pointed out that Lee had served with distinction as a young captain in the Mexican War and asked whether Colonel Martin had known him there. But Colonel Martin said their paths had not crossed. Exhausted from talking, we fell asleep upon our beds, still dressed. I awoke to Mrs. Selby's knock to see that my friend had departed but had left a note thanking me for "keeping the home fires burning" and suggesting that I mention his success with his regiment to "the right persons in the War Department."

His confidence in my influence flatters me, of course. I wish you could meet Colonel Martin. He is a fascinating gentleman.

Well, duty calls. I will write again to the entire family when time permits.

Your loving son, Jackson

June 16, 1862

Dear Father, Mother, Sisters Emmaline and Mary Bell, and Mattie:

This will have to be a quick note for we are busier than ever at the War Department. The situation here has improved somewhat since I wrote to you, Father, but the danger is far from over. You must have heard by now that General Lee has been put in command of our armies to replace General Johnston, who suffered a severe wound in a huge but indecisive battle fought two weeks ago at Fair Oak Station just seven miles from here.

We have been holding our breath ever since. Now I think McClellan may be holding his. The commander of our cavalry division, General Stuart, has just returned from a raid which carried him and over a thousand of his horsemen completely around McClellan's army, disrupting the enemy's communications and spreading confusion in his rear. And there are reports that Stonewall Jackson will be arriving soon from the Shenandoah Valley, to buttress the army with his magnificent "foot cavalry."

Fair Oaks Station was a horrible battle. The day before, i.e., May 30, a heavy thunderstorm drenched the city, after which the skies cleared and there appeared to the east of the city a full rainbow so lovely that we all went to our windows to admire it. We took it as a good omen that the radiant colors arched over the lines of General Johnston's army.

The sound of cannonading shook the building through the

*next afternoon. Secretary Randolph and other officials took
themselves off to watch the counterattack that Johnston was
making. We poor clerks were still laboring at our desks that
evening when we heard the direful news that General Johnston had been seriously wounded.*

*We remained at our posts during a long and anxious night.
Our gloom persisted until we learned our counterattacks had
stopped McClellan's advance and that General Lee had replaced Johnston, an excellent decision in my opinion.*

*That same day, the ambulances started rolling in from the
battlefield with their loads of wounded soldiers. Soon every
one of the several hospitals in the city was filled. The over-
flow of wounded now lie in improvised hospitals in churches
and other public buildings. I have seen at firsthand that war
is not so wonderful after all.*

*With the city no longer in immediate peril, Secretary Ran-
dolph ordered us to retrieve our War Department records
from the railroad box cars. McClellan's balloon still hovers
in the sky, however, reminding us that a huge enemy army
still lurks just outside the city.*

*He cannot be allowed to remain there, and I do not think
General Lee will long permit him to do so. I shudder to think
of the blood that will be shed, however.*

All my love, Jackson

SIX

• • • What we soon came to call the Seven Days' Battles opened on June 25 at Oak Grove, and every day for the next week the echoes of the guns rattled our windows at the War Department building. The fighting was fearful, by far the worst in the war to that date. Mechanicsville, Gaines Mill, Savage Station and Frayser's Farm became names written in blood, as Lee struck again and again, each blow driving the invader farther back but each also costing both sides enormous losses.

Now there weren't enough ambulances to handle the grisly cargoes of the maimed. Farm wagons, carts and carriages were pressed into service. High society ladies gave up their entertainments to nurse the wounded. Every church became a hospital. Retail establishments and tobacco warehouses were transformed into infirmaries. Surgeons went without sleep as they hacked off mangled arms and legs like slaughterhouse butchers. Ministers of the gospel could not keep up with the demand for funerals. Church bells tolled for the dead into the night. Hastily built coffins were hauled out to Hollywood Cemetery faster than grave-digging crews could prepare their resting places.

Still the fighting went on. It finished with a grand, but tragic finale on July 1 at Malvern Hill, fifteen miles from Richmond on the James River. There McClellan made a stand and there his massed artillery tore Lee's attacking ranks to shreds. Thereafter McClellan gave up his campaign to take Richmond and began withdrawing down the Peninsula. Lee had defeated him, but at a dreadful cost of Southern life, blood and suffering.

Even if my infirmity and my civilian dress had not made me diffident in my relations with the fairer sex, I was kept too busy to enter into the social life of the city, but I did occasionally attend services at St. John's Episcopal Church. I returned from there the first Sunday in July to find a note from the matron at a nearby hospital which had been established in a former drygoods store. It said that they had Colonel Evan Martin as a patient, and he wanted very much to see Mr. Mundy.

Forgoing Mrs. Selby's Sunday dinner, I rushed over to the hospital to find my friend in a large room reserved for officers. He lay propped up in a cot with a sheet drawn up around his shoulders. His face, partly hidden by a new beard, was pale, and his usually brilliant eyes looked dull and sunken.

He smiled when he recognized me and extended his left hand.

"Is it true, Mundy? Did we win?"

"Just yesterday, President Davis issued an official order congratulating General Lee on our victory," I replied.

"The cost was high, though, was it not?"

The casualties had not been made public, but I knew from War Department reports that they exceeded 20,000.

I nodded and said, "Very high, indeed, I fear." Then, before he could press me for specifics, I asked what had befallen him.

"My men fought gallantly," Martin said. "They made me proud of them. They followed me right up to the muzzles of the cannon, not once but three times . . ."

"At Malvern Hill?" I asked.

He nodded and closed his eyes.

"Colonel Martin," a voice boomed from behind me. "Let's see how that arm is doing."

A surgeon dressed in a filthy linen smock pushed me aside and drew back the sheet. I was shocked to see that the colonel's right arm had been taken off high up, near the shoulder. I turned my head as the surgeon unwrapped the bandages from the blood-encrusted stump.

"They did a good job on you in the field hospital. Much pain?"

"Terrible."

"I will tell the matron you may have laudanum. Don't take more than you absolutely require, though; stuff's habit forming."

The matron suggested that I return the next day, "when he is feeling better."

I came back the next day and every day thereafter, and on each visit found my friend looking stronger. He complained that the amputated arm pained him so he found it impossible to sleep at night without medication. And I observed that the matron and other hospital workers, captivated by his unusual accent and his outgoing personality, were making something of a pet of him. He seemed to thrive on their attention.

Although I did not press him, he seemed eager to talk about Malvern Hill. "They had their cannon lined in ranks up the long slope. We would have smashed McClellan's army if our artillery had done a better job, but they had us outgunned. They poured canister into our ranks without mercy. My brave, brave men. Do you know, Mundy, I fell not fifty feet from their batteries? A canister ball simply shattered my arm. My men pressed on and bayonetted some of the gunners. If we had been properly supported, we would have broken their lines and turned their guns on them. But my men refused to quit the field with me lying there. The last thing I remember was their picking me up. When I came to, I was in the surgeon's tent. Thank God for chloroform."

He asked what the newspapers were saying about the battles.

"General Lee has received some criticism for ordering the attack on Malvern Hill when he had McClellan on the run already."

He became agitated at this.

"They are wrong. General Lee had no choice. A good general does not let his adversary off the hook. It is not enough to say you won. You must destroy your enemy. We could have ended the war if our artillery had done its job, if I had been properly supported . . ."

On my next visit, I found my friend's bed surrounded by

soldiers of his regiment. He introduced "my young friend from the War Department."

The men left after expressing their admiration for the colonel and their wishes for his speedy return to his command of their regiment.

"Aren't they superb soldiers?" Martin said after they had left. "If only we had more of them. I would like to command an army the size of McClellan's with men like those we have. We would sweep the Federals from the earth."

On my next visit, the matron stopped me at the door. "He has a very important visitor. Perhaps you should wait here."

A slender, dark-complected woman was seated by his cot. Seeing me standing with hat in hand, Colonel Martin called, "Mr. Mundy, please come here."

"Mrs. Davis," he said. "I would like to present Mr. Jackson Mundy of the War Department."

I mumbled that it was an honor to meet the first lady of the Confederacy, adding, "I see your husband often at the office."

"He is too conscientious, I think, sometimes. I am pleased to meet you. And, Colonel Martin, let me say again how much I admire your courage, first to cross the ocean to fight for our country, and your valor on the field of battle. My husband joins me in thanking you."

His face glowed as she left. "I must write and tell my family of the honor our president's wife has paid me." He paused and laughed without humor. "I forget my disability. I will have to learn to write with my left hand now."

I offered to help but he shook his head in irritation. "I think I can manage a letter . . . when I feel stronger. Well, surely Mrs. Davis will recommend me to her husband."

"For what?"

He frowned in annoyance. "For a higher command, what else? I want a brigade, or in time, a division. That would make the loss of an arm worthwhile. Imagine, to command a division under Robert E. Lee, to become a figure of historical importance in the birth of a new nation. I can do it, Mundy. It is within my grasp."

He continued to mend after that, but I noticed that on some of my visits he seemed withdrawn and short-tempered; on others, full of enthusiasm. Soon he was allowed to dress and walk about the wards, chatting with other patients. He spent much time interviewing fellow officers and even ordinary soldiers about their experiences. He showed particular interest in the accounts of Jackson's men about their successful campaign in the Shenandoah. I asked whether he should exert himself so much until his arm had healed.

"Don't be absurd. I am learning about this war from these fellows. This information will stand me in good stead when I once more take the field. Now, tell me again about what Lee is doing with the army."

"He has renamed it the Army of Northern Virginia and he has reorganized it into two corps, one commanded by Jackson and the other by Longstreet, with Stuart as cavalry commander, of course."

"Good, good. Now we shall discover what Lee is made of," he said. "Let us see if he takes the offensive."

By August, the colonel was able to walk about the streets of Richmond. By now he had become a popular figure in the capital. He was stopped frequently by well-wishers. The more his health improved, the more he expressed his ambition for higher command and pressed me to direct his petition to Secretary Randolph. I asked Colonel Bledsoe if Mr. Randolph would see Colonel Martin, but the secretary declined. Perhaps Bledsoe was the wrong person to ask. Mr. Randolph despised him.

The colonel was downcast at my report. "You disappoint me, Mundy. I thought I could count on you. I suppose that I must take matters into my own hands."

My feelings hurt as much by his tone of voice as his words, I replied, "I am sorry, Colonel, but I am only a clerk, you know."

"Well, please do keep your ears open for me. I shall be released from this place soon."

"Good. Your bed in my room is ready for you."

"I am not sure I shall require it, but yes, thank you."

The next time I went to visit him, the matron turned me away, saying "He asked not to be disturbed. He is taking a nap."

The next evening I found that Colonel Martin's small

trunk and civilian clothing had been removed from "our" room. Mrs. Selby said that the colonel had come with two Negroes and a cart and taken them away.

"Our Captain Martin has come up in the world," she said. "He has found a private room at the Spotswood Hotel."

"Colonel Martin," I said. "He is a colonel now."

"Captain or colonel, he cannot rise above his Yankee upbringing. He had the nerve to ask me to return his advance on the room rental. Let me give you a word of advice, Mister Mundy. That man is an ingrate and an opportunist. Not even a word of thanks to me for all the trouble I took to find him shelter. Not even a civil good-bye. And that on top of asking for his money back. I am sorry I was taken in by his smooth talk. I hope you will not be offended by my frankness, Mister Mundy, but you would do well to avoid the company of that man."

"It would seem, Mrs. Selby," I replied ruefully, "that he has chosen to avoid my company."

I would have been more hurt by Colonel Martin's abruptly dropping me had I not been kept so very busy at the War Department. Having driven off McClellan, General Lee now turned his attention to a second army under General Pope, which the Federals had amassed to the north, up around Manassas Station. Lee dispatched Jackson's corps to keep Pope in check until he was sure McClellan was withdrawing his army by boat from the Peninsula. Jackson won a preliminary victory at Cedar Mountain on August 9. Lee hurried the rest of his army north and in the closing days of August achieved what might have been his greatest triumph of the War Between the States. Part of the great battle was fought on the same ground as had been the battle of Manassas. Just as in the first battle, the Federals were put to flight, this time with losses of more than 16,000. Once again, it seemed that the Confederacy was being offered the opportunity to win the war in a single bold stroke.

Not having seen Colonel Martin for some time, I inquired of Colonel Bledsoe if he had rejoined his regiment.

"The English chap? Why I saw him just last night. He was dining with Mr. Benjamin at the Spotswood. They looked to be thick as thieves. I have heard he has been received by President and Mrs. Davis as well. Friend of yours, isn't he?"

"He was, Colonel Bledsoe, or so I thought," I replied.

A worse blow to my spirits came a day or so later as part of a long letter from my mother. She related all the news of the family and the neighbors, complete with tedious details of how they were coping with the shortages caused by the war. Near the end of the letter, she wrote the words that pierced my heart:

"By the way, Cousin Horace stopped by yesterday to invite us to the wedding of their Lucinda to William Claymire, one of the Yardley County Invincibles, who is home on furlough. I suppose we will have to go, although to tell you the truth I have never cared all that much for Lucinda. She always seemed such a silly, shallow girl to me."

My captivating, lovely Lucinda married to "Billy Boy" Claymire? How could she give herself to such a loud-mouthed lout?

So it was a very downcast Jackson Mundy who sat at his desk on the second floor of the War Department building a few days later, composing a letter on Secretary Randolph's behalf to a North Carolina contractor who had complained he could not find the iron to manufacture the bayonets he had agreed to supply the army, when Colonel Bledsoe put his head in the writing room to say, "Mundy, you are summoned to present yourself at the State Department."

"What for? Who would want to see me there?"

"I don't know what for. All I know is that Mr. Benjamin himself has sent for you."

Had it not been for my lame foot, I would have skipped like a schoolboy over to the Old Treasury Building on Main Street where the State Department was housed. Secretary Benjamin must have remembered my writing skills and now wished to employ me in his department. That had to be it. I was ready for anything to escape the tedious rut in which I seemed trapped, anything to take my mind off of my loss of Lucinda to William Claymire.

At the top of the stairs on the second floor of the building, I told my name to a clerk, who ushered me directly into the office of Mr. Benjamin himself.

Wearing his usual faint smile, the man they called "the brains of the Confederacy" looked up from his desk. And in front of him, with his back to the door and the cuff of his right sleeve pinned to his shoulder, sat Col. Evan Martin.

PART THREE

ONE

London, England
October 5, 1862

Dear Father, Mother, Sisters Emmaline and Mary Bell, and Mattie:

I trust that my hastily written letter of September 15, from Wilmington, reached you. You must find it hard to believe, as did I, that Colonel Martin would choose me as his personal secretary for this mission to Great Britain, but here we are, happily ensconced in a narrow, three-storied house "in" (as the English say) Bishopsgate, not far from the magnificent St. Paul's Cathedral.

Just after I wrote to you from Wilmington, Colonel Martin learned that a blockade runner was taking on tobacco and cotton to slip past the Union fleet and over to Bermuda and that it would be leaving that very night, that is on September 16.

We boarded the Varina *late that afternoon. Painted a dull gray, she is a long, sleek, narrow-beamed side-wheeler with two low, backward raked stacks. Her hold was filled with hogsheads of tobacco and her deck was jammed with bales of cotton.*

The captain, a hearty Englishman on leave from the British navy, provided us with a so-called stateroom, which was little more than a broom closet. His crew is drawn from every nationality except American. They had already fired the boilers with anthracite (or hard) coal, which burns without leaving a trail of telltale smoke.

While it was still daylight, they cast off their lines and turned the sharp bow down the Cape Fear River, past Fort Fisher's high, sandy ramparts guarding the wide entrance into the river, and then dropped anchor to wait for full dark. Near midnight, we raised anchor and, with all lights extinguished and canvas flung over the paddlewheels to muffle the noise, steamed without incident until dawn, by which time we were more than fifty miles at sea.

Only after we were well clear of land and Yankee blockaders did I fully realize what was happening to me, who, until this war came along, had never been more than a hundred miles from Glenwood. Only after we were at sea did Colonel Martin reveal to me our true mission, which I will tell you in the strictest confidence.

As you know, we have emissaries in both England and France buying arms and arranging for shipping through the blockade. There we have been successful, as I am well aware from my War Department work. Also, we have agents working abroad to sway public opinion to our side, and there we have not been so successful, mainly because the European mind does not appreciate the place of "the peculiar institution" of slavery in our Southern way of life. I fear that the opinions of many have been soured by the literary efforts of Mrs. Stowe and others of her abolitionist stripe.

As Colonel Martin explained it to me, our mission is timed to coincide with certain pending military events. The mighty Robert E. Lee, in leading his superb army across the Potomac into Maryland, was to press on across that state into Pennsylvania and there, on northern soil, seek a spectacular victory. And, as a supplement to this invasion, General Bragg was marshalling a force to move across Tennessee and into Kentucky.

To make a long story short, Secretary of State Benjamin assigned Colonel Martin to employ his English background and military understanding to capitalize on our anticipated successes on northern soil by persuading influential persons in England—in particular, newspaper editors—that victory for the Confederacy is inevitable, thereby winning European recognition for our cause.

My perception of the importance of our mission was

clouded initially by a miserable attack of seasickness that overcame me the first morning out from Wilmington. As the old joke goes, the only thing that kept me alive was the hopes of dying, so bad did I feel. My ailment did not cease until three days later when we sighted the northern headland of Bermuda.

A Bermudian pilot came aboard and guided us into the picturesque harbor of St. George, which we found crowded with freighters from England and blockade runners like the Varina. We disembarked and walked up the hill to the Globe Hotel which serves as headquarters for the C.S.A. Agent, Maj. Norman Walker.

While Colonel Martin and Major Walker conferred, I strolled about the waterfront. The war has transformed Bermuda from a sleepy backwater into a tropical emporium where freighters from England unload medicine, salt, to-bacco, cloth, weapons and gunpowder, as well as various luxury items, and take on tobacco, cotton and other Southern commodities for shipment back to England. St. George's narrow streets are jammed with throngs of sailors and get-rich-quick merchants, just like Wilmington. It disgusts me to witness the profiteering that goes on while our boys and men are dying on the battlefield, but that is another story.

That night we rode with Major Walker and his young wife in a buggy to the home of another Confederate representative, a Mr. Bourne. At dinner, the two couples listened in fascination as Colonel Martin, in his eloquent way, described life in Richmond and told of his experiences in the Seven Days' Battles. I, in turn, was fascinated by Mr. Bourne's explanation of how the blockade runners operate. It is his job to pay the captains for their service. Lured by payments of $5,000 in gold or pounds sterling for a single run to Wilmington and back, many, like the captain of the Varina, have taken leaves of absence from the British navy.

The Bournes kindly put us up for the night. We slept under mosquito netting with the sweet odor of frangipani wafting through the open windows. Back in St. George the next morning, we went shopping for pens and ink and several reams of lined writing paper, which are scarce items back in Richmond. That night we went aboard a large steam-and-

sail freighter, the Mollie Brown, *to be ready for an early morning departure.*

We had barely set our heading for Southampton when the Colonel told me more about our mission and put me to work. My job is to help him produce unsigned articles, or in his words, "aides' memoirs," about various aspects of the war, for publication in English periodicals. Naturally, Colonel Martin cannot write with his untrained left hand, so he started out dictating them to me.

The work went very slowly at first. I was, and still am, surprised by this remarkable man's grasp of the details of the war, although he sometimes has difficulty expressing his thoughts in a comprehensible, well-organized form.

He knew the subjects he wished to cover: the methods by which Stonewall Jackson's men are able to march thirty miles a day; the education and character of Robert E. Lee; the military experience of Jefferson Davis as a former U.S. secretary of war; the constitution and organization of the Confederate government; the role of slaves in freeing up white manpower for military service; and an analysis of the Seven Days' Battles that saved Richmond.

Finally, he gave up trying to dictate his thoughts word for word. He merely talked freely, while I took notes. When he faltered, I would jog his memory with questions. Later, my seasickness only an unpleasant memory, I turned the information he had provided into comprehensible articles.

As you know from my letters, I was impressed by Colonel Martin from our acquaintance at Mrs. Selby's boarding house, but I realize now that I was seeing only his surface attainments. Beneath his easy charm and handsome appearance, he truly is a man of rare talents, talents which I would say approach genius. I am ashamed that I did not defend him when our dreadful landlady called him an opportunist who used people and cast them aside when they had served his purposes. It is an honor beyond my greatest expectations for him to have chosen me to serve as what he calls "my new right arm." He has given me the opportunity of a lifetime. I admire him more than any man I ever met.

The colonel does not suffer fools gladly, however. I made the mistake of asking if his selection by Secretary Benjamin *for this mission were not the culmination of his dreams. He nearly bit my head off for my impertinence, saying, "Don't be ridiculous. My preference would have been to lead a brigade or division, perhaps, even an army, in battle. But a soldier's first duty is to obey his orders, and mine are to return to England."*

I am not offended by his touchiness for I appreciate that he has not fully recovered from the amputation of his arm. Some nights aboard the Mollie Brown *I was awakened by his grinding his teeth in pain and moaning, until finally he would rise and fumble for his draught of laudanum, after which he would fall into a deep slumber, snoring on long past sunup.*

Father, this assignment means more to me than you and Mother may understand. I think that I have found my life's vocation. It is journalism. At sea, the pieces streamed from my pen at the rate of one or two a day. With each article, I have become surer of myself and my ability. I can just hear Mattie saying "That boy is getting too big for his breeches," so I will stop tooting my own horn and tell you a bit about our arrival.

Bermuda had appeared strange to me, but cool, damp England seemed even stranger at first. All my life I have read about the land of our ancestors, but reading is nothing like the experience of being here and listening to the rich accents of the people and seeing how they live.

In Southampton, the Colonel took a hack which hauled us and our belongings to the train station. Before I could catch my breath, we were riding in a first class coach with padded seats, on our way to London. What a contrast that ride was as compared with the hard seats and slow progress of our trip on a patched-up Richmond & Petersburg train down to Wilmington.

As we passed through the Southampton station, the Colonel bought a newspaper just arrived from New York. It contained a bulletin about Jackson's capture of Harper's Ferry. Wasn't that something? We bagged 15,000 Yankee prisoners, according to the paper. We read also that McClellan once more heads the Federal Army and that a major battle was expected in Maryland.

The colonel agreed with me that this was, indeed, welcome news, but he expressed his regret that the war might be over before he could realize his dream of leading a brigade or division in battle.

In London, we took temporary lodgings in a small hotel on Neale Street, near Covent Garden. The very next day, the ever-resourceful colonel began his rounds of the newspapers. Dressed in a suit of Confederate gray, almost like a uniform, and with his empty right sleeve pinned up, he cuts a picturesque figure. Journalists are vying for the opportunity to interview him. The articles that I wrote on the way over are appearing under various names. The colonel gets many invitations to dinner, one of them from a Confederate sympathizer willing to rent us this furnished three-story house. I have set up an office on the first floor and continue to spin out articles.

Dear family, I thought Richmond a large and bustling metropolis, but it cannot compare with London. I am in love with this city. Just to go stumping about its streets thrills me. But my work keeps me too tied down for much of that.

I must close. We have just received two pieces of news whose import I cannot yet evaluate. A New York newspaper dated September 22 just arrived, claiming that Lee's army has retired across the Potomac after a fierce one-day engagement near Sharpsburg, Maryland on September 17. And the colonel has received a letter from his wife in Liverpool. She and their daughter wish to join him here in London, and he seems distracted by this news. He never talks about them, so I do not know what to expect.

Meanwhile, I am safe and happy here in this queen of all cities.

Love to you all, Jackson.

P.S. Did Cousin Lucinda really marry William Claymire? He was at the academy with Fitz and me. Mother, I never regarded Cousin Lucinda as "shallow and silly," but I cannot say the same for her groom. It is none of my business, but I fear she has thrown herself away in marrying such an oaf.

TWO

• • • While the colonel and I waited with trepidation for the next report from America, the demand for our articles and company intensified. Since the colonel was away so often, I was forced to write my own material from scratch, which, to my pleasant surprise, came easily.

One afternoon as I was composing an article on the ineffectiveness of the Federal blockade, I heard carriage wheels halt in front of the house and then a knock. I opened the door and there stood a tall, handsome red-haired woman and a girl.

The woman's cold blue eyes made a critical appraisal of my person before she said in a haughty English accent, "Good day, young man. I am Mrs. Martin. Is my husband here?"

I explained that he was away on business, and then introduced myself as his assistant.

"His assistant?" She seemed skeptical. "Ah, then you will not object if we come in and wait."

I led them into the drawing room of the rented house and opened the drapes. She and the girl seated themselves.

I apologized for having no refreshments to offer. She looked as though she might have declined if I had.

"So you are Evan's assistant? Exactly what do you assist him with?"

I explained our work as discreetly and succinctly as I could.

"Not to put too fine a point on it, you are propagandists for the Southern slavocracy, I take it."

"Not at all," I protested. "We are trying to show the British public that the Confederate States of America is a legitimate nation with its own responsible government, that is all."

"Indeed. And this so-called government has made Evan a colonel of propaganda?"

"Oh, ma'am," I replied. "He holds a genuine military commission. He commanded a regiment in battle—"

"I am sure he will tell me all about that. But don't let us keep you from your work. . . ."

My attention had been so fixed on Mrs. Martin that I did not look closely at her daughter until I was leaving the room. About fifteen, she had dark hair and eyes. When she smiled at me, two dimples appeared.

Hearing the colonel at the front door, I intercepted him in the hall to tell him that his wife and daughter were waiting in the drawing room.

The colonel seemed flustered for a moment, then examined his image in the hall mirror, ran his fingers through his beard, straightened his coat, and opened the drawing room door, leaving me outside, listening.

"Miriam, my dear. And Sarah, how you have grown."

"What has happened to you, Evan? Where is your arm?"

"My dear, I did not want to cause you concern, but as you can see, I was wounded."

"You have gotten yourself maimed. And that awful beard!"

"Mama, don't be cruel. Oh, Papa. I am so sorry. I have missed you dreadfully."

"Why did you not write me about your disfigurement?"

"Now, Miriam. Are you not glad to see your husband?"

"Yes, Mama, give Papa a kiss. Our family is together again."

During the few days we had occupied the house, the colonel and I had been taking our meals, usually separately, at cafes and hotels. The colonel seemed to have plenty of money. Although I drew no salary, I was given a living allowance.

Mrs. Martin quickly took over the household. By the next

day, a cook had been installed in the kitchen and a parlor maid employed. And the colonel had shaved off his beard.

I got to know Miriam Martin better than I wished during the next year, and my memories of her are not pleasant. She continued to treat me with the sort of disdain that only certain British women can manage. I tried to like the woman but gave up the effort after overhearing her telling her husband one day that she wished "your assistant would learn to speak our language properly. I can't bear that atrocious accent."

I was standing in the hall, about to enter the drawing room with the latest New York newspapers, when I heard this.

"My dear, Mundy is a well-educated young man from a prominent family. He is a talented writer, as well."

"I don't wonder that you like him. He fawns on you like a spaniel. Let me tell you that if your objective is to sway public opinion, I must wonder what sort of impression the two of you make. A one-armed so-called colonel and a club-footed secretary who talks as though he has a mouthful of porridge."

Ordinarily my feelings might have been hurt by her harsh judgment, but the importance of a story in the newspapers I bore outweighed the opinion of one discontented woman. And whatever sting her words might have caused were erased in the following seconds. Just as I raised my hand to knock, I heard a voice behind me saying softly, "Mr. Mundy."

As I turned, Sarah put her finger to her lips and whispered, "You must not mind Mama. She says hateful things sometimes, but she does not mean them. I find the way you talk charming."

And she flashed me a radiant smile.

"You are most kind, Miss Martin."

"Please call me Sarah. I would like for us to be friends. Is that possible?"

"Yes, oh my, yes. I would like nothing better. And please call me Jackson."

Whereupon I entered the drawing room and gave the newspaper to the colonel.

It was bad news. The battle of Antietam, as the Federals called the engagement near Sharpsburg, Maryland, was now reported to have been the bloodiest single day's fighting in the war, some 12,000 or 13,000 casualties on each side. Although Lee had stood with his back to the Potomac and fought off each of McClellan's several attacks, he had been forced to pull his army back into Virginia, thereby writing finis to his invasion of the North. But the Federals were calling this tactical draw a great strategic victory, and Lincoln had taken the occasion to announce that at the end of the year he would declare all slaves in Confederate territories to be free.

Colonel Martin now had his work cut out for him. I was kept too busy concocting responses to this ploy of Lincoln's to brood over whether Mrs. Martin liked or despised me. Anyway, her scorn was more than balanced out by the knowledge that her lovely, sweet daughter valued my friendship.

My love affair with London deepened each week of my residence in that marvelous city. It was a short way from our house to St. Paul's Cathedral. After services I liked to walk down to the Embankment and stroll beside the Thames. I also became a habitué of the book stalls in Charing Cross.

The colonel made one attempt at entertaining at home, but his wife put a damper on the occasion by making sarcastic remarks about the Confederacy to our newspaper editor guests. Thereafter he did his official entertaining outside the home. However, Mrs. Martin saw to it that he ate well at their regular meals, which I shared with the family.

The colonel soon hit upon a new idea for us to earn our keep and that was for me to write articles for the Richmond and Charleston papers about the English reaction to the war in America. I prepared these for his scrutiny and he then sent them back under his own name via Bermuda and Wilmington. Not everything we sent got through the blockade, but that which did was well received.

An English journalist, learning that I was the author of the articles the colonel handed out to London and provincial papers, invited me to attend a Saturday evening house dinner in Drury Lane, sponsored by a new literary gentlemen's club whose members called themselves "the Savages." There I ate a splendid meal and afterwards enjoyed a program which included comic vocalists and imitations of politicians.

It was one of the most pleasant evenings of my life, but I drank too much wine. At the encouragement of my new journalist friend, I mounted a table and recited Marc Antony's "Friends, Romans, Countrymen" speech from Shakespeare's *Julius Caesar*.

The next morning, awakening with a splitting headache, I shuddered to think what a fool I had made of myself. My fears were baseless. The Savages had been so taken with my Southern elocution that soon thereafter, I received an invitation to become a member of the club and through it developed a small circle of friends of my own.

I cherish the memory of a Savage meeting at which the celebrated Charles Dickens himself came as a guest and read from his latest book, *Great Expectations*. I summoned the courage to speak to the author, who gravely shook my hand and said that he was pleased that I liked his novels so much. Although I cannot recall his exact words, he appeared to favor the Confederate cause, or perhaps I should have said he criticized the Northern side's behavior toward the South. My conversation with Mr. Dickens pleased me mightily, as did my report of our meeting to Colonel Martin.

Sarah Martin was much amused that I had become a Savage. "No one could be less savage than you, dear Jackson," she said.

That Christmas was only the second I had ever spent away from home. On Christmas eve, I accompanied the Martins in a carriage down to Trafalgar Square to sing carols. At one point, when her parents' attention was diverted, Sarah took my hand and leaned her head against my shoulder. No female outside my own family circle had ever shown me such affection and it went to my head very much like the wine with which the Savages had plied me.

Thereafter London became a magic city for me, and Sarah Martin a magic person in my life. I had never been happier.

In my mind, the war had faded into an abstraction. Three thousand miles away, across the Atlantic, the fate of the American nation was being decided by real men carrying real weapons, by flesh-and-blood men enduring hardships in camps and facing the threat of death and dismemberment on battlefields stretching from Virginia across Tennessee and beyond the Mississippi. Both north and south of the Mason-Dixon line, factory workers toiled to produce muskets, cannon, tents, blankets, uniforms, canteens and other military paraphernalia. In capital cities separated by a mere hundred miles of increasingly bloody ground, officials of the two rival governments conferred with military leaders through anxious nights about the conduct of the vast and growing war. More than three million human beings of African descent remained in bondage, the civilization to which I had been born resting upon their backs. But to me, happily spewing out empty words in London, the war had become something as remote from reality as a Sir Walter Scott novel.

THREE

• • • Our New Year's day was much cheered by reports in the New York papers of a great Confederate victory on December 13 at Fredericksburg in Virginia. Once again the colonel and I churned out articles touting the military superiority of the Southern soldier and his commanders. This helped somewhat to offset the Emancipation Proclamation's effect on the English.

Mrs. Martin made much of this proclamation.

"It exposes the hollowness of your cause," she said to the colonel at dinner.

"Not at all my dear. It exposes the speciousness of Lincoln's coercion of the South. Note that he does not offer to free the slaves in Maryland, Kentucky or Missouri. No, those states have not left the Union. He declares slaves to be free only in those states controlled by the Confederacy."

"It sickens me to hear you defend slavery. I saw a slave auction in Mobile. It is a spectacle that still haunts me."

My ears perked up at that remark. I had not known that she had ever been in America. I had assumed the Colonel had met her after he moved to England.

Now she was making one of her rare statements to me. "Mr. Mundy, your father is an owner of slaves, is he not?"

"We own five families, about twenty slaves in all," I said.

"So many that you are not sure of the number? And do you buy and sell your human chattel often?"

"My father inherited most of them. He did purchase a husband and wife from the estate of a neighbor when I was a baby. The wife is our family cook, Mattie. She helped rear me. Her husband is our blacksmith and cares for our livestock. His name is Ben. He taught me to hunt and fish, and to ride, also."

"And does your father whip his slaves when they displease him?"

Swallowing my resentment, I said evenly, "My father treats our darkies with great kindness, Mrs. Martin. They are almost like members of our family."

"I expect that he does not whip his horses or dogs, either."

"When I left home, Mattie wept along with my mother and sisters, Mrs. Martin. I fail to see the comparison with horses or dogs."

"Yes," the colonel said. "You are being rather hard on Mundy."

"He says his family cook wept when he left home. How touching. I recall the tears of a slave girl who was being auctioned off in Mobile. I wonder whose tears were the more bitter."

I felt ready to erupt at the woman's calculated rudeness. I was saved further embarrassment by the colonel's excusing ourselves to return to our work.

"You mustn't mind Miriam's remarks, Mundy," the colonel said. "She doesn't understand the situation, I fear."

When her mother went out shopping, Sarah would often come into my little office and chat. She was much interested in life in the South. She wanted to know all about Glenwood, our family and the slaves. She also was a great reader of Mr. Dickens's novels and we had many a cosy talk about his characters. She was captivated by my somewhat embellished account of Dickens's visit to the Savage Club and my conversation with the great author.

This charming, unspoiled girl was six years my junior, but in many ways she seemed more mature than I. She loved her father dearly but, it seemed to me, only tolerated her mother.

I mentioned my surprise at learning that her mother had been to America.

"Oh, yes, they were married there, in 1847, in Mobile."

"Are you sure about that? Your father left West Point at

the outbreak of the Mexican War in '46 and the war did not end until 1848."

"I was born January 5, 1848. I don't know anything about the war."

"How did your mother happen to be in Mobile?"

"Grandfather went there on business. He imports cotton, or he did until your war. He took his family, and Mama met Papa, who had just returned from West Point."

I did not further press my inquiry. It would be some time before the confusion of dates was cleared up for me.

I cannot say exactly when I fell hopelessly in love with Sarah Martin. It may have been that time in the hall when she and I overheard her mother ridiculing me. That certainly started the process. Or it may have been when she held my hand at Trafalgar Square. Anyway, by the summer of 1863, I lived for the stolen but innocent moments of her company. Jackson Mundy, who had guarded his heart against Cupid's arrow for fear of being rejected, went weak at his knees and got tears in his eyes when she smiled. But, whereas I had been tongue-tied in the company of Lucinda, I found it easy to speak freely to Sarah. Compared to her, Lucinda was indeed, as Mother said, "a silly, shallow girl."

Neither could I say precisely when Sarah began to reciprocate my feelings. But it was one of the happiest moments in my life when I realized, belatedly, that she felt somewhat the same about me.

The streets of London were much frequented by prostitutes, many of them quite attractive girls from the north of England who had lost their jobs at textile mills closed down by the shortage of cotton from the United States. Although I sometimes stopped to chat with them at night, when I thought no one would recognize me, I declined their offers of "a bit of comfort, dearie." To succumb to the temptation they represented, I felt, would be to despoil my platonic relationship with Sarah Martin.

On the whole, I enjoyed my year in London more than any period in my life. But like all good things, it had to end. The reality of the war back home finally intruded into my dream world across the sea.

Around June 1, 1863, we learned of Lee's smashing victory over the Army of the Potomac at Chancellorsville and a week later of the equally depressing news of the death of Stonewall Jackson as a result of a wound suffered in that epic battle.

"Now is the time," Colonel Martin declared. "Now is the time to invade the North again. Surely, President Davis and General Lee will not let this opportunity pass. We need another victory."

"I should think we had won ourselves time," I replied.

"By we, I meant you and I and our mission. Our funds will not hold out much longer and it is unlikely that the State Department will replenish our coffers."

Our mission and the Confederate cause were dealt a double blow toward the end of July when the New York newspapers arrived telling of Lee's defeat at Gettysburg, Pennsylvania, July 1–3 and of the almost simultaneous surrender of Vicksburg. Each fresh report from New York further dashed our hopes that English public opinion would swing our way and that the British government would recognize the Confederate States of America. Lee's losses at Gettysburg exceeded those in the Seven Days' Battles, and the South was beginning to scrape the bottom of the manpower barrel. U. S. Grant's capture of Vicksburg and its large garrison opened the Mississippi River for northern boat traffic and split the Confederacy in two.

I hated Mrs. Martin for the way she gloated over these reports. But she went too far at breakfast one morning.

"Surely, Evan," she said, "you will give up your so-called commission now and settle down to a responsible job. You are a fool if you do not. The South is beaten."

"I have taken an oath of loyalty," he replied.

"Like the Federal oath you took in 1846?"

"Why do you say things you know will hurt me?"

"It is good for you to hear the truth. You have always chosen to believe myths."

"Enough of that now, my dear. We can discuss it later."

"I will not be told to keep quiet."

He arose and threw his napkin on the table. "And I will

not be humiliated at my own table in the presence of my assistant and my daughter."

He strode from the room. The front door slammed. Mrs. Martin sat for a moment, with a look of fury on her face, then quit the room, leaving Sarah and me alone at the table.

"I am sorry about my parents, Jackson."

"Please don't apologize. I suppose every married couple has their differences. . . ."

"Mama and Papa have nothing in common. I think that is their problem."

"Has it always been so between them?"

"Mama always acts disappointed in him, no matter what he does. He was in business with Grandfather, you know, in the cotton importing business. But there was a dispute of some sort and soon after that Papa left for America."

"Oh? And your mother did not wish him to go?"

"Certainly not. They had a dreadful quarrel. She called him a coward who ran away from his problems instead of facing them. Papa broke down and cried. It was terrible to hear him crying. I was afraid he would never return to us. He never wrote us a line from America, you know. We only heard from him when he got back here in London."

Thereafter the atmosphere at mealtimes was civil but strained. To fill the awkward silences, Sarah chattered about her studies and books she was reading, while I sat in silent adoration.

My health began to falter as that summer of 1863 faded. I was often confined to my bed with chest colds, which the doctor attributed to the London fog and dampness.

Exhausted from a fit of coughing, I was lying in my little room on the third floor with my eyes closed one afternoon, when the colonel opened the door without knocking.

"We have important news from Richmond," he said.

He held a letter with a broken seal.

"Have they sent us fresh money? Is our assignment to be continued?"

"No, we are ordered to return."

I was puzzled by the exultant look in his eyes. "I am sorry. I like it here so very much."

"It is all right. I have been notified that my promotion to brigadier general has been confirmed. The War Department asks that I return to Richmond to serve as an advisor to President Davis. Isn't that the grandest news you ever heard? I am to become a brigadier general at last."

Our English friends gave us a grand going away dinner at a gentlemen's club in St. James Place. The colonel, or rather the general, had let slip the news of his promotion. Many toasts were drunk to his good health "and that of his worthy assistant." The general drank far more of the grape than he should have, and so did I. Singing "Dixie" and "The Bonnie Blue Flag," we rode back to our house in a hansom. A disapproving Mrs. Martin and Sarah came to the door in their nightgowns. It took the three of us to help the general up the stairs and into bed.

During all this Sarah held her hand over her mouth and giggled. I stood outside in the hall with her while Mrs. Martin remonstrated with her husband.

Perhaps it was the wine, but at any rate I summoned all my courage and said, "Sarah, I am sorry. . . ."

"About what, Jackson?"

"About having to return."

"I am sorry, too. It has been wonderful having dear Papa back again, and having you with us, too."

It was now or never. I drew her away from the door of her parents' bedroom and out of the sound of her mother's strident voice.

"I know that you are only fifteen," I began.

"Almost sixteen," she replied.

"But I am twenty-two now, and Sarah, our war in America can't last forever. I am not so sure anymore that the South will win, but however it comes out, I know one thing."

"What is that, Jackson?"

"I want to return here to England someday."

"Oh, I do hope that you will."

"And I hope that you will wait for me."

"Wait for you, Jackson?"

For a moment I feared that I had gone too far, but damn it, I could not hold back the words any longer.

"Is it too much to hope that one day you might marry me?"

She took both my hands in hers, stood on her tiptoes, and kissed me lightly on the lips.

"You are the kindest, sweetest boy I have ever known. I can't promise to marry anyone just now . . . let's wait and see."

Her mother was coming. There was nothing for me to do but limp off to my own bedroom. At least Sarah had not turned me down.

The next morning, as I was dressing, I heard the Martins quarrelling downstairs. I cracked my door open and heard:

"General? So you call yourself a general now?"

"Damn it, Miriam, I am a brigadier general in the Confederate army. You have seen my commission."

"And because you are a general, you now feel it your duty to once more desert your wife and child. Once again you are to throw us back on the charity of my poor father in Liverpool."

"Your father is far from poor, Miriam, and you know it."

"I also know the shame I feel depending on his charity. He tried to warn me that you would never settle down at anything worthwhile."

"Your father may feel differently when he hears that his son-in-law has become a brigadier."

Her voice changed to a more conciliatory tone. "Look, Evan, you have sacrificed your arm to the Confederacy. You have done as well as could be expected in advancing its cause. Father would forgive you for the missing funds, he would let bygones be bygones and take you back into the business, if he thought you were giving up a generalship to remain here. I will make the overture. Won't you at least consider doing that?"

"Trade an opportunity like this to return to a cotton brokerage office in Liverpool? Don't be ridiculous."

"Is it not far more ridiculous to abandon your family in pursuit of a childish dream for military glory, and in service of a threadbare, doomed way of life?"

"Let's get something straight, Miriam, about what you call 'the missing funds.' I used company money in what turned out to be an unwise speculation. Your father would have been glad enough if the investment had lived up to its promise. As for my personal ambitions, I gave up one opportunity for military attainment when I followed you back to England. If you had remained in Mobile and waited while I went to Mexico—"

"What? You would have come back as a captain and done what? Continued as an army officer? Returned to West Point? That is your notion of glory? Don't be silly."

They lowered their voices when they heard my footsteps on the stairs. By noon, we had completed our packing.

Mrs. Martin's father, whom I never got to meet, had arranged to send a carriage for her and Sarah the next day. As our own hired hack waited at the curb, Mrs. Martin suffered herself to be embraced and kissed by her husband.

Sarah slipped a note into my hand and whispered, "Dear Jackson, I shall miss you. Don't read this until you have boarded your ship, promise?"

"I promise. And I shall miss you, Sarah."

"And I shall miss you. Please look after my poor Papa."

The general turned and put his arm around his daughter. "Now, kitten, be a good girl. Look after your mother. You will be proud of your papa when you hear what he has done in America."

"I am already proud of you, Papa."

"Evan?"

"Yes, Miriam?"

"Your post with Davis will keep you out of danger, I hope."

"I have never heard of an advisor getting killed, Miriam."

"Well, that is some consolation. I shall miss you, even if you are a fool."

As our hack neared the end of the street, I looked back. Mrs. Martin was holding her handkerchief to her eyes. Sarah's merry face wore a smile and she blew first one kiss and then another.

God protect me if Martha Jane should ever read these words, for she can be fiercely jealous, but I carried that image of Sarah Martin in my heart for many a year, long after the war had ended and even after my own marriage. Indeed, I carry it still.

FOUR

• • • True to my promise, I did not open Sarah's letter until the ship had cleared Southampton Harbor and was steaming through the Solent past the Isle of Wight. Every word she had written was like a precious gift. I read and re-read that letter all the way across the Atlantic, until the pages came apart, by which time I knew it by heart.

My dear sweet Jackson:

You must not let Papa see this letter. I am not sure he would approve and I know Mama would not.

I am very sad that you are leaving us. You have become the best friend I ever had and I shall miss you even more than I shall miss poor Papa.

This past year has been the happiest in my life, partly because our family has been together again but also because you have been here. Haven't we had some wonderful talks? Every night when I went to bed I looked forward to seeing you the next morning.

We have never spoken of your poor foot and I would not mention it now, but Papa has said that he thinks it bothers you more than you may realize yourself. He says you have a very bright mind and that you would have made a splendid soldier.

Well, I just want you to know that although I think you are handsome, I like you for your true self and not for your outward appearance, and I want you to know also that it is my fondest hope that you will return to England after the

*war so we can resume our friendship and see where it might
lead us.*

*I have been thinking a lot about what friendship means,
because as you know, Mama and Papa have not been acting
very friendly toward each other. I would never marry a man
if he and I were not first good friends who could talk to each
other in an easy way as you and I have been doing.*

*I wish my parents were really good friends. It makes me
sad when they quarrel. It is mostly Mama's fault, of course.
She is always so critical of Papa. She wants him to be rich
and successful. Grandfather, also, has been very hard on
Papa. I wonder sometimes if Papa isn't trying to earn their
respect with all this soldier business.*

*Please write to me when you get to America. And don't
forget your promise to return to England after your war is
over in America.*

Love, Sarah

It had never occurred to me that I might be attractive to the
fair sex, and here I had received a letter from a lovely young
girl in which she seemed to stop just short of accepting my
drunken proposal of marriage.

I developed a fever that night, caused in part perhaps by
excitement over Sarah's profession of, if not love, at least an
affectionate friendship. My chest cold turned much worse
and I remained in my bunk. The freighter's doctor listened
to my cough and diagnosed the trouble as pleurisy.

Sick or well, "the general," as he now wanted to be called,
was determined to complete a number of written memoranda
for President Davis and Secretary Benjamin before we
reached Bermuda. So while I lay abed with my note pad, the
General paced back and forth, dictating his thoughts on various subjects having to do with the war.

"Lincoln hopes to make slavery the Achilles heel of the
Confederacy, and I must admit that the masses of Europe
find the institution a stumbling block to official recognition.
Yet, paradoxically, the slave population of the Confederacy
is a great asset, providing labor which frees the white male
population for military service. Now that the white male population is being depleted, why not strike a double blow

against the Northern government by enlisting Negroes in the Confederate army?"

I was able to turn these rambling ideas into a cogent, thoughtful memo which the general said he intended to present to President Davis. In the memorandum, freedom would be offered as a reward for faithful military service. Also, it was suggested that the Confederate government compensate slave owners for the loss of their property.

The general had an idea for the rapid movement of troops which I found intriguing. He suggested that each army collect a train of light wagons, each to be drawn by two mules, and that the packs and weapons of soldiers be transported in these vehicles, and that the troops themselves take turns riding.

He calculated that soldiers would be able to travel much faster and longer that way. They would arrive on the battlefield in fresh condition, ready to fight, and in greater numbers, since straggling would be reduced.

He also suggested much wider use of mounted infantry. He argued for the formation of several "strike forces" of 3–5,000 mounted troops, each of which would conduct small invasions of the North, raiding targets such as Pittsburgh, Baltimore and Indianapolis. And he wanted to flood the North with saboteurs who would destroy railroad bridges and set fires to docks and any other facility that aided the Northern war effort.

Each morning he would pace back and forth, dictating these memoranda. Each afternoon, I would struggle from my bunk and turn them into comprehensible form.

I was impressed by the scope of the general's thinking and the fertility of his mind. His ideas and his way of expressing them continued to excite my admiration.

However, as we neared Bermuda, his imagination seemed to slacken. He acted depressed. At night I could hear him grinding his teeth and thrashing about in his bunk.

"General," I asked one night, "are you in pain?"

"Yes, damn it. My arm still hurts."

"Have you no more laudanum?"

"I am giving up the stuff. I purposely brought none with me. Mind your own business and go back to sleep."

The general must have regretted his rudeness, for the next day he went out of his way to praise my work.

That night he obtained a bottle of brandy from the ship's doctor and proceeded to drink it in our cabin. He started out talking rationally about the war and his ambitions now that he was a brigadier.

The more he talked, and the more he drank, the more his speech became slurred.

"Know something, Mundy, you're a pretty smart young fellow."

"Thank you, sir."

"No, no, I mean you see things other people miss. I mean it. You put things in my memo . . . memoranderums. I mean memoranda, which is it? Anyway, things I know but don't say just right . . ."

"The ideas are always your own, sir."

"You see things . . ."

He paused to replenish his glass.

"Fer instance, you know my wife and me, we don't see eye to eye about my military career."

"Yes, sir, I will not deny that I am aware of that."

"Don't misjudge Miriam, Mundy. Don't. She was a beautiful girl. Met her in Mobile after I came back from West Point. I was helping raise a company to go and fight the Mexicans. The men elected me captain. I was nineteen, and they chose me to be their captain. What do you think of that?"

"That is remarkable, sir."

"Poor Miriam. Hate to go off and leave her back in England. Out of the question for her and little Sarah to come along. You can see that, can't you?"

Trying not to think of how pleasant it would be with Sarah accompanying us, I said, "It would be very hard on them."

He drained off his glass and stared at the bottle. I saw that he was getting drunk but did not interfere, thinking we both would sleep better that night with him intoxicated.

"Didn't want to leave her in '46, either."

"When you had to go off to Mexico?"

He looked at me as though he did not comprehend, then continued, "See, Miriam's parents did not approve her marrying an American, particularly an American with no money, no family except for an uncle . . ."

He seemed to lose his concentration for a moment.

"Did she wait while you went to Mexico?"

He looked at me in a way that made me wish I had not asked the question.

"Her parents wanted her to return with them to England, without me." He laughed harshly and wiped his mouth. "We got married anyway, without their permission."

"And then you went on to Mexico?"

"Why you keep talking about Mexico? I didn't go to Mexico."

"What about the company you help raise? I thought they elected you as their captain."

"Had to chose between Miriam and Mexico. Don't dare ever tell this, damn your eyes. Sneaked aboard ship . . . the ship Miriam and her parents were taking back to England. After we got to sea, I came up from the hold."

He laughed, now bitterly, and lifted the bottle to his lips, draining it.

"Should have seen her father's face when I appeared, but what in the hell could he do? Son of a bitch never forgave me. I'll show him though, God damn it. He'll see. Accused me of stealing from his precious company. Treats me like dirt. I'll show him and Miriam, too."

He swept his bottle and glass from the table, and lurched to his feet. Fearful that he would fall onto the broken glass, I took his elbow and helped him to his bunk. He collapsed into it and put his hand over his eyes.

"What would I do without you, Mundy?"

"Oh, you would do fine, sir."

"Mundy, tell me. You think I can get along in Richmond? Lee was advisor to Davis before Seven Pines, remember? Then Johnston was wounded and Lee took over the army. You think Davis would promote me if same thing happened to Lee? Wouldn't that be something? By God, Miriam and her family would snap to attention over that, wouldn't they, Mundy? Wouldn't that be something? By God, I could handle the job, too. Don't you think I could?"

"Yes, sir," I replied. "I expect you could do anything you

put your mind to. Now try to get some sleep."

Later, when I had time to think about them, the general's drunken ramblings helped me make sense of some gaps in his personal history that had puzzled me. But I put his revelations out of my mind and fell asleep imagining a life spent with his daughter.

In my fantasies, the Confederacy reached some sort of negotiated peace with the Federals. Some plan for the gradual empancipation of the slaves would be worked out between the warring sections that would satisfy even the Miriam Martins of the world. And I would become an international correspondent for an English newspaper, and would return to London and claim the hand of Sarah Martin in marriage. Her mother, seeing my success, would realize how wrong her appraisal of me had been. The general would welcome me into his family as the son he never had. I would be a warm and tender husband to Sarah and father to our children.

I do not think the General remembered what he had said to me that night. Now I understood why he did not talk about the Mexican War. He had chosen love over duty, and, it seemed, he now was trying to rectify his mistake, if mistake it was. Anyway, I was too ill to brood over his revelations. Back in the harbor at St. George, the General had me carried directly from the freighter to the blockade runner that would transport us back into Wilmington.

I asked one of the sailors who carried my litter what had happened to the *Varina*.

"She was run aground by the blockaders just last month. The crew set her afire to keep the Federals from capturing her."

"Too bad. What happened to the captain and the crew?"

"They got ashore. She had made so many trips she paid for herself several times over. But it's getting tougher and tougher. The Federals have tightened up the blockade considerable. We're having trouble finding hard coal to burn so our smoke don't give us away."

Just as the sailor warned, it was not so easy to get through the blockade anymore. Our narrow little blockade runner lay to in a heavy sea, with the North Carolina coast barely discernible on the horizon until nightfall, and then, with all lights extinguished, started feeling its way toward the entrance to Cape Fear. I covered my face with a pillow when I had to cough. The general talked in a low voice.

"I just had an idea. You'll have to write this up for me tomorrow before we take train to Richmond. We ought to arm a few fast side-wheelers with lightweight rifled Whitworth guns. They are small caliber but they can throw a bolt up to five miles. We could annoy the blockaders from their seaward side and distract them while our blockade runners slip past."

Suddenly the ship's engines stopped throbbing. We lay to, rocking in the swells. Then the engines started again and the ship reversed course. The general went on deck and returned in a few minutes to say, "We blundered into a blockader. We're running back out to sea."

Over the noise of the now-pounding engines, I heard the boom of a cannon from astern. The ship suddenly changed course and again I heard a cannon's boom.

"Not to worry," the general said. "They're firing blindly."

After a third boom, there were no more cannon shots. The engines worked away furiously and by dawn we were out of sight both of the land and the blockading Yankee fleet.

I can recall little about our try the next night, when the ship sneaked into Cape Fear from the south, past Fort Caswell. My fever rose even higher during the night, and much of the time I was out of my head.

They had no room for doctors aboard blockade runners. There was little need for them on a vessel built to flee, not to fight. In my delirium I imagined that Sarah appeared by my bunk, smiling, to bathe my face. Then her mother pushed her aside and glowered down at me.

"Are you sure your father is always kind to your slaves?" I imagined her saying. "How do you know they love you as much as you think they do?"

"Yes. Yes, they do. . . ."

"Keep quiet, for God's sake, Mundy," the general said.

I opened my eyes. The general stood beside my bunk with a cloth and a basin of water.

"Where did Sarah go?"

"Why, we left her in England, do you not remember? Now, keep quiet. We must make no noise."

Somehow, we slipped past the Yankee vessels that night, and the next morning in Wilmington, the general arranged for me to be delivered to a local military hospital.

He said good-bye in a distracted, perfunctory way on the dock as I was being loaded onto an army ambulance.

"When you regain your health, let me hear from you. There should be a place for you in Richmond."

With that, he thanked me for my service, and left me lying on a litter, waiting for a C.S.A. ambulance to haul me away.

I remained in that fetid hospital for a month. The doctor there warned if I did not take a complete rest for the next six months I very likely would develop consumption.

"You have been working hard, haven't you? Under a lot of nervous strain?" he asked.

"I have been too busy to think about that."

"You have a home, a family?"

I told him about Glenwood.

"Then that is the place for you, not Richmond. If you try to return to your post, I wouldn't give two cents for your chances of living for a year. No, home is the place for you, young man."

Before I departed Wilmington, I wrote a long letter to Sarah Martin. In it I professed my great admiration for her and promised to do as she wished, i.e., return to London someday and resume our friendship. I assured her that I, too, regarded friendship as a prime ingredient of a good marriage and, that it pleased me to think that she and I had begun a relationship which might mature into one of lifelong duration. It was a long letter which stopped just short of repeating my drunken proposal of marriage. A blockade runner captain promised to see that my missive got sent on to England from Bermuda.

A chilly November wind was blowing when I boarded a rickety car on the Wilmington & Manchester Railroad, bound for Columbia, South Carolina. The rolling stock of that and the other railroads I rode on for the next three days had deteriorated since I had traveled up to Richmond in June of 1861. There were long delays at Columbia and Atlanta. Confederate soldiers on leave crowded the unheated cars. From some of them I learned that the battle of Gettysburg the previous July had been an even bigger and bloodier affair than it had appeared from the papers I had read in London.

A sergeant with one leg missing below the knee held me riveted with his account of the fighting. "It was a near-fought thing, I tell you. We came damned close to winning her on the afternoon of the second day. Aye God, we would have took Baltimore and Washington if we would of won that fight. The war would be over by now, I reckon."

Even though the South had lost at Gettysburg and Vicksburg, there was much boasting about Bragg's victory at Chickamauga Creek in northern Georgia in September. Now, Bragg had a Federal army under virtual siege at Chattanooga, Tennessee. Everybody I talked to on the trains assumed the Confederacy would win eventually, but in the words of one captain: "It is just taking a little longer than we thought, that's all."

Once again, reality was being rubbed in my face. Except for my train ride from Montgomery to Richmond two and a half years before, I had had very little contact with the lower orders of Southern whites. My family's friends were all well-established planters or local politicians and professional people. Growing up at Glenwood, I had much contact with the slaves who, of course, always treated me with deference. Because I was the only son and handicapped, my family had coddled me. In Richmond and London I had rubbed elbows with educated, even sophisticated people. Now, for the first time, I was forced into intimacy with men who could not read or write, who chewed tobacco and ate raw peanuts with equal gusto, and who expressed themselves in earthy prose.

Strangely, though, I enjoyed their company. They were the real folk of the Confederacy. It was they who were sacrificing their lives and their limbs for the sake of a new nation and, unwittingly, in support of the rights of men like my father to own other human beings. As one of my traveling companions put it, "This is a rich man's war and a poor man's fight, but we're in it, by God, and I don't intend us to lose it."

Those words belong on the tombstone of the Confederacy.

DIED IN A RICH MAN'S WAR AND A POOR MAN'S FIGHT. My admiration for the rare courage of the white yeomanry of the South was quickened by my experiences of that train ride as were also my doubts about my own courage. Sure, I had been eager to go to war at the beginning but was thwarted by my infirmity. Now, as I looked into the faces of my less fortunate fellow Southerners, I wondered whether I would have made a very good soldier. Did I have what it took to fight and suffer? Or had my zeal for war been that of an armchair warrior? I had yet to experience war up close and dirty. My bravery on the battlefield had yet to be tested. Indeed, I had no reason to think that it ever would.

PART FOUR

ONE

• • • "Massa Jackson, over here!"

Ben, towering over the crowd at the station in Yardley City, was waving his hands and shouting to get my attention as I climbed off the train.

"You looking mighty poorly," he said as I shook his hand. "Yo folks been worried sick about you."

I must have been a pretty sorry sight. Mother and my sisters burst into tears when they saw me emerge from the crowd, holding Ben's arm. I could read Father's concern in his eyes. They hurried me home to Glenwood and put me straightway to bed. Old Doctor Long, the same physician who brought me into the world, ordered first a month of complete bed rest and thereafter a regimen of moderate exercise and afternoon naps.

Father had aged more than I expected. Not only did he oversee the plantation, he also had to do patrol duty for the home guard. He had invested all his gold in Confederate bonds written to mature upon the "successful cessation of the war." In order to increase the production of potatoes, corn and other food stuffs, the Confederate government had decreed a ban on growing cotton. Glenwood had used up its supply of salt, so they could no longer cure hams and bacon. Molasses and honey were being substituted for sugar. The slaves had to make do with their old clothing and to go shoeless. My sisters wore dresses made from window drapes and feed sacks. I recalled ruefully the article I had written in London about the ineffectiveness of the Federal blockade.

Even so, I was glad at first to be back in our comfortable old house and the center of attention for everyone from Mattie to the editor of the *Yardley County Leader*, who asked me to write several articles about my experiences in England. In those days the *Leader* was a mighty thin product, so scarce was paper to come by. It was an honor to be allowed to take up part of that precious space along with accounts of battles and lists of the dead and wounded of Yardley County.

As I was looking over the list of local casualties suffered during the Battle of Chattanooga, the name of William Claymire jumped out at me. It was followed by the notation "died of wounds in hospital at Atlanta." I had scarcely thought of him or of Cousin Lucinda since leaving London. As a convalescent, I could have been excused from going with my family to Cousin Horace's house to pay our respects but, partly out of curiosity, I bundled myself up against the chilly weather and went along.

To my surprise, perhaps even disappointment, Lucinda's beauty had not faded. Indeed, her grief had added a touch of needed character to her face, and the blackness of her dress accentuated her fair hair and pale complexion. She really made an attractive-looking young widow.

"Dear Cousin Jackson, it is so thoughtful of you to rise from your sickbed to come," she said after I had mumbled my condolences. "I would so like to hear all about your experiences in England. My poor William once said how much he admired your intellectual attainments."

It was news to me that William Claymire had ever taken any notice of me, but I assured Lucinda that at some appropriate time I would be glad to tell her about my overseas adventures.

On the way home from our visit, Sister Mary Bell slyly asked if I had noticed how lovely Lucinda looked, and, after I had said yes, she inquired whether I had not been "sweet on her before her marriage."

I replied that, if it were any of her business, I had admired Lucinda.

Emmaline giggled, and said, "We always thought so, but Mama would not let us tease you about her."

Mary Bell chimed in with, "Well, the coast will be clear for you now, Jackson."

"Mary Bell!" Mother said. "What a thing to say."

"I meant after a decent period of mourning, Mama. Anyway, the war has changed all that about the proprieties."

"Standards of good manners do not change," Mother said. "Besides, Lucinda is a stupid girl. Jackson is far too intelligent for her."

"You are always going on about how intelligent Jackson is. Do you ever stop to think how that makes Emmaline and I feel?"

"Me," I said. "You should say 'Emmaline and me'. Makes is a verb and it should not be used with a subjective pronoun."

"Oh, listen to the international correspondent. He has learned to put on airs in England, hasn't he? Besides, he is just trying to change the subject."

"Or, perhaps he found himself a girl back in London."

"Yes, Jackson. Tell us about your love life in England."

I kept quiet, but as my sisters chattered away, I wondered what my family would think of Sarah Martin. Although I had never mentioned her to them, she was nearly always in my thoughts.

By the spring of 1864, the color had returned to my cheeks. Ben altered the right stirrup of a saddle to accommodate my special boot and Father turned over Nellie, a gentle mare, to me. I rode about the plantation and supervised the field gangs, but my heart wasn't in my duties, nor was theirs, for I often had to chide them for their slipshod work.

I dreamed of being back in London, in the company of Sarah Martin, yes, and of her father, too, for I missed them both. The slaves presumably dreamed of their freedom for, although they did not read newspapers, it was obvious that the Confederacy was being hard pressed, and they must have known that a Federal victory would end their servitude.

Soon after returning to Glenwood, I wrote to General Martin in Richmond but never received a reply. I often wondered what he thought of the news from the war front. It wasn't very good. Bragg had let slip the advantage he had gained from his costly victory at Chickamaugua Creek; U. S. Grant reinforced the Federal army at Chattanooga and drove Bragg's army into the hills of Georgia. Now the papers told of Bragg's replacement by Joseph E. Johnston, and of U. S. Grant's promotion to commanding general of the Federal armies and of Sherman's elevation to command of an army assigned to take Atlanta.

In May, Grant began his drive on Richmond. Lee balked him in the Wilderness, but instead of retreating as previous Yankee generals had done, Grant moved around Lee's flank and they fought another horrible battle at Spotsylvania Courthouse and yet another at Cold Harbor. Lee inflicted awesome casualties on the Federals, but they filled up their ranks and kept pressing until Richmond and Petersburg came under siege.

I wondered what it was like in the Confederate capital now. Was Mrs. Selby still running her boarding house? How were my fellow clerks in the War Department? Did they like James A. Seddon, who had replaced Randolph as the secretary soon after I left for England? But most of all I wondered how the general was getting on as an advisor to President Davis and what Sarah was doing back in England living with her grandparents. Did she think of me as often as I did of her? Did she daydream of being my wife?

Riding my mare about the lands was good therapy for my chest. In fact, I grew so robust that I thought of returning to my post in Richmond.

Father was aghast at the idea. Mother nearly had hysterics, and my sisters pleaded with me not to go.

"But I feel that I must serve," I said.

"In that case," Father replied, "Let's see about procuring you a commission in the state militia. You can get about well enough on Nellie. And you know how to organize things."

Since the war, people have called me Captain Mundy, the same as if I had been a Confederate officer and not just a militia captain, a sort of inspector for Yardley County's home guard. The honor was not unmerited, I suppose, for I did a good enough job to win a letter of commendation from the governor.

There were Yankee raids and rumors of raids across the northern half of the state but Yardley County, with its deep black soil and fertile plantations, escaped these incursions. The militia gathered for drill every Saturday afternoon. The ranks were filled with men from the ages of seventeen to fifty, many of them able-bodied enough but exempted from conscription by reason of carrying mail routes, teaching school, running printing shops, or owning twenty or more slaves. A few escaped the draft because of real or feigned physical infirmities, but none was as little fit to serve as I. Still, with the use of good old Nellie, I did my bit for the Confederacy, but there was no glory in what I was doing. Certainly my role required little of the courage I had so much admired in General Martin and in the soldiers on my train ride home.

Part of the militia's duties was to round up deserters or men who failed to report for conscription. My heart wasn't in this work, just as theirs increasingly were not in the war itself. They were mostly from families who owned no slaves and who no longer saw any point or justice in fighting to protect the human property of those, like my family, who did.

As I was to discover, slavery was the South's Achilles' heel as well as the root cause of secession and the war itself. And sad to say, we in the South, white as well as black, still suffer from its consequences, and, who knows, perhaps always will.

Even today, as I write these words, that cloud of slavery and the inhumanity of one race toward another still hangs heavy over my head and my conscience.

TWO

• • • My attitude toward the Negroes at Glenwood was benevolent and trusting, as I assumed theirs was toward us. It never occurred to me that, behind those subservient black masks, they might be hiding strong opinions and emotions about their bondage. The scales were removed from my eyes late one night after I had returned from a night patrol with the militia.

Ben came out to the stable to help me unsaddle Nellie and feed and water the mare. When I complained of being weary, he suggested that I leave the care of Nellie to him and take myself off to bed.

To avoid disturbing my family, I removed my boots in the hall and crept in stockinged feet up to my room. But after I had donned my nightgown and lain down, I remembered that I had not eaten since early afternoon. A struggle ensued between hunger and fatigue. At last, hunger won out. I tiptoed down the stairs and out to the kitchen, which was connected by a covered walkway to the rest of the house.

Ben and Mattie enjoyed a special status at Glenwood. They did not occupy a cabin in the slave quarters as did the other Negroes. When Father purchased them he had built a large lean-to across the back of the kitchen for them, and they ate the same food as did our family.

I found a pan of corn bread on the hearth. Mother had an ironclad rule against carrying food to our rooms, so I sat down and leaned my back against the kitchen wall to eat a chunk of the bread.

Although sounds passed easily through the wall, Ben and Mattie must not have heard me sneak into the kitchen. I heard Ben say, "Mattie?"

I was at the point of making a commotion so he would realize that someone was in the kitchen, when he called again, more loudly.

"Mattie?"

"What you want, Ben?" she replied at last.

"You asleep, baby?"

"I wouldn't be answering you if I was."

"I been thinking."

"What about, sweet man?"

"About this war. About the way they treat us, white folks, that is."

Now, I am not by nature an eavesdropper, but suddenly I became one.

"Why, Ben, we is treated better than most. We eats the same thing they do. They girls gets on my nerves sometimes, bossing me around when they so lazy, but that is just the way white folks is."

"I ain't talking about this plantation. I am talking about the general condition of how things is."

"Things is just the way they is. That is the way they always been."

"Yeah, but you know something, Mattie, honey, they try to hide the truth, but the white folks is losing this war. Sooner or later, freedom gonna come."

Now I was frozen to my seat on the hearth. Suddenly my mouth went dry and I could not swallow my corn bread.

"Where you getting notions like that?"

"When I go into Yardley City to pick up the mail and the newspaper, I stop by the livery stable and talk to old Mose. Don't you never breathe a word of this but Mose can read. He can read the newspaper, and he says they fussing and fighting among themselves up in Richmond. He says the Northern armies is getting bigger and stronger every day."

"That is way off from here. It ain't got nothing to do with us. Now, Ben, don't you go talking that kind of talk to nobody else."

"What you mean?"

"I mean we is lucky to be together. Don't you never forget that Old Massa took particular pains to buy us together so we wouldn't be separated. If he hadn't of done that, you could be off in Texas or somewhere . . ."

"With another woman, maybe, yeah."

"Yeah, and maybe I would be with another man, maybe a man with good sense, for a change."

"Here, now, Mattie, come back over here. I didn't go to make you mad."

"I ain't mad. I just want you to be careful how you talk."

"Well, surely a man can say what he wants to to his own wife. I got to say what is in my heart to somebody."

"What is in your heart, then, sweet man?"

I turned my ear toward the wall so that I could hear more clearly.

"Suppose Old Massa was to die. You know what happened to us before. We had just jumped the broom and bam, there we was to be sold like we was nothing more than livestock. It ain't right to live like we has to live, to be worried all the time about what somebody can do to you, if they want. I am tired of being property instead of a human being, like God meant." "Yeah, but young Massa Jackson, he would look after things. His heart is in the right place. I helped raise that boy and there ain't a mean bone in his body. He wouldn't never do nothing to hurt us."

"Aw, he don't care about Glenwood, I could tell that when he come home from college. Anyway, what I said still holds. Freedom is gonna come. And when it do, we gonna leave this plantation and I am gonna set up my own blacksmith shop and we gonna buy ourselves some land."

"Maybe, some day freedom will come, Ben. Now hush up and go back to sleep."

"I ain't sleepy. I need something to put me to sleep and you got what I need. Come here, baby."

"I don't feel like it tonight, Ben."

"Come on, Mattie, don't go turning your back. Put your arms around my neck and tell me if you love me as much as I love you."

"Aw, Ben, you knows I do. You means everything to me."

"Ah, that be more like it. You know you just about the sweetest woman that ever drew breath."

They say an eavesdropper never hears anything good about himself. While Mattie's comments warmed my heart, Ben's chilled it. Feeling a sense of shame and confusion, I waited until the sounds of their bed creaking would cover my footsteps and slipped out of the kitchen and back up to my room to finish my corn bread there.

I never mentioned the incident to Father. But the next time I went into Yardley City, I made a point of riding by Lowery's livery stable and scrutinizing Old Mose, who was sitting on a bale of hay and whittling. His hair had turned cottony white. He looked surprised when he saw my gaze but recovered quickly and said, "Morning, young master. I hopes you is feeling well today."

"Well enough, Mose," I replied. "How about you?"

"Oh, I is tolerable. Just tolerable," he said, and returned to his whittling as I rode on.

I wondered how he had learned to read. But I said nothing to his master or anyone else. Several weeks would pass before I regretted my silence.

Thereafter I felt less comfortable around Ben. He was as diligent as ever in caring for Nellie. The sounds of his hammer against his anvil rang as vigorously as ever. But his talk with Mattie which I had overheard continued to worry me. I was too fond of both of them to relate the incident to Father.

Just a couple of weeks after my overhearing Mattie and Ben I arose one morning and ate a hurried breakfast with my family. Mattie seemed unusually quiet and cheerless but I attached no importance to it.

I strapped on my revolver and walked out to the stable, expecting that Ben would have Nellie all saddled up and waiting for me. She was still in her stall and whickering from hunger.

Ben had always been so conscientious about caring for our horses that I could not believe he had forgotten to feed Nellie. I walked over to the blacksmith shop to remonstrate with him. The shop was silent. The charcoal in his furnace had grown cold.

Father frowned at my report of Ben's laxness. "It's not like him. Mattie! Come here."

She entered the dining room with bowed head and puffy face.

"What in heaven's name has got into Ben?" Father demanded.

She raised her apron to her face and began sobbing. Mother got her calmed down enough to tell us that she had awakened during the night and discovered that Ben had left their bed.

"I just thought he had gone outside to do his natural business and I went on back to sleep, but then when I woke up this morning, he was gone. He done took his clothes and everything."

"He has run away! Why in God's name didn't you tell us as soon as we got up?"

"I was hoping he would come back."

Father proceeded to put Mattie through a rough cross-examination but she steadfastly denied any foreknowledge of Ben's intentions or where he might have gone.

"Well, he is an ungrateful wretch. I paid $800 for him and another $500 for you, just so you would not be separated. And this is how I am treated in return for my kindness."

He turned to me, as if Mattie had no ears or feelings. "I tell you, never trust a darkie. I have been too easy on ours."

At this, Mattie broke into tears again. It was plain to see that she was just as hurt and bewildered by Ben's abandonment of her as Father was outraged. Mother put her arms around her and chastised Father for his callous remarks.

Still, I did not tell anyone of what I had overheard through the kitchen wall. That afternoon I saddled Nellie myself and rode her into Yardley City to the *Leader*, where I wrote out the following notice to appear in the next edition:

RUNAWAY

Negro man about 40 named Ben. Dark Brown complexion. About 6 feet tall and well formed. Burn scar on left forearm. Worked as blacksmith and driver. Intelligent and well spoken for a Negro. Reward for information leading to his apprehension and return. Notify Capt. Jackson Mundy, Glenwood Plantation.

The editor of the *Leader* was kind enough to set the notice in type on the spot and make me several proof copies. After posting these about the town at places such as the train station and hotel, I rode over to Lowery's livery stable. Mr. Lowery was busy with a farmer haggling over a very poor piece of horseflesh. He interrupted the transaction to give me permission to nail a notice on his door.

"Could your Mose help me?" I asked.

"If you can find the worthless old scoundrel."

After the proprietor had bellowed his name several times, Mose emerged sleepily from the feed room.

Lowery greeted him with, "Make yourself useful and give Captain Mundy a hand."

Mose walked up to where I sat astride Nellie.

"I want you to tack this notice on the door where everyone will see it," I said.

"Sho, young master."

I leaned down and handed it to him.

"Read it," I said.

After he had glanced at the notice, he looked up at me in puzzlement.

"How you expect a poor old nigger like me to read?"

"Don't try to hornswaggle me, Mose. I don't give a damn whether you can read or not. What I want to know is, where can we find him?"

"Find who?"

"If you don't tell me straight out, I will inform Mr. Lowery that you know how to read. And then I will arrest you for inciting slaves to rebel against their masters. You could be hanged for that, you know."

I hated myself for bullying the old man so, but I desperately wanted to get Ben back.

"What make you think I told Ben to run away—"

He caught himself, too late.

"I never said a word about Ben. And I said nothing about a runaway. You crafty old liar. Now, tell me where he may have gone."

"Captain Jackson, sir, I never told Ben to run away. That is the Lord's truth. I can't help it I know how to read."

"How did you learn?"

"I kind of learnt myself. My old master's children taught me my ABC's and I studied the little school books they left lying around. You not going to get me in trouble for that, are you?"

"I will not get you in trouble about anything, if you will tell me the truth about Ben."

"Look, Captain, I knowed Ben wasn't happy. He said he wanted to work for hisself and that is all I know."

"I don't believe you."

"It ain't going to help bring him back for you to get this poor old nigger in trouble. I begs you, please don't say nothing about this to nobody."

"Mose, I am going to ask you one more time. Where do you think Ben ran off to?"

"You promise you won't get me in no kind of trouble?"

"If I am sure you are telling the truth."

"Now, I don't know this for dead certain, Captain, but I 'spect Ben has took off for the hill country up to the north. He told me he wanted to lie low and trap deers and bears so's he could sell their skins and earn enough money to buy his freedom and his wife's, in case the war keeps on and the South don't . . ."

"The South doesn't lose?"

"Now, I didn't mean it that way, Captain."

It did not make sense to me that Ben would think that, as a runaway slave, he could earn money by taking animal skins, but before I could cross-examine Mose, his owner completed his trade and came walking out of the barn to ask, "Did Mose help you?"

Mose's eyes were wide with fear as he waited for my answer.

"Mose has been helpful, yes sir."

Actually, he had not been all that helpful, but I saw no purpose in exposing the old man. Besides, as a lover of literature, I could not bring myself to cause anyone distress because he knew how to read.

THREE

• • • Ben's absence made life at Glenwood even harder.
Old Slocum had to do double duty as stable groom and foreman. We had to borrow Cousin Horace's blacksmith to keep
our horses shod. Other such work simply went undone. Beyond this, we all missed Ben. Mattie most of all, of course.
She was desolate without him. Father did not talk about him
once it was clear he had gone for good. As for me, I felt that
I had been betrayed by an old friend.

In July of that year, our hopes were buoyed briefly by
word of Jubal Early's invasion of Maryland, in which he
seized the city of Frederick, won the battle of the Monacacy,
and came within a whisker of capturing Washington, D.C.
But Early had to withdraw back into Virginia's Shenandoah
Valley. Then came word that Jefferson Davis, exasperated
by the failure to check Sherman's relentless advance upon
Atlanta, dismissed Johnston and replaced him with General
Hood, the fighting Texan.

Hood was chosen to fight and fight he did, losing many
irreplaceable men, only to be forced to abandon Atlanta in
the end to Sherman. That was in September. I saw no hope
for the Confederacy after that and made the mistake of saying
so to Father.

"No hope? We must have hope. We are not beaten, not
yet. General Lee still holds firm at Richmond. Hood's army
remains intact and free to maneuver now that it is not tied
to the defense of Atlanta. Wilmington is still open."

"How can we win against such odds, Father?"

"Lincoln is coming up for election in November. The Yankees are as sick of this war as we are. They thought it was going to be over with in a few months, just as we did. McClellan is popular with the Yankee troops. He wants to settle this war and end the killing. All we have to do is hang together until November and see if the Yankees don't vote that baboon Lincoln right out of office. We can make peace with McClellan."

"I hope you are right, Father."

"I am right, Jackson. Now let's hear no more defeatest talk."

Far from encouraging me, his views only deepened my despair. It seemed to me that our very civilization was collapsing around us. Ben had run away. The other slaves were turning surly, almost defying us to punish them for their slackness. Mother lost her customary cheerfulness and my sisters whined about their hardships.

During that same period, I had another conversation with Father, a very curious one. Following me from the house, out of the hearing of my sisters, to where I had tied Nellie, he said, "Jackson, I had an interesting talk with Cousin Horace yesterday." He looked at me closely before he added, "We talked about you and your future, among other things."

"I didn't know Cousin Horace was concerned about my future, Father," I replied.

"Well, he is. He holds you in high regard. He and his family. All of his family."

"I am glad to hear that. After all, we are kinfolks."

"Quite so. Grandfather Mundy came here from North Carolina when this was still Indian territory. It would please him to see two of his grandsons owning large and successful plantations so near to each other."

I headed him off with "If I don't check on our hands, this plantation may not remain successful," and started to mount Nellie.

"Not so fast, Jackson, let me finish. Cousin Horace told me that you wrote quite often to Lucinda when you were in Richmond."

"I did write her a few letters. But she was not what you would call a faithful correspondent."

"Your sisters think you were interested in Lucinda."

"You know how Mary Bell and Emmaline love to gossip."

"Now, don't hurry off, Jackson. I have not finished telling you what Cousin Horace said."

I resigned myself to hearing him out. Father went on to say that Cousin Horace was concerned about the future of his plantation because he had no sons and, with William Claymire now dead, not even a son-in-law. He also was concerned about the future of Lucinda now that she was widowed.

I did not not like the drift of Father's talk, so I broke in with "What was the point of his telling you all this?"

"He mentioned the possibility of putting our two plantations together someday. He has four hundred acres and we have three hundred. He has about thirty slaves and we have twenty—"

"With old Tibbie dead and Ben run away, we only have eighteen," I said.

"Don't quibble, Jackson, this is serious."

"Well, Father, it is your plantation. I don't see how merging Glenwood with Cousin Horace's would be any advantage to you, however."

"I was thinking about you, Jackson. You are the only son in either family."

"If we lose the war, it won't matter."

You could always tell when Father was getting angry. His ears would turn red and his lips tighten.

"Damn it, Jackson, shut up and listen to what Cousin Horace was trying to say. He likes you and more important, Lucinda does. He thinks that you would make her a good husband."

I nearly dropped Nellie's reins at this. "Lucinda is still in mourning for her husband. And she is my cousin."

"Oh, for God's sake, Jackson. She is only your second cousin. And come December it will be a year since her husband was killed. Anyway, Cousin Horace and I, we thought that a Christmas wedding might be in order."

It took a moment for me to react to this.

"Let me get this straight, Father. You and Cousin Horace

have been making wedding plans for Lucinda and me without consulting us?"

"What has got into you? I am consulting you now. And Cousin Horace sounded Lucinda out before he broached the subject to me."

"And what did Lucinda say?"

"She is willing. Now, don't take that the wrong way, Jackson. I know your mother doesn't think highly of Lucinda, but she is a fine-looking young woman and you would make a grand couple. And with the two plantations put together, your children would be sitting pretty, no matter what course the war may take. What are you laughing at? This is a serious proposal."

I laughed so hard that it brought on a fit of coughing. I clung to Nellie's saddle and leaned my forehead against her flanks until I recovered my breath.

Father frowned as he tried to understand my reaction.

"This is serious, Jackson. It is not a joke."

That set me to laughing all over again. But then I saw that I had hurt his feelings, so I choked down my mirth and said, "Father, I know you and Cousin Horace meant no harm. But do you really think I want to play second fiddle to William Claymire? And even if I did, what Mother says about Cousin Lucinda is true. She really is a stupid, shallow girl. I can do a lot better than that, I assure you."

"You just think about the proposition before you turn it down. I am going to tell Cousin Horace that you are thinking about it."

"Father, I have thought about it all—"

"Can we at least discuss it tomorrow, after you have had time to sleep on it? You would be master of seven hundred acres of prime land. You would be one of the biggest landowners in Yardley County."

"We can discuss it tomorrow, certainly, Father, but I am no longer interested in marrying Lucinda."

His eyebrows went up at my inadvertent admission that I had once been seriously interested in Lucinda, and his face lost its angry, puzzled look.

"There is not a more beautiful young woman in all the

world," he said. He had never met Sarah Martin or heard her sweet voice.

Poor Father. He did not know that I daydreamed constantly about London, that I wondered how I might escape from the ruins of the Confederacy and make my way back to England. Once there, surely my friends in the Savage Club would help me find journalistic employment, and then I could win Sarah Martin's hand in marriage. Having lost hope in the Southern cause, I seized upon this fantasy. Without it I might have committed suicide, so deep was my despondency. But, as Father liked to say, it is always darkest just before dawn.

The next morning, after setting the slaves to their tasks in the fields, I returned to the house to breakfast with my family. We had just sat down to our corn mush and molasses when Mattie cried from the kitchen, "Oh, my goodness, Master. The Yankees is coming!"

Father's face turned white. He scrambled for his double-barrelled fowling piece and I strapped on my Colt navy revolver.

Sure enough, a band of well-mounted soldiers had turned off the road to Yardley City and was coming down the lane.

"Put down your gun, Father," I said. "They are Confederates."

"They could be bushwhackers," he said.

"No, they are properly uniformed. Let's go out and see what they want."

We stood on the porch as the five horseman approached. At first I thought my eyes were playing tricks on me but the closer they drew the surer I felt that the bearded man on the snowy white horse was none other than Evan Martin, now wearing the two stars of a major general.

All doubt faded when he halted his horse and raised his hat.

"Jackson Mundy," he said in that rich non-Southern voice I knew so well. "Do you not recognize me?"

Mother and Father were flabbergasted. General Martin said they had not eaten breakfast and yes, they would be pleased to break bread with our family.

Mother sent Mattie to saw slices from the ancient ham she kept hidden under corn cobs in the store room. Sister Mary Bell was assigned to forage for eggs; Sister Emmaline, to rescue the family silverware from its hiding place under a kitchen hearthstone.

While this went on, the General introduced his comrades, two of whom wore the insignia of brigadier generals.

"General Wiggins and his brigade have seen long service under Bragg and Johnston and Hood," he said as he nodded toward a heavyset, balding man with sidewhiskers. "I am delighted to be associated with such an able, experienced officer."

When I shook General Wiggins's hand I was surprised at his flaccid grip.

"And General Bristoe has seen long service with his brigade along the coast."

Bristoe was a lanky fellow with sandy hair and a sardonic expression. He shook hands vigorously with first Father and then me.

The general turned to the third person in his party, a fellow of dark, intense mien, and introduced him as "Major Calkins, who has come with me from Virginia as a supply officer."

The fourth man, dressed in the blue-and-red uniform of a militia staff officer, looked sickly. "And this is Colonel Turnbull, who is on leave from his post as commandant of the Francis Marion Military School to serve as deputy commander of the state militia."

Turning to face them, he said, "Gentlemen, Jackson Mundy was my special assistant during my sojourn in England. He became my right arm after I lost that part of my anatomy at Malvern Hill. I could not have achieved a fraction of my success in England without his assistance."

I was dying to know what the general was doing in Yardley County but he offered no explanation. He showed great enthusiasm for Father's appraisal of where the war seemed headed.

"Quite right, Mr. Mundy, quite right. I cannot imagine the North choosing Lincoln and four more years of killing. I visited the field at Cold Harbor back in June with President Davis. The Yankees lost seven thousand men there in not more than half an hour. We reckon that during the month of May alone, they suffered more than fifty thousand casualties. We are bleeding them white, indeed we are."

His discourse was interrupted by Mother's timid call to breakfast. It was a repast such as Glenwood had not seen for many months, and apparently neither had the general and his comrades, for they wolfed down the ham, hominy grits with red-eye gravy, fried eggs, biscuits and honey as fast as Mattie could bring the food from the kitchen. My sisters hovered in the background, captivated by the general's easy flow of talk. Mother turned red at his compliments of her food. Father basked in the honor of entertaining three Confederate generals. Never before, even in Richmond or London, had I so enjoyed a meal.

I had seen the general charm a table of Mrs. Selby's boarders in Richmond. There he had been the earnest, modest prodigal son returned to serve the South. In London he had held the often cynical members of the press in the palm of his hand as he spouted information about the war in America. Now he spoke as an experienced military man of authority, freely quoting Davis and Lee to back up his opinions.

Father finally asked the question that had been nagging me. To which General Martin replied: "The purpose of my visit to your part of the country, Mister Mundy? I would tell you if I were allowed to. But military security demands that we remain close-mouthed, does it not, General Wiggins? General Bristoe? Colonel Turnbull?"

Those three men nodded.

"However, having extended such lavish hospitality to us, you are entitled to the explanation that we are en route to Yardley City to confer with your Governor Timmons and Colonel Turnbull's superior, state Adjutant General Postlethwaite. That is our purpose for passing through these parts but I have a particular reason for seeking out this house, and that is to talk to your son."

He turned and smiled at me.

"Tell me, Jackson, how is your health?"

Taken aback by the general's unaccustomed use of my Christian name, I stuttered "I am completely recovered, sir."

"Indeed, he is," Father chimed in. "He serves as an overseer for Glenwood. And he is a captain in the militia."

"You have a horse and are able to ride?"

I told him about Nellie and my special stirrup.

"Good, good. Then there is no reason why you cannot accept an assignment as my aide de camp."

My parents, who had been so adamant against my returning to a civilian post in Richmond, offered not a single demurrer about my acceptance of the general's offer. While he and Father continued to talk about how, contrary to all appearances, the South was winning its war of attrition against the North, I packed my belongings in two old carpet bags. Nellie, still saddled from my morning ride about the plantation, was ready. Mother wept as she kissed me. So did my sisters and Mattie.

Father shook my hand and said with a catch in his voice, "I see why you speak so highly of General Martin. It is an honor for a member of our family to serve on his staff." Then in a lower voice, he said, "Now, son, there is no need for you to expose yourself in battle. General Martin is not engaging you to fight, just to assist him with his correspondence, as you did in England. He says you will be in no danger at all. I trust the man. In fact, I wish I could be going in your place. By the way, that little talk we had yesterday— we'll just keep that under our hats for the time being."

"I certainly don't intend to tell anyone," I replied.

"Quite so. I am sure that the offer will stand until you return."

As we rode down the lane toward the Yardley City pike, the field hands looked up from their labors and sullenly watched our party. I raised my hat to them. Only Old Slocum, the foreman, returned the salute. The others laughed, it seemed to me with derision, and then turned their heads to talk, but I was too elated to allow the scorn of field hands to bother me.

Once on the road, the general summoned me to ride beside him and proceeded to explain his mission.

"You know of my ambition for field command of an army, Jackson. I expressed my desires to President Davis and he seemed receptive. In fact, he gave me to understand that I was under consideration to replace Johnston in front of Atlanta but then Hood received that honor, for political reasons. Ah well, that was a mistake. Atlanta is gone. I might have saved it. Now Hood is undertaking the sort of campaign I advocated long ago and that is to leave Sherman in possession of Atlanta and invade Tennessee. Carry the war to the enemy. That is sound policy and I approve of it."

"And what exactly is your mission?" I found the courage to ask at last.

He lowered his voice so the others could not hear. "My primary mission is to protect this state against raids and incursions, but I obtained the option to press northward into Tennessee on my own, should there be no threat to this area. Yes, I might descend on Nashville itself, from the west, that is, while Hood closes in with his larger force from the south. If we seize the Federal base at Nashville in time or win a grand victory in Tennessee or even Kentucky, that would have a powerful influence on the Northern elections, don't you see?"

"But where are your troops?"

"Wiggins and Bristoe each command a full brigade, more than four thousand seasoned troops in all. I could not tell your father this, but they are en route to Yardley City by train. Then two regiments of Texans have been ordered to slip across the Mississippi and rendezvous with us, so add another eight hundred to a thousand men there. And Walther's brigade of mounted infantry, some fifteen hundred in all, is to be placed under my command. They are operating to the north, keeping an eye on the Yankees over the line in Tennessee. But that is not all. My purpose in meeting with Governor Timmons is to gain temporary command of your state militia, whose three thousand men would swell my numbers to nearly ten thousand, a not inconsiderable corps d'armée, wouldn't you say, Jackson?"

"Very impressive, indeed, sir. But our militia is not allowed to serve outside of the state."

"We will have to see about that. At least one Federal division has been moved east from Memphis and it may be their intention to invade this state. The best defense is a strong offense; you know my philosophy of warfare. It will be up to me to persuade your governor that it would be better for the militia to fight outside the state rather than inside. I tell you all this in confidence, of course. Let's discuss it further when we reach Yardley City."

It took me a while to get up my nerve, but finally I rode up beside the general again and managed, "I've been wondering about your family. How is Mrs. Martin . . . and Sarah?"

"Well enough, Jackson, well enough. At least they said so in their last letters to me. Which reminds me: Sarah inquired in particular about you. When I write again, I must tell her of the renewal of our relationship."

"In particular" about me! My heart sang with hope and happiness as we rode on toward Yardley City. I was back at the side of my hero, in a new capacity. No matter how the war turned out, my entree to the Martin family circle had been revalidated. It would not be an impossible step to take from aide de camp to son-in-law. Or so I thought at the time.

PART FIVE

ONE

• • • There has always been only one hotel in Yardley City, the same long, two-story brick building with a second-story porch across the front that still dominates our town square. The general promptly commandeered the building as his headquarters, and likewise took charge of the telegraph office that lay between the hotel and the railroad station. He summoned the mayor of the town and persuaded him to help Colonel Turnbull, the militia officer, round up slave labor from nearby plantations to dig latrines and make the county fairgrounds ready as a campsite.

I marveled at the energy of General Martin and his powers of persuasion. He stayed in constant motion, either inspecting the campsite, or—through Major Calkins, his supply officer—leasing wagons and teams for transport, placing contracts for spades and picks, and purchasing rations for several thousand men.

The first trainload of Wiggins's men arrived on the second day, and a tough lot they looked to be as they jumped down from their boxcars. Bearded and unwashed, these lean, battle-tested veterans wore ragged gray-and-butternut uniforms, and many were barefooted. Their patched and tattered tents soon dotted one end of the fairgrounds. By the end of the next day, three trainloads of them had arrived, five regiments averaging about three hundred men each.

The next morning Bristoe's brigade of five regiments started streaming in from the south. They had not seen hard fighting and marching as Wiggins's had, having been on coastal garrison duty. They looked better fed. Their uniforms were not so tattered, and nearly all had shoes.

The first night these two brigades bivouacked together a fight broke out between soldiers of two of their regiments, many of whom had been drinking. The general was summoned. I followed on Nellie. He rode his white horse right into the melee, bowling over the scrapping soldiers and roaring for them to stop. At last he got their attention and spoke in a loud, deep voice.

"For the first time in my experience, I am ashamed of Confederate soldiers. You came here to fight the enemy, not each other. Listen to me and mark me well. If anyone else of any rank insults another man of any unit or strikes a blow, I will have him shot."

"Well, sir, they called us cowards," one of Bristoe's men said. "Said we wasn't real soldiers."

"They started it," a soldier from Wiggins's brigade replied. "Said we run from Sherman, and they made fun of our uniforms."

"Enough of that," the general roared. "You have heard me. No more name-calling. And that goes for the militia when they arrive. Fomenting quarrels in the ranks henceforth will be severely punished. Now return to your tents."

As we rode back toward the hotel, General Bristoe overtook us on his horse. "General Martin," he said in the nasal drawl that I was beginning to find irritating, "I would appreciate it if you would leave the disciplining of my men to me. I fear you will undercut my authority—"

"Damn your authority, sir!" The general's voice was like a whiplash. "If you had been properly exercising your authority, you would have been in control of your troops. First thing tomorrow morning, I want you to inspect your men and confiscate all whiskey. And that goes for you, as well, General Wiggins. I will not have liquor in our camp. Pass the word to your colonels."

I had not seen this side of the general before. The squabbling between the brigades stopped after this. And on subsequent days when the state militia arrived in driblets from across the state, the regular Confederates expressed their scorn only with scowls and muttered insults.

THE BATTLE OF MILROY STATION   119

By the time Governor Timmons's train arrived from the capital, Martin's "corps d'armée" was in place, in a well-ordered camp. The troops were drilling every morning and afternoon. Wiggins's veterans were not happy about this but they were being so well fed by the efficient quartermaster service the general and Major Calkins set up that they went through their drills without mutinying.

The governor came by special train and with him he brought General Ephraim Postlethwaite, his adjutant general and commander of the state militia. Governor Timmons was a nervous little potbellied states-righter who despised Jefferson Davis almost as much as he did Abraham Lincoln. The general treated him with forced deference, even going so far as to promise him a review of Wiggins's and Bristoe's brigades with all the militia.

"My instructions are to spare no effort to defend the population of your state against the enemy, Governor. And your state is in mortal danger."

"We have had these alarms, before, you know," Timmons said.

"But this time the danger is real. My intelligence advises me that a considerable Federal force is being gathered just across the Tennessee line, with a view to despoiling this area."

State Adjutant General Postlethwaite, nearly seventy years old, had been a private in the War of 1812 and had served as a quartermaster officer in the Mexican War. His snowy white hair stuck out in all directions and he carried a hearing trumpet. Too infirm to mount a horse, he had brought along a buggy and a pair of roan mules and two Negro liverymen, the sight of which caused much merriment among the regular Confederate ranks.

"I was at New Orleans with Jackson, you know," this old worthy interjected in a quavery voice. "We beat them there and we can beat them again, I reckon."

The general looked at the old man with a pained expression. "Quite so, General Postlethwaite, quite so."

That night the general prevailed upon the manager of the hotel to scrounge up a welcoming banquet for the governor and his militia commanders. The repast was of surprisingly good quality and quantity, including a supply of very sweet scuppernong wine. The general made a stirring speech about how he had come to protect "this fertile breadbasket of the Confederacy." And he introduced Generals Wiggins and Bristoe. The governor responded with a harangue about the importance of shielding states' rights against the tyranny of any central government, "be it Northern or Southern."

General Postlethwaite tottered to his feet and rambled on for half an hour about the Battle of New Orleans.

After his guests retired, the general settled down with me to dictate a comprehensive plan for organizing the collection of troops he was bringing together.

"In my view," he said, "Lee had the ideal organization when his army was divided into two corps, Longstreet's and Jackson's. Longstreet was the anvil and Jackson the hammer with which he forged his mighty victories in '62 and '63. Wiggins will be my Longstreet and Bristoe my Jackson. I have observed the two men closely and have analyzed their temperaments. Wiggins is the more professional soldier, a graduate of Virginia Military Institute. As you may have noticed, he is phlegmatic but steady. I think he lacks imagination, but that is no bad thing. Bristoe is more mercurial; he has fire in his belly, and I like that. The man is conscious of his lack of military education and I think wants to prove himself on the battlefield. He will have his chance, I promise you."

"What about the militia, sir?" I asked.

Making a face he said, "I like Turnbull, but if Old Postlethwaite tells me once more about the Battle of New Orleans I shall strangle him. There may be some good fighting material in that lot. So I will divide them into two brigades, one to be assigned to Wiggins and one to Bristoe."

"And the two regiments of Texans?"

"The same there. When they arrive, I shall assign one of the colonels to command half of the militia, as a brigade under Wiggins, and the other to Bristoe with the rest of the militia. That way I will command two full divisions of nearly four thousand each. The leavening of the Texans should improve the quality of the militia. I have not met General Walther, but I hear nothing against him or his mounted infantry except that his manners are a bit rough. He knows this country and he has seen more than his share of fighting. He shall be my Jeb Stuart, but I will detach the better mounted men of the militia and use them for light scout duties and courier service."

He proceeded to dictate far into the night. The orders poured from his lips, and they all made sense to me at the time as I wrote them down at a furious rate. In the matter of hours, he was whipping together from odds and ends of the Confederacy's fading forces a small army to be reckoned with, at least on paper.

The general arose early the next day to greet the last of the militia to arrive: the cadets from Colonel Turnbull's Francis Marion Military Academy in the southern part of the state. All between the ages of fifteen and eighteen and dressed in smart blue-gray woolen uniforms, they came by passenger cars and carried spanking new Enfield muskets.

The general was slack-jawed when he saw that flatbed cars on the rear of the train bore six bronze Napoleon cannon complete with caissons and ammunition. This was the militia's artillery battery and it was manned by a company of men in their thirties and forties from the area around the state capital.

"Look there, Jackson. Lee is desperate for artillery in Virginia and they have been hoarding Napoleon guns and putting fine Enfield rifles in the hands of schoolboys. No wonder the war has gone as it has. Well, sir, we will soon put a stop to that. These pampered militiamen will be able to tell their grandchildren that they were a part of Martin's army. Ah, Jackson, I have been preparing for this event all of my life. My own army. Stonewall Jackson must have felt like this in the Shenandoah when with fifteen thousand troops he outwitted and defeated three separate Federal armies, each larger than his own. We have the opportunity to eclipse Jackson's campaign. You will be a part of military history, Mundy, I promise you that."

He stopped pacing and sat down opposite me, looking suddenly very weary. He massaged the stump of his right arm and grimaced, then leaned across the table.

"Jackson, I need you as my aide de camp, but there is

another, higher use, to be made of your talents."

"Indeed, sir?"

"You must be my Herodotus. Observe carefully all that takes place. The day may come when people on both sides of the Atlantic will want to read of what we are about to accomplish. You shall be my historian, my biographer. How does that strike you?"

"I am not sure that I have the gifts—"

"Nonsense. Never deprecate yourself. Think on a large scale. Dare to be great. Now let's to bed. Tomorrow will be a grand day. Perhaps our Texans will show up. Then I can get rid of Governor Timmons and we can organize our march north."

I was not present late the next morning when the general met with Governor Timmons to review the plan for organizing the forces. But afterwards I saw from Martin's stormy expression that it had not gone as he planned.

"That damned fool has his head stuck in the sand," he growled. "He insists on keeping the militia in one unit. He says that politics demand that Postlethwaite command it as a separate force. What's more, he gratuitously told me that he forbids me to take his precious militia out of the state."

Pacing back and forth as he fumed, he stopped and slumped his shoulders in the habit of the governor, then said in a whining imitation, "We shall defend to the death our own homes and hearths, but I will not countenance the use of a single man beyond our own borders. Surely, this great state has given the Confederacy enough of the flower of our young manhood."

"What does he expect of you, sir?" I asked.

"If the Federals do not cross into the state within the next thirty days, he wants to send his milksops home and leave it to our two brigades to guard his borders."

"What will you do, sir?"

"I have not decided, but I will do something, Jackson, you may count on it. Damn it to hell, why don't those Texans show up? If I had them, I could get by without the militia. Confiscate their artillery and their Enfields and move north, while they skulk at home and guard their precious slaves."

By noon, he had calmed down enough to treat the governor with feigned civility, and to proceed with the grand review of all his forces planned for that afternoon.

He had envisioned a spectacular parade of nearly 8,000 men, assuming that each brigade would have a strength of 2,000 men, plus the militia's 3,000. Actually, the returns from Wiggins's brigade totalled only about 1,600; Bristoe's about 1,900, so that with the Texans still absent, he had 6,500 troops available for review, counting the militia.

He also had the militia's six Napoleon cannon and a four-gun battery of three-inch ordnance rifles attached to each regular brigade. The artillerymen, with their fourteen cannon, gave a grand demonstration of their prowess as their well-drilled crews charged onto the field with their horses, unlimbered their caissons and quickly fired off five blank charges.

I had only heard the boom of cannon in the distance from Richmond. It was thrilling to feel the blasts at close range and to smell the odor of burnt gunpowder. Even to my un-practiced eye, it seemed that the militia crews handled their guns with greater zest and skill than did the regulars. They were directed by a redhaired, rawboned militia major named Addison Bolick, who controlled them with the ruthless efficiency of a plantation slave driver—which, as it turned out, was what he had been.

Following the artillery demonstration, all 6,500 of the troops lined up, regiment by regiment. They made a magnificant sight if one did not look too closely at the garb of Wiggins's men. The general rode his white horse at the head of a parade of inspectors. The governor rode in General Postlethwaite's mule-drawn buggy. Generals Wiggins and Bristoe followed. And I brought up the rear on Nellie. A militia band played "Maryland, My Maryland," "The Bonnie Blue Flag" and, of course, the ubiquitous "Dixie," which provoked a mighty Rebel Yell and caused the cadets to toss their caps into the air.

It was a marvelous experience. By the end of the review, a look of confidence had replaced the general's scowl. He seemed bent on charming the governor, asking him if he were not proud of "our splendid little army." Pressing business back in the capital required that the governor leave late that afternoon. The general accompanied His Excellency to the station where a locomotive with a single car awaited him.

"General Martin, I am impressed by our army, I am indeed, sir," the governor said. "Just remember that my job and General Postlethwaite's is to defend the inhabitants of this state, and not to engage in military adventures. Right, General Postlethwaite?"

Old Postlethwaite put his trumpet to his ear. The governor repeated his question.

"That's it, Governor. Now don't you worry about a thing. General Martin and I will hold the line. God help them if they come this way. We'll be ready for them."

As the sun was going down, the general and I were eating supper in the hotel dining room with Generals Wiggins and Bristoe. From the dining room window, I observed pulling into the station yard from the direction of Milroy Station, a handcar propelled by two Negroes and carrying a strange passenger, a bedraggled-looking fellow wearing a battered stovepipe hat. The man jumped down and spoke to the stationmaster, then strode toward the hotel. Coming directly into the dining room, he marched up to our table.

"General Martin, I have been asked by General Walther to give you this."

He handed the general a sealed note. The general passed it to me. I broke the seal and read the ill-formed writing:

This here fellow is Cyrus Hooker. Listen careful to what I have told him to tell you. Monroe Walther, Br. Genl, CSA

The general arose from the table and excused himself. The man followed him out of the dining room, leaving me alone with Wiggins and Bristoe.

"Well, Wiggins," Bristoe said, "what did you think of our grand review?"

"I didn't see the point of it. We did not have time for reviews in the Army of Tennessee. We were too busy fighting."

Bristoe laughed. "I did not bring five regiments up here to

drill with a batch of pusillanimous militiamen myself. What does the man mean to do with us?"

"I am not sure he knows himself."

Bristoe turned to me. "Captain Mundy, you spend much time with him. Does he mean to keep us here parading for the likes of that pipsqueak governor for the rest of the war?"

Bristling at the sarcastic emphasis Bristoe placed on "Captain," I replied, "I would rather the general spoke for himself."

"I wonder if he knows what he wants to do, or is he just playing soldier?"

"The general knows as much about soldiering as anyone I have met," I replied with some heat.

"I wasn't talking about theory. I appreciate the fact that he is well versed in military theory, for he has told us so."

I could not let his remark pass unchallenged. "General Martin fought with great distinction in the Seven Days' Battles. He lost his arm at Malvern Hill. And he has been a close observer of the fighting this year in Virginia, as President Davis's advisor."

"And that qualifies him to command what he likes to call an army?" Bristoe raised his eyebrows and smirked at Wiggins.

"I have nothing to say against the man," Wiggins replied. "Hood is such a damned reckless fool I was glad to get away from him. So, I'm for giving General Martin the benefit of the doubt. The review did us no harm."

"I suppose you are right, but I can't see why Davis couldn't have sent us a real Southerner, and not a Yankee by way of England. Do you know what my officers call him?"

"No," Wiggins said.

Bristoe snickered and leaned across the table. "They call him General Martinette."

I was beginning to dislike General Bristoe more and more, but before I could think of a response the general summoned us into his office.

A map of the state was spread across the table. Cyrus Hooker still wore his stovepipe hat. He looked and smelled as though he had not bathed in weeks.

After introducing us, the general said, "Gentlemen, Mr. Hooker has been dispatched by General Walther to give us some important, I might even say alarming, intelligence, information too sensitive to trust to the telegraph wires. He has ridden one hundred miles to Milroy Station and from there has taken a railroad handcar. He is weary but I hope he can bear up long enough to report what he has found. Mr. Hooker, the floor is yours."

TWO

• • • Hooker was a far brighter and more articulate fellow than one might have judged from his mode of dress. A native of eastern Tennessee, he posed as a Unionist cotton speculator operating behind Federal lines; indeed he made a living buying up cotton and shipping it north, but his true vocation was scouting for military intelligence on behalf of his boyhood friend, General Walther.

His story—pieced together from his conversations with Federal army sutlers and telegraphers and talk overheard in bars—held us transfixed for half an hour. The hostile force gathering just beyond our state's border was far larger than just one division, as the general had thought.

"I tell you, it is a full corps," Hooker said in his mountaineer's twang. "Three infantry divisions, with twenty-four cannon. I counted them. They are getting ready to move somewhere. Just waiting for a cavalry brigade to come down from Nashville."

"How many men in all?" Bristoe asked.

"I didn't count the men," Hooker said, "but I calculate they got close to fifteen thousand, or will have when the cavalry arrives."

As Hooker described how he had gathered this information and slipped through the northern hill country to report to Walther, I studied the faces of the others in the room.

Bristoe's initial expression of skepticism had turned to one of excitement. He bent forward so as not to miss a word of the spy's report. Wiggins sat back impassively, with his arms folded. The general stood erect, with his hand on his chin. His eyes gleamed and he wore a faint smile.

Wiggins remained silent, leaving the questioning to the general and Bristoe until Hooker paused to accept the drink of brandy the general offered him. Then he said in his matter-of-fact way, "What about these three divisions? What's the size of each and who commands them?"

"The corps commander is a fellow from Ohio, name of Alexander McIntyre. Big fat chap with a loud voice. I hear he was a state senator and he wants to be governor. He commanded a division at Vicksburg, I think. Anyway, this is a big promotion for him."

"What about the divisions?" Wiggins persisted.

"The biggest one is McIntyre's old division with more than five thousand men. The commander is Francis Beltham. Don't know much about him except he's from Boston and is a brigadier general. His division includes a brigade of niggers, most of them runaway slaves with not much training. The second division has in the neighborhood of four thousand men, they say, and it is commanded by Brigadier General Thomas Patterson, an Irishman from Chicago—"

"What about the cavalry?" Bristoe interrupted.

"That will be Morrison's brigade. About fifteen hundred mounted troops. I got that from a sergeant who works their telegraph."

"I know of Morrison," Wiggins said. "He is a Southerner. From Virginia. A steady chap but no match for Walther, I would say. What about the third division of infantry?"

"It was just coming down from Ohio as I was leaving. Only has about three thousand men. Got shot up at Chickamauga and is getting a new commander. Fellow named Kane, from New York City, they say."

"I never heard of him," Wiggins said.

"They say he is a West Pointer, but I don't believe it, for he is only a colonel. Anyway, he hasn't shown up yet."

General Martin suddenly stiffened and his mouth dropped open. For a moment, I feared that he was suffering some sort of attack.

"Would that be Jonathan Kane?" he asked.

"That's the name. I am not sure about the West Point part. Why, do you know him?"

"Oh, I know Jonathan Kane, all right. What else do they say about him?"

"He was a lawyer in New York City before the war. My friend said everybody was wondering what sort of fellow he is."

The general, the color having returned to his face, smiled. "I know what kind of fellow he is, I assure you. Now, Mr. Hooker, you must be bone tired. Captain Mundy, please ask the hotel manager to set a plate for Mr. Hooker and find him a bed for the night. He has earned a good night's sleep."

There was no difficulty getting supper for Hooker, but there were no vacant rooms. So somewhat reluctantly, I offered to share mine. When I returned to the conference, the general and his two lieutenants had spread a map across the table and were orienting themselves.

The Youghaloosa River cuts a diagonal slash across the state, curving at Yardley City and running fifty miles almost due north to Milroy's Landing. In that day, large boats could come up as far as the rapids near Yardley City. Above that point, smaller boats could continue clear to Milroy's Landing, where the hill country begins. Beyond there, the river was too rocky for navigation all the way up to where it was joined by its main tributary.

Until the railroad was extended from Yardley City to its terminus at Milroy Station, there had been a lively boat traffic on that stretch, but the iron horse put a quick end to it.

The general ran his finger along the railroad to Milroy Station. "Now, Hooker says Walther has his headquarters at Chinckapin Furnace, about twenty miles north of Franklin's Ferry on the east branch of the Youghaloosa. Ah, here it is. What would you say, Captain Mundy, another seventy miles above Milroy Station?"

"Yes, sir, and in some very rough, hilly country, with poor roads."

"Quite so. And McIntyre and his Federals are a good day's march beyond, over in Tennessee. So, I would say that we have time enough to move up and meet him."

"If he comes this way at all," Wiggins said.

"What do you mean?" the general asked.

"They must know of Hood's intentions by now. I would think the Yankees would be pulling in everything they have to protect their base at Nashville. It makes no sense for them to move in this direction."

"What do you think, General Bristoe?"

"We have all this force. It doesn't make sense not to go after them. I sure wouldn't wait for them to make the first move."

"I would prefer to have the Texans here before we leave this base," the general said.

"That would be my view," Wiggins said. "Then move up and meet them on ground of our own choosing, if they come at all."

"I say the enemy is there and that is where we should meet him." Bristoe smacked his palms together. "Catch him off guard and pitch right into him."

The general looked first at one and then the other man, then at me. I assumed that he wanted me to speak.

"What about the militia?" I asked.

The general frowned and shook his head at me. "We have talked long enough. We will sleep on this and I will decide in the morning how to deal with this information. Stay behind a moment, if you will, Captain Mundy."

When the others were out of earshot, he fixed me with a fierce glare and said, "Jackson, I welcome your questions and comments in private but please remember that an aide de camp does not participate in councils of war. I did not want the question of the militia's role to be raised just now."

"I thought you were soliciting my opinion."

"I merely wanted to make sure that you were noting the opinions of Wiggins and Bristoe. For future reference, that is. They are very different men, are they not? Wiggins is full of caution while Bristoe itches for a fight. Bear that in mind when you help me write my memoirs." Seeing how his rebuke had embarrassed me, the general paused and smiled. "You must forgive me. I am still angry at your governor for his obdurancy. And this spy told me something that was most upsetting."

"You mean that the Yankees have massed so many men?"

"No, I am rather relieved at that. It would have been of little honor to outwit or defeat a single division, but an entire corps, now there is a task worthy of Stonewall Jackson. No, I was taken aback to hear that Jonathan Kane commands a division in the enemy camp."

"The man you said you knew?"

"Yes. He was a classmate at West Point. It was a shock to learn that we may face each other on the battlefield. But the more I think about it, the better I like the idea. In fact, I wish he commanded the corps rather than McIntyre."

"Why is that, sir?"

"I know how Kane's mind works. I have played poker with him. I could make a fool of him. And it would give me the most exquisite pleasure to do so. Ah, that would be something. But he is a mere colonel, in temporary command of a very small division. Now, good night, and say nothing of this to anyone."

Taking pains not to disturb Hooker, I tiptoed into my room and began to undress, in the dark.

"That you, Captain Mundy?"

"Yes, I hope I did not awaken you. You must be very tired."

"I am too tired to sleep for a while. So you are General Martin's aide de camp? How long have you known the man?"

I explained about meeting him in Richmond and assisting him in London.

"He seems like an elegant gentleman, a cut above the other two, I reckon. Has got them under his thumb pretty well, too. I hope he and Walther will get on."

"What makes you think they will not?"

"I growed up with Monroe Walther. We're both ridge runners. He quit school after the third grade. Can barely read and write. I went clear through the local academy and taught school myself. He went to work and got rich trading mules all across Tennessee. I remained home and stayed poor, until the war, that is. Monroe Walther is one tough son of a bitch, let me tell you. Always was, even as a boy. We used to fight. I was bigger and older than him and I could throw him three times out of four, but know something? He never would stay throwed. We quit fighting and became friends when I seen it was impossible to win a fight with him. He has since outgrown me in more ways than one."

"Well, General Martin gets along with everyone he meets."

It dawned on me that Hooker's comments about the cavalry commander could be useful to the general, and so I drew the scout out. He talked on and on until his speech became slurred, slowed and finally stopped, to be followed with deep snoring. By that time I had learned a great deal about the man who commanded the mounted infantry assigned to Martin's command.

I drew my pillow over my head to muffle the sound of snoring and tried to make sense out of the events of the day. It was to be the last night I would spend in a comfortable bed for a long and very chaotic while.

Near dawn, I was awakened by a heavy knock on the door.

"Captain Mundy, get dressed right away," the general shouted. "Meet me in the conference room."

As I drew on my clothes, I could hear the general down the hall, rousing Wiggins and Bristoe.

Holding a piece of paper in his one hand, he was striding back and forth and muttering to himself. He ignored me until both his lieutenants appeared.

"Gentlemen, the time for action is upon us. I have here a telegram from Milroy Station. Walther says that the Federals have crossed the state line. He has had a sharp fight with their cavalry. He is trying to delay their advance, but he needs reinforcements. The invasion is under way. I wish to God we had got started yesterday."

This time there was no council of war. He did not ask for comments or questions.

"Wiggins, feed your men their breakfast and start them on the road to Milroy Station within two hours. Yes, yes, you can do it. I know we have a railroad but get started anyway. As soon as we can get a train up that way, you can use it to relay your men by rail. It is fifty miles up there. Here, look at this map. See here along the Youghaloosa just north of

Milroy Station. There is a long ridge starting just two miles to the east of the river. Pass on beyond and send out scouts to make contact with Walther. Leave your artillery behind. I will put all our guns under the militia artillery commander. Don't argue, man. Get moving."

He turned to me. "Summon Turnbull. No, let old Postlethwaite sleep. Get Calkins in here. You, Bristoe. Come look at this map and hold your tongue while I tell you what to do . . ."

At first some of the general's orders seemed illogical, but there was method in what seemed to some to be his madness. As he explained it to me later, "I wanted our first contact with the enemy to be made by Wiggins. He would do nothing rash. He has been in battle and he knows how to skirmish and delay the enemy's advance. Whereas Bristoe, in his inexperience and zeal, would bring on a general engagement prematurely. . . ."

His decision to mass all fourteen pieces of artillery under the command of the militia gunnery major had a double purpose. "First it is a sop to the militia to have control of the artillery, but, more important, the fellow knows his trade. What's his name?"

"Major Bolick. Addison Bolick."

"Yes, the big redheaded chap. Did you observe him and his men at our review? Not only are they better armed with their Napoleons, they are better drilled. His men may not love him, but certainly they obey him. The man has a ruthless quality that could stand us well. The regular artillerymen strike me as poltroons."

While Wiggins's men were breaking camp to start their northward march and Bristoe was supervising his regiments in packing up their gear to follow at a more leisurely pace, the general turned his attention to Turnbull, the second in command of the militia, who had been rejected by the Confederate army as a consumptive.

"At your military academy, Colonel Turnbull, do you teach your cadets the elements of military engineering?"

"Indeed we do, sir. Vauban and subsequent French engineers are all covered in our curriculum."

"And which of your staff teaches these courses?"

"Why, I do, sir. I was a civil engineer in my younger days. In fact, I worked on the Yardley City and Milroy Station line."

The general's face lit up. "Then you know the terrain up there. Here, let's look at the map. But first, Captain Mundy, go and send a telegram down to Governor Timmons. Tell him I want all available locomotives and cars hurried up here."

In the telegraph office after the operator had tapped out the message, I waited for the Governor's reply to be received. As I waited, the militia men streamed over from the fairgrounds and were packed, at Colonel Turnbull's direction, shoulder to shoulder in the street in front of the hotel. Three thousand men, all the military reserves of the state aside from older home guards like Father, were assembled there.

Telling the operator to call me as soon as the Governor's response was received, I went out and climbed on a cart at the rear of the crowd to hear and see what was going on.

The general, wearing his best hat and uniform, stepped out onto the second-floor porch. Colonel Turnbull stood on one side and General Postlewaithe on the other.

"Brave guardians of this rich and wonderful state," the general said in a voice strong enough to be heard by everyone, except for General Postlethwaite. "The time for proving your manhood has arrived. Now we shall see what stuff you are made of. Just last night I received some shocking intelligence. I was informed that a large Federal army has been massed on your border to invade and despoil your native state. It is a large force, well-equipped and able to do great damage to your homes.

"I did not wish to raise a needless alarm and so let you sleep last night, thinking that we had plenty of time to complete our preparations. Just three hours ago, I was awakened to receive a telegram from General Walther, who commands our mounted infantry up at Chinckapin Furnace. He informs me that the invasion has begun. He and his brave horsemen are resisting the enemy's advance and will continue to do so until we can arrive to succor him.

"I have been in battle. I have heard the roar of artillery. I have had the blood of brave men splattered on my person. My right arm was shattered at Malvern Hill and had to be amputated. I have heard the screams of the wounded as the surgeon's saw rasped through their bones. I know the pain and horror of battle. I have stood with brave Confederate soldiers in the rain, have slept with them on the cold, wet earth. Yes, I know the horrors of war . . ."

"What the hell is he telling them all that for?"

Hooker, the spy, had climbed up on the cart beside me.

"I don't know."

"He sounds as if he is trying to scare them into deserting."

The general continued on about the agony and confusion of battle and then stopped for a moment to catch his breath.

"Now we come to the moment of decision for you as members of your state militia. Under the terms of your enlistments your first duty is to protect your own homes. General Postlethwaite is your commander and he is answerable to your governor. Colonel Turnbull is your second in command but within the past hour he has offered his services to the Confederate States of America, and I have accepted his enlistment. Colonel Turnbull will leave by the next available train for Milroy Station to supervise field fortifications. It may be that some of you prefer, for reasons of family or health, to remain behind as a reserve to protect against servile insurrection and keep order, but certainly I would not deter those of you who wish to follow your Colonel Turnbull to Milroy Station. Now General Postlethwaite wishes to address you."

As the general had been speaking, I could tell from the puzzled look on General Postlethwaite's face that he did not know what was going on. But he understood that he was to speak.

His voice was surprisingly loud and carried amazingly well for one so old. "My fellow patriots," he began, "it gives me the greatest pride to see you standing before me this morning in your splendid uniforms. I was thinking as General Martin spoke to you of a day back in January of 1815 in the city of New Orleans. There we were with the British advancing from the south . . ."

As Postlethwaite rambled on, Turnbull disappeared from

the porch and then came out the front door of the hotel and walked over to his regiment of cadets. I could not hear what he said to them, but suddenly they gave a mighty cheer and broke ranks to follow him back toward their camp.

Meanwhile, Postlethwaite continued. "The British were arrayed in their red uniforms rank upon rank. They were armed with mighty cannon and batteries of rockets. We waited behind hastily built breastworks of cotton bales and overturned farm wagons . . ."

Certain of the older cadets were passing along the rear ranks of the other militiamen. I saw heads turning to hear what they said. This passed from regiment to regiment, until only those men in the front ranks gave any appearance of listening to General Postlethwaite. The others either were listening to the cadets or arguing among themselves.

Slowly at first and then faster and faster, the ranks of the militiamen melted away, following the cadets back toward their camps. Postlethwaite, whose eyesight was nearly as bad as his hearing, gave no sign that he realized what was happening. The longer he talked, the stronger his voice seemed to carry, and the more his audience dwindled.

"We bore up to their bombardment and held our fire. At last the British fixed their bayonets and began their advance against our lines . . ."

"By God, that Martin is something else," Hooker said.

"How so?"

"The son of a bitch is stealing the best men from the state militia. Look at the fellows still in the ranks. Did you ever see a bigger bunch of slackers and pissants? They'd be nothing but a burden to him in the field. He has took their artillery and now he is taking them that is most likely to be of any use. What would you say, at least half?"

"Captain Mundy," the telegrapher called. "I have a reply from the governor for General Martin."

He handed me the telegram.

YOUR REPORT ACKNOWLEDGED. STOP. I WISH TO BE INFORMED OF YOUR PLANS TO REPEL THE INVASION IN EVERY DETAIL. STOP. KEEP ME FULLY INFORMED OF DEVELOPMENTS. STOP. IMMEDIATE REPLY REQUESTED.

The telegrapher was still standing, with another piece of paper in his hand.

"I got another telegram here, for General Postlethwaite."

"I will deliver it for you," I said.

I read that telegram as I walked toward the hotel through the thinning ranks of the militia.

IS THE REPORT OF AN INVASION REAL OR IS MARTIN CRYING WOLF? STOP. I REQUEST A FULL REPORT ON THE SITUATION FROM YOU AND TURNBULL. STOP.

Meanwhile, from his place on the hotel porch, General Postlethwaite was winding down. "We shot them down like so many rabbits. When they finally gave up their attempts to break our lines, the ground was littered with the red-coated bodies. And that is what we will do with the Yankees. The ground in front of our defenses will be littered with blue-coated bodies, mark my words. Now, let us prepare ourselves for the campaign."

The general snatched both telegrams from my hands.

He read the one to General Postlethwaite first. His face turned dark red. He thrust the telegram into his pocket and read the one addressed to himself.

"Timmons is a damned fool. I am not going to waste my time reporting to him."

He flung himself into a chair and closed his eyes. For a moment I thought he had fallen asleep. Suddenly, he opened his eyes and, seeing Hooker standing in the doorway, smiled.

"Mr. Hooker, do you know anything about telegraph systems?"

"I would have to answer yes, to that. From hanging about with Yankee telegraphers and such."

"Would you know how to, let us say, interrupt the telegraph wire between here and the state capital, perhaps in such a way that the difficulty would take some time to locate and repair?"

"I could manage that, yes, And I might suggest that the wires be broken at more than one place. One obvious one and perhaps two where the difficulty would take some time to locate."

"How soon?"

"I'll need a good horse. Then give me a half an hour for the first interruption. I'll need a bit more time for the others."

"Tell Major Calkins to provide you with a horse. Then on your way, man."

Turning to me, he said, "Fetch Postlethwaite."

When the old man, looking pleased with himself, came in from the porch, the general took his hand and and shouted in his ear.

"That was a noble address, General. I am sure that your men will never forget your stirring words."

"I appreciate your saying so."

"Now, General Postlethwaite, we have just got a telegram from Governor Timmons asking you to report to him in person on the situation here. He regards your presence as urgent, I gather."

"It is a long way down there. It would take me several days to make the trip. I am needed here, with our men."

"It isn't necessary for you to make the trip by buggy. We have a handcar available and two strong Negroes. You could cover the distance in a half day, I should think. And the governor did ask for a personal report, did he not, Captain Mundy?"

I had been brought up always to tell the truth, but I set aside my scruples and replied, "Yes, that is correct."

"Very well, I will send a telegram advising the Governor that he can expect you by nightfall. I can understand why he relies so much on you, General Postlethwaite."

"Are you certain that you can get along without me that long?"

"War often requires us to make sacrifices. Now do you need any help?"

"What about my boys? My mules and buggy?"

"They will be safe right here."

He smiled when the old man left the room. "All's fair as they say, Jackson. Thank God, I am getting that millstone from around my neck. Now, sit down in a quiet place and compose a detailed report on what has happened this morning. Alert the telegrapher that you have a message to be transmitted to the governor. But wait until he tells you there has been a breakdown. Then give him the message and tell him to send it as soon as the wires are in operation again. Oh, yes, and Jackson . . ."

"Yes, sir?"

"This business about the telegraph lines needn't go into your history of the campaign."

With that he winked, put his hand on my shoulder, and propelled me toward the door.

The best way to tell what happened in those next few hectic days preceding the battle of Milroy Station is to quote from a letter I wrote in confidence to Father. In rereading it, I am embarrassed by my own naïveté, but will let my former words stand as I wrote them.

THREE

Milroy Station
October 17, 1864

Dear Father,

Please assure Mother, the girls and Mattie that I am well and happy, but otherwise this letter is for your eyes only. After reading it, please put it away in a safe place for my future reference.

General Martin has paid me the supreme compliment of asking me to act as official historian of his army, and I thought a letter to you would serve as a record of what has transpired up to the present.

Father, I am convinced that General Martin is a military genius. In just two days he has relayed about 5,000 men with all their equipment and three batteries of artillery fifty miles from Yardley City here to Milroy Station. He has accomplished this feat by skillful use of two decrepit locomotives and a collection of rickety boxcars, with some help from shank's mare.

This movement is all the more remarkable when you consider that General Bristoe's brigade has long been on garrison duty and his men are unused to long marches and our militiamen are little better than recruits.

General Wiggins's brigade of veterans got here in just one day. They marched north for about ten miles at which point a commandeered train picked up one of his regiments, hauled them up here to Milroy Station, then backed down and met a second regiment, and so on until the entire brigade was transported.

Meanwhile, Bristoe's brigade—dispatched several hours later—was hoofing it, followed by a wagon train carrying tents and rations. The general thought Bristoe's men needed to be toughened up for what lies ahead.

They did much grumbling because a second train, brought up later from the capital, carried Turnbull's cadets and a large supply of spades and picks right past them as they marched along the road. They assumed the young blue bloods were getting preferential treatment. But the trains shuttled up Bristoe's men to Milroy the next day.

After a night's rest, acting on General Martin's very explicit instructions, General Wiggins moved north from here to search out and support a brigade of mounted cavalry, which is facing an entire corps of Yankees up near the Tennessee border.

The general and I left Yardley City on horseback the day after Wiggins moved up here. We were accompanied by our artillery crews and their weapons, which the general has placed under the command of a militia major named Bolick. We also are accompanied by a contingent of mounted militiamen chosen as couriers for the quality of their horses rather than their own military abilities.

We were met at a fuel-and-water station about halfway here by one of the two trains. They loaded our horses and artillery onto the cars, and we chugged up to find a camp in place alongside the railroad. Our very efficient quartermaster, Major Calkins, has already started accumulating forage for our animals and other supplies, and our chief surgeon is setting up a base hospital. I am amazed by the general's grasp of detail and his masterful way of handling officers and men.

Milroy Station is a poor excuse for a town. There is one Baptist and one Methodist Episcopal Church South, a lumberyard, a stockyard and livery stable, a drygoods and feed store, a telegraph shack and about a dozen houses. Oh yes, and the terminus station of the railroad.

The land around here is better suited for growing trees, broom sage, and corn than cotton. The farms are smaller,

*and you see fewer darkies. I am amazed at the spectacle of
white women actually working in the fields alongside the
men. Can you imagine what Emmaline and Mary Bell would
say if you asked them to take up a hoe or a scythe?*

*This morning, the general and I rode seven miles to Mil-
roy's Landing, the village on the bank of the Youghaloosa.
There we found Colonel Turnbull and his three hundred cadets earning their easy train ride by laboring away with pick
and shovel, something to which they are unaccustomed, but
which, to my surprise, they are doing without complaint.*

*Colonel Turnbull congratulated the general on his choice
of ground to fortify. A ridge, called Stony Mountain—far too
steep and wooded for a military body to cross—begins just
two miles from the river and runs about ten miles to the
northeast. The ground along the river is impassably marshy
and that along the base of the ridge very rocky and over-
grown with brush.*

*Turnbull has his cadets digging a line of rifle pits and
breastworks to cover the gap between the mountain and the
river, but they will need a great deal of help to do the job
properly. As he explained to the general, he plans to create
six star forts as strong points spread along the line—one at
each end, two along the road leading north and two more
midway between those four.*

*Each of the six forts will include embrasures for our ar-
tillery, allowing three cannon in the two center strong points
and two in each of the other four.*

*The general says that in the Army of Northern Virginia,
they reckon that one man fighting from behind well-prepared
field works can stand off at least three attackers, citing the
battle of Cold Harbor last June as an example. He says that
if we had learned that lesson earlier in this war, many more
of our men would still be alive.*

*Returning to Milroy Station this afternoon, he gathered
the militiamen, of whom there are about a thousand, and
explained to them how much safer they will be manning
breastworks while the regulars seek out the enemy to the
north. After he had driven home that point, he told them that
they were assigned to help Colonel Turnbull and the cadets
complete the fortifications up at Milroy's Landing. You*

should have heard them complain about being expected to do what they called "nigger work." But, as usual, the general's will prevailed and they are on their way as I write.

The general cuts an impressive figure, mounted on his white horse. I shall always be grateful to him for the opportunity to serve as his aide de camp. I wish that I had half of his extraordinary courage and qualities of leadership. My own courage has not yet been tested in this war and I doubt that it will be in my present role. So have no fear for my safety, Father.

Except for her skittishness at being loaded onto a boxcar, Nellie is adjusting well to military life, as am I. I am sure we both will return to Glenwood victorious and in good health. Must close. The general is ready to give Bristoe his marching orders.

Your loving son, Jackson

FOUR

• • • The general summoned Bristoe and ordered him to be ready to move at first light in the morning.

"I want us to move north to join General Wiggins and General Walther. Have your men cook up rations for three days. And make sure each has sixty cartridges on him."

Late that afternoon, Hooker came up from Yardley City on his handcar to recover the horse he had left there and to report that part of the militiamen the general had left behind had skedaddled for home; others were marching back to the state capital.

As for the telegraph lines, a squad of militiamen had located the obvious break and repaired it, but they were still searching for the ones where he had grounded the wires.

"Is there anything else I can do for you?" he asked the general.

"Yes, ride back to General Walther. You will overtake General Wiggins on the way. Tell both of them that I am leaving in the morning with Bristoe's brigade. Tell General Walther that I am counting on him to hold on until I get there."

The road from Yardley City forked at Milroy Station. The right fork angled off to the northeast, past a sort of wilderness of second growth timber called "Mueller's Woods" after the German immigrant who had long operated a sawmill in the area. That road then curved around the eastern base of Stony Mountain to a village shown on maps as Croxton's Crossroads and continued to the state line. The other fork led due north, past Milroy's Landing and through the gap between Stony Mountain and the river, through the Fleming's Store community and up into the hill country clear to Franklin's Ferry on the east branch of the Youghaloosa, near the state border.

The general and I set out on the direct route for Franklin's Ferry, the same road Wiggins had taken two days before.

The leaves on Stony Mountain's trees were just beginning to turn red and yellow. Smoke from the breath of Bristoe's men arose in the chilly autumn air. The general sat on his snowy white horse and watched them march past. As the leading rank of each of the five regiments came abreast of the general, the colonels shouted "Eyes right!" and "Present, arms!" The general raised his left arm in answering salute.

"They make a pretty sight, do they not, Jackson? An army is such a satisfying entity. Everyone knows his place. Its life is regulated. It is full of a tremendous latent power, like a terrible engine. It is a shame to risk such a beautiful, intricate thing in battle. And yet, that is its purpose, to do battle."

Looking back from the vantage point of middle age, I realize that what Martin called "my army" was really a collection of ragtag units thrown together by a "nation" already on its last legs. But I had fallen so far under the spell of his personality and had become so besotted with love for his daughter that I saw those soldiers through his eyes, and so, declared, "It must give you great satisfaction to have organized such a grand force."

"Enormous satisfaction. A week ago, this army existed only on paper. Now it is a reality. And it is a wonderful thing to behold."

After the last regiment passed, he said, "Come along, Jackson. Let's go to meet our foe."

He put his spurs to his horse, which broke into an easy canter. I could not blame the soldiers for laughing at my struggle to catch up. After the general had overtaken the head of the column, he slowed to a fast walk. We halted near Milroy's Landing and the general had a final conference with Colonel Turnbull.

"I was thinking last night, Colonel. When your line here is complete, move forward about a quarter of a mile and throw up a line of shallow breastworks, just sufficient to provide cover for a strong line of skirmishers. And be sure to cut down all the underbrush to provide a clear field of fire."

"When shall we join you, General Martin?"

"I will send word if I need you. If I do, drop everything and rush to the point I tell you to."

"And the artillery?"

"I will tell you when and if it is needed. Meanwhile, Major Bolick understands that he is under your command."

"Ah, yes, Bolick. I wish you had consulted me before you put all our guns under his control."

"Is he not an excellent artillerymen?"

"He does know his artillery, yes sir."

"And do his men not do his bidding with alacrity?"

"Yes. They fear him. The man has an unsavory reputation, however, and I just thought—"

"I know enough to feel secure with him supervising our artillery. Let's hear no more about reputations."

North of the crossroads at Fleming's Store, the country got even scrubbier. We passed more and more cabins of poor whites. Children raised their hands in timid greeting, but the adults, mostly women and older men, simply stared.

We halted at noon, to allow Bristoe's soldiers to eat their cold rations and fill their canteens from a clear stream. We pushed on for three more grueling hours, and the general allowed the men a half hour's respite before trudging on. As the sun sank behind a line of hills to the west, he called a final halt and told Bristoe to allow no fires and to be ready to break camp at dawn.

The next day there were so many blistered feet and strained ankles that the general allowed the worst cases to take turns riding on the wagons following the column. But he warned that anyone who dropped out of the line without permission was subject to being shot as a deserter.

Early in the afternoon, I heard what sounded like thunder to the north.

"That is artillery," the general said. "We must quicken our march. No more time-out for rests today."

The faster pace created more stragglers than the wagons could carry, but most of Bristoe's men kept doggedly on until we met three ambulances coming from the direction of Franklin's Ferry. The general stopped them and learned that they conveyed several soldiers wounded in a bombardment that had gone on intermittently since dawn.

A sergeant from Wiggins's brigade, suffering from a shell fragment in his thigh, explained that his unit and Walther's mounted infantry faced the Yankees, who were gathered in force across the river at Franklin's Ferry.

"All we got is the cavalry's two little mountain howitzers, and the Yankees must have two dozen regular cannon. Been giving us holy hell."

After speaking to each wounded man and assuring them that good medical care awaited them back at Milroy Station, the general put his spurs to his horse and led us forward again.

Late in the afternoon, we heard once more the sound of cannon fire. The general shouted at Bristoe to give his men a brief rest and then "bring them along at the double step. I am riding to the front."

As the sound of cannon fire grew louder, we came to a clearing in the woods which I recognized as an old camp meeting ground. A large arbor with a shingled roof sat in the middle of the grounds, surrounded by a circle of rude huts. The open space was littered with knapsacks and blanket rolls. Two surgeons had set up a field hospital behind the pulpit. The front pews were occupied by wounded men awaiting their turns.

Now we heard the sound of musketry. We rode on until a shell whined through the treetops and exploded a hundred yards to our left. Nellie shied so that I nearly fell off. The general's horse reared, and he had to bloody his spurs in its flanks before it would continue.

The road curved up to the top of a ridge, and there in the edge of the woods, mounted on his horse with a pair of field glasses in his hand, waited Brigadier General Wiggins.

"The Yankees are across the river. See, the ferry is down there. Their guns are lined along the ridge on the other side.

It got so hot, I have withdrawn my men from the riverbank and spread them out in the woods."

"What is the musket firing all about?"

"We are taking potshots to keep them back from the river bank. I hope you brought our artillery along."

"No, I left it back at Milroy Landing. Where are General Walther's troops?"

"He has posted them on my flanks. The river is up above normal. We are covering about a mile above and below the ferry. There are a couple of places where the Yankees could ford when the water goes down. I don't see how we can hold them when that happens. They outnumber us five to one."

"Bristoe is coming up fast. We will have two brigades in place by morning."

"That still leaves the odds at three to one in men and twelve to one in artillery."

The general took out his field glasses, surveyed the ridge across the river, and then handed them to me.

At that point, the muddy east branch of the Youghaloosa was about two hundred feet wide. A ferry house and dock stood on either side of the stream, with two cables running between to guide the now sunken ferryboat, whose side rails and pilot house could be seen sticking above the swirling water. Along the crest of the slope on the other side, I saw men in blue standing around or sitting on horses, making no effort to conceal themselves. Their gun crews lolled about their cannon as though defying the Confederates to start another artillery duel. And I was surprised to note that the faces of many of the infantry were black.

After surveying the scene once more, the general said, "Where is General Walther? I am eager to meet him."

Wiggins guided us along a lane through the woods to a large cabin with a deep porch, the home, he said, of the Mr. Franklin who owned the ferry. The yard was full of horses, one of which I recognized as Cyrus Hooker's nag.

As we approached, two rough-looking chaps with carbines jumped to their feet and cocked their weapons. They relaxed when Wiggins greeted them and asked the whereabouts of Walther.

"He is inside trying to calm old man Franklin down about

us sinking his ferryboat." Then, in a louder voice, "Hey, General, they's somebody out here to see you."

The clear bass voice that answered was one I would get to know intimately. "Well, if it is a Yankee, shoot the son of a bitch. If he is a Confederate, ask what the hell he wants."

"Tell him Major General Evan Martin is here to see him."

"Martin?" the voice roared from the cabin. "Why the hell didn't you say so? By God, I want to meet him, too."

FIVE

• • • Cyrus Hooker had told me much about his boyhood
friend, Monroe Walther, and I had related this information
to the general on our ride up from Milroy Station. But neither
of us was prepared for the man who emerged from the ferryman's cabin; no, not a man, more like a great force of
nature.

He was large, at least 6-foot-2, big-boned, with wide
shoulders and long arms. I estimated that he weighed about
190 pounds, without an ounce of fat. With his thick blond
hair and fierce blue eyes, he looked more like a Norse ad-
venturer than a Tennessee mule trader. He wore a Confederate gray jacket, a checked shirt and the conventional boots
of a cavalryman. Strapped to his narrow waist were two enormous revolvers and the sheath of a bowie knife.

He looked appraisingly at General Martin. The general,
still mounted, stared back, a faint smile on his face.

"General Martin, I have been wanting to meet you ever
since Cyrus told me how you handled that little half-assed
Governor Timmons. Cut his telegraph wires and stole half
of his militia. By God, I want to shake your hand."

I had seen the general in many situations with very different people. With the suave Judah Benjamin, he had been
urbane and glib. With the press in London, he had behaved
in a modest, but forthright manner that earned their trust.
With the brawling soldiers of Bristoe and Wiggins, he acted
like a tough top sergeant. I had feared that he might treat

Walther with icy English reserve or in a patronizing way. Either would have been a mistake.

The general dismounted, took Walther's proffered hand and hung on to it as he looked up into the giant's face and smiled.

"And by God, General Walther, I have wanted to meet you so much that I have ridden for two days through this miserable countryside just to make your acquaintance. I understand that you don't object to a drink now and then. You wouldn't happen to have a drop to spare for a weary traveler, would you?"

Walther, his hand still held captive by the general's, threw back his head and laughed.

"We've sunk Mr. Franklin's ferryboat. We might as well drink up his liquor while we are at it."

Walther insisted on hearing the full story of how the general had wrested the artillery and the better militiamen from Postlethwaite's control. He expressed surprise that we had moved two brigades nearly one hundred miles in four days.

"Enough about what we have done," the general said. "Tell me what you have been up to. Captain Mundy, bring out the maps."

Walther did not need maps. "I did my God-damnest to delay them up the road and leave Mr. Franklin's ferry open so's you could cross. Now I could have handled their cavalry. In fact I did, but McIntyre is a better general than I figured. Every time we got ready to kick his cavalry's ass, he would roll his artillery up and shell us, or swing his infantry around our flanks. Best I could do was check his cavalry and put him to the trouble of deploying his guns and infantry, then fall back to a new position. I never had no chance to strike him a real blow. He kept pressing me, trying to get twixt me and the ferry. I didn't want to get cut off from you, so we left campfires burning one night and slipped back to the river in the dark. The water had come up too high for us to ford, so we imposed on Mr. Franklin here, and borrowed his ferryboat."

The ferryman made a rueful face, but before he could respond, Walther boomed on with, "I barely got our rear guard across the next morning before here they come with their artillery. We sunk Mr. Franklin's boat after our last crew got across. Hated to destroy a man's property like that but I have signed a note obligating the Confederate States of America to pay him the value of his boat. Ain't that right, Mr. Franklin?"

"I wouldn't go so far as to say it was right, but that is what you done," the ferryman said glumly.

"Howsomever, Mr. Franklin, he seemed to lack faith in the paper's worth. So, to keep him happy, I have given him another note to cover the toll for crossing eleven hundred horses and men. He will be a rich man if we win this war."

Walther laughed loudly at his own joke.

"How do you see our present situation?" the general asked.

"We are all right as long as the river stays up, but that can't last forever. When the water drops, they will be able to cross one ford about a mile and a half upstream or another about two miles below the ferry."

"I considered bringing along our artillery but concluded that it might be a hindrance in this rough country with only one road," the general said.

"I would of give my right arm this morning to have your guns," Walther said, "but I reckon it would just be a waste of powder and shells. Artillery can be more trouble than it is worth. Least it is the way I fight."

During this conference, Cyrus Hooker stood cleaning his fingernails with a penknife and listening while Franklin, a sour, nervous-looking fellow, kept an anxious eye on his whiskey jug.

Finally, the general said, "General Walther, let me suggest that you and I stretch our legs outside and explore some possibilities, in private."

When they were gone, Hooker looked up from his nails and said to me, "Didn't I tell you Monroe Walther was just about the damnest fellow you would ever want to meet?"

Mr. Franklin broke his sullen silence. "You wouldn't think he was such a grand fellow if he had destroyed your property and put you out of business. I wished I had never laid eyes on Monroe Walther or his bunch of cutthroats."

"What are you complaining for?" Hooker demanded. "You

have got Monroe's promissory notes, ain't you? After the war you can use them notes to wipe out all your debts."

"I can't think of but one thing to wipe with them two worthless pieces of paper," the ferryman said. "And I reckon you know what that is. Besides which, who is going to pay me for the liquor you fellows have drunk up?"

"You will have to ask General Walther about that."

"He would just give me another one of his damned notes."

When the general and Walther returned from their stroll, it was plain to see that they had come to a meeting of minds.

"Very good," the general said. "I will instruct Bristoe to wait in reserve back at the camp meeting grounds and to stay out of sight."

"It makes sense to me, General Martin. I got to tell you though, McIntyre is not the windbag politician I took him to be. This ain't going to be easy."

"General Wiggins says that McIntyre has not shown much respect for you up to now. You know what I said?"

"What's that?"

"I told him he would learn to respect us before we are done with him. Now, General Walther, I hope you will not be offended if I rephrase my comment to General Wiggins in earthier terms."

"You can't get too earthy for me, General Martin."

"Good. Before we are done with Alexander McIntyre we— you and I acting together—we will make his ass suck wind."

For a moment Walther looked as shocked as I was at this crude expression. Then he roared with laughter again and said, "By God, Cyrus thought we would get along and I reckon he knowed what he was talking about."

From that point on, the two men were a mutual admiration society. They continued to call each other General Martin and General Walther, but the titles sounded almost like nicknames rolling off their tongues.

Again I marvelled at General Martin's ability to influence others and bring them around to work his will.

Exhausted from the unaccustomed marching, Bristoe's men straggled in throughout that night. They occupied the huts around the camp meeting arbor for the next two days.

Walther posted one of his artillery pieces and half his mounted infantry at points covering each of the two fords while Wiggins's brigade continued its watch over the ferry landing itself. The Yankee artillery tossed a few shells across the river every hour or so, as the water gradually subsided.

Through odds and ends of conversations, I gathered that the general had confided to Walther his ambition to carry an offensive into Tennessee. I overheard the horseman saying:

"I know my native state like the palm of my hand. There ain't a road I have not traveled in my mule business. And I have conducted three raids into the state in the past year. But first we have to do something about McIntyre. We need to draw him deeper south before we slip away from him, or else deal him such a blow right here that he can't follow us."

After the first day at Franklin's Ferry, I noticed that Cyrus Hooker no longer was hanging about but attached no significance to his absence.

The plan the general and Walther had worked out finally was divulged in a council of war including Wiggins and Bristoe. The general spoke first.

"It could happen any time now that the river is down. McIntyre will cross over one of the two fords, maybe feint at one and then pile across at the other. Our advantage is that he thinks we have only General Walther's cavalry and one brigade. If we catch him at the right time, when he is only part way across, we can hit him with both our infantry brigades and drive him back across the river. Do you follow me?"

Bristoe spoke up. "Why not slip across the river and attack them first, in their camps? Say early in the morning when they least expect it."

Walther made no attempt to hide his contempt for Bristoe's opinion. "That would be a good way to commit suicide. They got twelve thousand infantry and fifteen hundred cavalry, plus God knows how many artillerymen. And you want to cross a river with thirty-five hundred infantry and attack them?"

"We have nearer to five thousand with your cavalry."

"My fellows ain't cavalry. They are mounted infantry.

Cavalry is them idiots that gallops about waving sabers and firing off pistols in the air. That don't mean doodly squat. My fellows do their traveling on horseback and their fighting on the ground, with carbines and shotguns. We can move in and out of a fight quick. Show up where the enemy least expects us. But there's one thing I don't never do, and that is attack a infantry formation from on horseback."

"You might catch them in the camps, asleep," Bristoe said.

"Might? General Bristoe, my men provided their own horses when they enlisted. I paid for their carbines and revolvers out of my own pocket. We have made a considerable investment and I ain't going to throw my investment away crossing a river and tackling a whole Yankee corps."

Perhaps to save Bristoe further humiliation, the general asked for Wiggins's opinion.

"At Chickamauga, Bragg made the mistake of doing nothing when he had the opportunity. Then I served under Joseph T. Johnston. He took care to save lives, but Hood replaced him and came out of Atlanta's defenses and piled into Sherman. I lost a lot of good men following Hood and I don't want to lose any more in a foolish attack like crossing a river against heavy odds."

Bristoe glowered at his colleague. Still, he would speak, saying with ill grace, "If we had brought along the militia and our artillery, we would have had a lot more to work with."

The general said, calmly, "I doubt very much that we could have done much more than frustrate the enemy's efforts to cross the river for a while."

"That is right," Walther joined in. "If McIntyre thought we was too strong here, he would just leave a rear guard and move down the river and try to get behind us. The trick is to make him think we are weak enough to be attacked here."

"Then we have discussed this matter sufficiently," the general said. "I will review once more just what we will do."

That night, after we had retired to our tents, Walther awakened us. I struck a light and hung a lantern from the general's tent pole. The general slept in his trousers. Not taking the time to don his shirt, he opened his tent flap.

"Hooker is back," Walther said.

"Bring him in," the general replied.

The spy was wet from his waist down, and his stovepipe hat was missing.

"Tell him, Cyrus."

"Well, I swam my horse across the river way downstream and slipped through the woods and got on the road well to their rear. Then I rode straight toward the river, like I didn't know they were there—"

"Damn it, Cyrus, you don't need to go into all that. Get to the point."

"They have brought up a pontoon train. And they plan to cross first thing in the morning."

"Where?" the general asked.

"Couldn't find out. Provost ordered me to turn around or he would arrest me. I like to have drowned getting back across the river. But I got some good information on this Kane fellow . . ."

The general held his forefinger to his lips to stop Walther from interrupting Hooker.

"What kind of information?"

"West Pointer or no West Pointer, the men in his division are not too happy about serving under a fellow that has come to them straight from the New York militia. The only fighting he has done in this war was in the streets of New York last year during their draft riots."

"Very interesting," the general said. "Jonathan Kane has been practicing law and shooting down Irish immigrants in the streets? What else did you learn?"

"Some of the fellows in McIntyre's old division are not too happy either, because they have saddled them with a brigade of colored soldiers. They figure it is a waste of uniforms and equipment, that the niggers will break and run in a real fight."

"It is good to see into the mind of your enemy," the general said. "What else did you learn?"

"They are getting fed up with marching through this sorry hill country and are eager to work their way to the south where they can live off the land while they tear up our railroads and such. Oh yes, and there is a lot of speculation about you, General Martin. The report has got out that you were sent here by Jefferson Davis. That seems to be giving them some concern."

We slept no more that night. By dawn Bristoe's brigade had been moved up just behind the crest of the slope leading down to the ferry, and most of Wiggins's men were pulled back to join them, waiting to learn at which ford McIntyre would attempt a crossing. Sharpshooters had taken up positions in the breastworks overlooking the landing.

The sun had not yet appeared when the Federal guns opened up across the river and fired at the rate of about two blasts a minute for the next half an hour. The air was filled with strange whines and whistles. I had never been under a bombardment before and found it a terrifying experience. Dismounting, with trembling legs, I took refuge behind an enormous oak tree. Shells exploded all around me, sending their fragments shrilling through the air. Some of the missiles burst in the treetops, bringing down showers of limbs. A mist of acrid white smoke spread through the woods. Then, as suddenly as it had begun, just when I thought my nerves could take no more and that I might soil my trousers, the bombardment stopped.

Soaked with sweat, I thought ruefully of what I had written to my father, that my courage had not yet been tested and that I doubted that it would be in my present role as an aide de camp. But I recovered my composure when I thought of what General Walther had said: The bombardment had been a waste of ammunition. Only a handful of Wiggins's men had remained behind their breastworks as sharpshooters, and these had hugged the ground so closely that none were injured. The general had dismounted during the bombardment, but had not taken cover. Now he mounted his horse and ordered me to follow. We rode to the crest of the slope and peered across the river. Crews of bluecoats were rolling special wagons down to the water's edge, and each wagon was laden with a pontoon. The top of the ridge was obscured by smoke from the Yankee cannon.

"They can't be planning a direct crossing," the general exclaimed. "That makes no sense at all."

Yet, despite the musket fire of Wiggins's sharpshooters, they continued to roll the pontoons down the slope by hand.

And a string of their infantry—black men for the most part—lined the bank and began taking potshots at us across the river.

General Walther galloped up on his horse to consult with the general, who asked, "Should we have left Wiggins in his place?"

"I don't think so. Them niggers can't get across without a lot more help. What has McIntyre got up his sleeve?"

His answer was not long in coming. First we heard a cannon shot from the right, a pause, and then another.

"That's my gun at the upper ford. Wait! Hear my chaps' carbines? They must be trying to cross there."

His evaluation was quickly confirmed by a horseman who raced up to report that "the Yankees are coming across the river fast. We can't hold them long. . . ."

"I think the time has come to strike our blow, do you not agree?" the general said to Walther.

"I would say so. I'll stay here for a bit to see what them niggers are up to."

Before the general could mount his horse, we heard the sharp, high boom of a howitzer from the other direction.

Walther cupped his hand to his ear. The cannon sounded again and again.

"Great Jehovah, they are starting up at the lower ford. Damn McIntyre anyway. He is threatening us at three points."

I later learned that the Yankees had divided their forces, leaving their large Negro brigade at the ferry to fix attention on the pontoon boats, while sending about half the remaining men to cross each of the fords simultaneously. If Martin had had a larger army, he could have held the enemy at one ford while destroying the other column, then could have marched back and struck the other. But with their preponderance of strength, each Federal wing was strong enough to defend itself, if not defeat our force, and the other meanwhile could have swept inland and cut us off.

The general and Walther conferred hurriedly. The Federals chose that moment to open up with a fresh bombardment, and the Negro soldiers began sliding their pontoons into the water.

Shortly, another horseman came dashing from the lower ford to say that "the place is crawling with blue bellies. Looks like two divisions at least."

Walther looked at the general and said, "Do you play poker?"

"I used to."

"Then you understand that you got to know when to hold and when to fold. The time has come for us to fold and wait for a new hand. McIntyre has got us where the hair grows short. We had better clear out."

"I fear you are right. I will instruct Wiggins and Bristoe to fall back to the camp grounds and form a line of battle. Will your people be all right?"

"We will be fine. I'll pull my artillery out first and send it back to you. Then my fellows will fall back and screen you."

In a nutshell, that was the affair at Franklin's Ferry. Later I heard Bristoe complaining that we could have won a great victory if we had brought up the artillery and militia from Milroy's Landing and if Martin had allowed him and Wiggins to launch a sneak attack across the river. Actually, McIntyre's army was too fresh and strong for our little force at that point. But the campaign was far from over, as was my own part in it. My courage, character—whatever you want to call it—had yet to be tested.

SIX

• • • It had taken General Martin only two days to march his two brigades nearly fifty miles up from Milroy's Landing to Franklin's Ferry. It took General McIntyre a full week to cover the same gloomy, barren ground. And working together with great skill, the general and Walther made him pay for every mile of his advance along the single good road in the area.

Forming a line of battle a half mile wide, we made a stand at the camp grounds, five miles from the river. This gave our wagon trains time to head south, out of harm's way. And it provided Walther's hard-pressed mounted infantry with a rallying point.

First his two little mountain howitzers rolled back down the road from the ferry and were positioned to cover the front. The sound of carbines and muskets grew louder and louder and, suddenly, there came a rush of Walther's horsemen, led by their general himself. These rough-cut warriors rode right through our infantry ranks and reformed to the rear. While they reloaded their carbines and shotguns, Walther stopped and conferred with Martin.

"We got off just in time, and it's a good thing we did. Huh, oh, here comes their cavalry."

The thunder of hooves and shouts of Yankee horsemen rang through the woods. They blundered to within easy range of our infantry, who rose to their feet and gave them a blistering volley. Walther's cannon joined in with two rounds each. The Yankee cavalrymen stopped in their tracks, fired off their revolvers and, hit with another volley, quickly retreated, leaving behind a dozen or so stricken horses and a score of fallen soldiers.

Walther's men dashed out on foot and stripped the horses of their saddles and other accoutrements. Then, acting out of mercy rather than brutality, they shot the maimed animals in their foreheads. That grisly chore completed, they hauled in the wounded Yankee cavalrymen for questioning by Walther.

His method of interrogation was harsh but effective. With the muzzle of a cocked revolver pointed at a Yankee's forehead, he said, "Now, son, this thing I have in my hand may look like a pistol to you but what it really is is a truth machine. I'm going to ask you a few questions. The machine won't go off unless you tell me a lie or refuse to answer. You understand? Good. As soon as I am done with asking you questions, we'll turn you over to a doctor and he will have a look at that there arm."

In this way, he found out exactly who was who in McIntyre's force.

This was my first battle experience, and the sight of fresh blood and the cries of the wounded left me shaken. The general was not affected. Looking amused, he stood beside his white horse and watched Walther's interrogation of a wounded corporal.

"Ask him about Kane's division," he said.

"They are in the rear of the column," the corporal replied. "Have been all along."

"Ask him who guards the pontoon train."

"Some of General Beltham's colored troops. They help the engineers, too."

We held our position until the Yankee infantry came up, but, forewarned by the cavalry that a strong line of foot soldiers lay in wait, they wisely delayed an attack until after they had brought up their artillery.

"They must of got their pontoon bridge across," Walther said. "Damn them Yankees, anyway. Why did God make so many of the bastards?"

The general leaned close to Walther and said in a voice so low I could barely hear, "What if you were to send a few of your men off into the woods with their horses to hide until the Federals have passed? Could they then not retrace our steps and destroy the pontoon bridge? You know, cut their communications."

"It would take more than just a few men. McIntyre ain't no fool. He'll have a strong guard posted at the crossing. How many men was you thinking of?"

"About as many as the number of blue uniforms we could strip from our prisoners."

A huge grin spread across Walther's face. "By God, General Martin, I am glad that you have not let your West Point education cloud your military judgment. That is just what we will do."

"But instruct your men to wait at least three days before they attempt the undertaking. We don't want to discourage General McIntyre from advancing."

Shortly before twilight, the Yankees shelled the woods, but without much effect. Our men lay on their arms until near midnight and then slowly and silently we arose and slipped back down the road. We passed the camp of Walther's mounted infantry and by dawn had put several miles between ourselves and the enemy.

Later we learned that McIntyre had hurled two of his divisions into a dawn attack on the unoccupied camp grounds. Around noon, his cavalry again caught up with Walther, who stood his ground until Yankee infantry came up, and then fell back a mile or two and set up a new line.

I wondered at first why, having gained a head start on McIntyre, the general did not hasten his retreat back to the safety of our fortifications at Milroy's Landing. Gradually I divined the purpose. Martin was dangling bait in front of the Yankee general, leading him farther and farther south and, in the process, giving Colonel Turnbull even more time to perfect our fortifications at Milroy's Landing.

We passed up several places where we might have made strong stands. Even General Wiggins wondered why we did not throw up a line of breastworks and challenge McIntyre to attack. Bristoe was all for Wiggins's holding an entrenched line while he and Walther launched a flank attack but the general said no, so we fell back another few miles and waited for the Yankee infantry and artillery to catch up and deploy again.

By this time, the Federal cavalry had learned its lesson. Their horsemen dared not press Walther too hard, for fear of blundering into our infantry again.

At night the general ordered each brigade to provide one regiment to throw up a line of shallow rifle pits. Then he retired the other regiments several hundred yards to erect a second, stronger line of defenses. It was tiring work, but the soldiers seemed to understand its necessity.

As the general said to Walther, "the stronger the enemy, the more precautions we must take. That is one of the great lessons of military history."

Walther nodded and replied, "General Martin, I have not had your educational opportunities, but as a country boy I learned a long time ago not to ever let yourself get caught with your pants down. I reckon it's the same thing."

When the two men first met, I had feared that Walther, used to operating independently with his half-civilized horsemen, would not accept the authority of a Philadelphia-born, West Point–educated gentleman. My fears were baseless. Somewhat as a clever horseman trains a high-spirited stallion, so the general seemed to win the respect and admiration of Monroe Walther, no small accomplishment. But with the passage of that worry, a new one arose.

On our way to England in 1862, I had been concerned at what seemed to be the general's dependence on laudanum to control the pain in his amputated arm, and had been equally relieved on the return trip when he confided that he was determined to break the habit.

We slept, the general and I, under a large spread of canvas, the general on a folding cot and I on a bed roll. On the march up to Franklin's Ferry, the general had appeared alert and vigorous during the day, and at night he dropped off to sleep quickly. On the retreat, however, one night I heard him sit up in his cot and make little grunting sounds of pain.

"Is there anything I can do for you, General?"

"Must be going to rain. My stump hurts so. I can't sleep."

I asked if he wished me to summon Major Ferebee, the

surgeon for Bristoe's brigade. At first he refused but just as I was about to drop off to sleep again, he said, "You had better fetch the surgeon. I must get some rest."

Major Ferebee was none too happy about being awakened, until it sunk in that the general wanted to see him. Carrying his black bag, he stumbled behind me through the dark to the tent.

"There's just one thing that will give you rest," the doctor said. "These pills."

"What is in them?" the general asked.

"They contain a little opium but not enough to be concerned about. Just try one and see if it don't help. You can keep the box."

The pill did help. The general dropped off to sleep, so deeply that I had trouble arousing him at dawn. True to his prediction, a cold rain had started. The general donned an Indian rubber cape and made a show of riding along and encouraging the troops as they slogged southward through the mud.

"Remember, men," he said. "This rain is falling on the enemy, too. How would you like to be hauling their cannon in weather like this?"

We moved back only about five miles and camped in an oak grove beside a log church appropriately named the Oak Grove Primitive Baptist Church. There, the general called another council of war.

"Gentlemen, I want to congratulate you on the conduct of this operation," the general said. "Thus far it has been a flawless performance."

As ever Bristoe was critical. "All we have done is retreat. When are we going to fight?"

"We will fight when the time is right," the general replied. "When we hold a clear advantage. I saw too much needless bloodshed in Virginia by both sides making attacks on the off chance of success."

Wiggins offered one of his rare comments. "I don't think Joe Johnston himself could have handled a withdrawal any better than we have. But I agree that we got to make a stand somewhere. I just wish we had our artillery with us."

"I am just as glad you don't," Walther said. "Even my little pop guns get in the way sometimes. I expect McIntyre wishes sometimes he had left his cannons in Tennessee."

The rain stopped during the night. To the sound of skirmishing between Walther's mounted infantry and Morrison's cavalry, we again moved south, through more open country, until, to my delight, we could see the crest of Stony Mountain looming through the trees.

The crossroads settlement of Fleming's Store lay just three miles north of Milroy's Landing. The road to Franklin's Ferry was intersected there by a narrow lane that stretched about twelve miles east, along the northern shadow of Stony Mountain to Croxton's Crossroads. On the last night of the retreat from Franklin's Ferry, the general ordered Bristoe's brigade to deploy east of the settlement and Wiggins to the west, between the road and the river. One regiment from each brigade was held around the store as a reserve. Half of Walther's horsemen were sent forward as skirmishers and half were posted on Bristoe's flank, with the two artillery pieces stationed near the road in the center of the line.

At the conference that took place the next morning in Fleming's store building, the general made it plain that he was there to give orders and not seek advice.

But first he announced, "Gentlemen, General Walther has received some good news. The party he left behind in Federal uniforms to destroy the enemy pontoon bridge across the river at Franklin's Ferry has carried out its mission."

"That's right," Walther chimed in. "They just got here last night by way of Croxton's Crossroads. Took the long way around through the hills. Said they waited in the woods for three days after we retreated from the camp grounds and then rode right up to this side of the ferry. Some nigger pickets challenged them. They pulled out their shotguns and killed them. Then they dashed across the bridge and cut the ropes and let the current carry the pontoon boats down the river. They got away without losing a man."

"I shall offer them my congratulations in person," the general said. "Now to our present business. Gentlemen, we have reached a crucial point in our campaign. If the Federals get wind of the fortifications that lie just to our south, it would be most serious."

"Why do you say that?" Bristoe asked.

"Look at the map. This road leading over to Croxton's Crossroads—the one General Walther's party just traversed—it gives me much concern. I should not like McIntyre to change his route and follow that lane around Stony Mountain."

Walther smote his hands together. "That's exactly right. We got to let him chase us down the road where we can bottle him up."

Even Wiggins showed excitement as he bent over the map. "If Turnbull has done his job properly, with our artillery in place, that line should be impregnable."

"But gentlemen, we must make a show of standing up to McIntyre, here, without extensive fieldworks," the general said. "We will act as though challenging him to battle in an arc, just north of here. We let him bombard us, and then when he sends forward his infantry, General Wiggins, you draw back your men first, then you, General Bristoe, will give way, and both of your brigades will retire into the works prepared by Colonel Turnbull. Now, General Walther, explain what you will do."

"After Bristoe has cleared out, we will fall back and help the two reserve regiments cover your withdrawal."

"That is the plan. Do you all understand?"

I tried not to be unduly sensitive, but it seemed that the general had very little time for me after we had reached Franklin's Ferry and met up with General Walther. He treated me almost as a servant, never explaining his thinking, simply saying, "Captain Mundy, do this or that" in front of others. Of course he had his hands full managing the retreat of some 4,500 men in the face of a well-equipped corps of three times that number. And he did not need me to write out orders since his three brigadier generals remained close at hand. Still, nobody likes to be ignored, especially a self-centered twenty-three-year-old.

Thus I was doubly pleased when the general invited me

to accompany him up to the bell tower which stood atop Fleming's store. The general having only one arm, and I, being lumbered with my awkward boot, we found it difficult to climb the ladder to the tower, but the view was well worth the effort.

With several young militiamen sitting on their horses in front of the store, ready to relay the general's messages to his brigade commanders, the bell tower made an ideal command post. As McIntyre's corps maneuvered across the fields and through the woods to the north, the general opened his heart and mind to me as he had done only once before, on the night he got drunk aboard ship on our return from England.

"I hope that you have observed closely our movements of the past several days," he said. "It has galled me to avoid a battle, to always give ground. Very soon we will see whether our patience bears fruit. I am confident that it will, but we must never take anything for granted in this game of war. Often during the past week, I have tried to put myself in McIntyre's shoes, to think as he might think. I must admit that he has made few mistakes. He perhaps should have hurled his infantry at us there at the camp grounds, without waiting for his artillery to move up, but we must remember that his men were weary from crossing the river and driving off our mounted infantry. Also he was uncertain about the terrain. Unless I greatly misjudge the man, he is very cautious, wouldn't you say?"

"It would seem so to me, sir."

"Then you will want to say so when you write our account of this campaign."

He paused to survey the countryside to the north through his field glasses.

"Those Federal uniforms make a pretty sight. They move toward us so ponderously, in columns like blue juggernauts. My grandfather served in the Revolutionary War. He was present in Boston when the British attacked the colonial lines on Bunker Hill. He wrote a vivid account of seeing the redcoats advance against the American positions. As a boy, I was much impressed when I read his description. But I can-

not think it could have been a more impressive sight than
what you and I are witnessing. War is splendid. Dangerous
but splendid."

He raised his field glasses to his eyes again.

"I wonder where McIntyre is just now. I wonder what he
is thinking. He seems to be a deliberate man, not likely to
take chances. It is important to know your enemy, to see into
his mind and divine his thoughts and aims. One should know
one's own lieutenants as well. Our Wiggins is phlegmatic,
practical, in every way dependable, but lacking in dash. Bristoe is mercurial, too swift to make judgments, given to rash
statements and over-eager to do battle, but intelligent. Then
there is General Walther. I was not sure how to handle him,
but now I am confident in our relationship. He is truly a man
of action. He is without fear yet he calculates every risk. He
and I are in perfect agreement about our objectives."

"So I gathered at the council of war," I said.

The general turned to me and smiled. "I don't mean just
the conduct of this battle, Jackson. This is only a preliminary
phase. We must injure McIntyre and pin him down."

"And drive him from the state?" I asked.

"That would only restore the status quo. No, my friend
Jackson Mundy, when you record all this for posterity, say
that even as we drew McIntyre's corps into battle, I was
thinking ahead to our ultimate goal . . . Nashville. Earlier in
this war, I feared that the Confederacy would win its independence before I had the opportunity to command my own
force in battle. Now, despite what I said to your father, time
is running out for the Confederacy, which means that it is
running out as well for me as a military commander. It is
now or never for me. I shall not have another opportunity
such as this."

He peered again through his glasses, then handed them to
me.

"Look along the main road. See how that division is
wheeling off toward the river? I wonder if that is Jonathan's
unit."

"Jonathan, sir?"

"Jonathan Kane. I haven't seen him for nearly twenty
years."

The division completed its maneuver and then advanced toward our positions. At last they paused and fixed their bayonets. Their artillery opened fire. Walther's two little cannon soon stopped even trying to respond. Shells burst all around the store. But the general went on talking as calmly as though he were chatting over dinner.

"I have spent a lifetime dreaming of this moment, Jackson. This game of war is terrible but splendid. I would not miss its glory for all the world."

Now a second of McIntyre's divisions had left the road and was maneuvering across the broken ground to menace Bristoe.

Blocking their advance, the butternut-and-gray–clad men lay shoulder to shoulder behind hastily built breastworks of logs, fence rails, and piles of dirt. The Yankees halted, fixed their bayonets and moved forward at a dog trot toward Bristoe.

Bristoe's men opened fire first. A long line of smoke erupted along his line. The mass of blue rolled forward and halted. A sheet of flame erupted along their front, as they returned the fire. Bristoe's men gave them another volley and then let out a piercing Rebel Yell.

On the left, Wiggins's men held their fire until it seemed they were about to be inundated by the Yankee horde. The blue advance faltered as the battle-tested Confederates, crouched behind their skimpy breastworks, delivered a tremendous volley.

McIntyre had advanced the 3,000 men of Kane's division, his smallest, against Bristoe, as a feint it turned out, for they fell to the ground and kept up a steady harrassing fire. His real blow was directed against Wiggins and it was delivered by Patterson's larger division. No longer could I distinguish volleys, as soldiers on both sides fired as rapidly as they could. For a few minutes, it appeared that we might be winning, but then the general pointed down the road.

Like a battering ram of massed humanity, in a long column perhaps a hundred men across the front, here came the 5,000 men of McIntyre's old division—his largest.

The general shouted down to a mounted messenger to tell Wiggins to give way. Wiggins reacted with surprising speed.

His men quit their line of breastworks and raced to the rear. Their departure was so sudden and the smoke so dense, that Patterson's men seemed not to realize that they now faced unmanned breastworks.

The general's face went chalky white as he peered through his glasses to the right. "Damn that fool, Bristoe. He is hanging on too long. He must get out of the way before that third division strikes our center."

He shouted down to another messenger, "Tell General Bristoe to give way, or he will be trapped." Then to me, in a normal tone, "We had better clear out."

We scrambled from our vantage point and mounted our horses.

Wiggins's men streamed around us toward the rear. From beyond the settlement we heard the hoarse "hurrahs" of the Yankees.

Later I would learn that General Walther had collared Bristoe and threatened to shoot him if he did not fall back as the General planned. As it was, Bristoe's brigade came perilously close to being cut off by the main attack against the center of the line. Walther's two little cannon, firing canister, held up the attackers just long enough for them to clear out.

Walther's horsemen stemmed the blue tide for a few precious minutes, giving Bristoe time to follow Wiggins to the south. It was a close call but the affair ended as the general wished, with the Federals in pursuit, heading south toward Milroy's Landing.

Wiggins's regiments reached Turnbull's outer works first and dropped behind the welcome wall of dirt thrown up by the militia to shelter a skirmish line. First Bristoe's brigade and then Walther's mounted infantry passed through their ranks to the safety of the main fieldworks to the rear.

It was impossible to determine at that point, but later the general calculated that his stand at Fleming's store had cost him between one and two hundred casualties. He had inflicted perhaps twice that number on his enemy.

"I expect or anyway hope that McIntyre thinks he has won a victory by driving us back. He has won the field, but this campaign is far from over, wouldn't you say, General Walther?"

"I agree. As you said to me up at Franklin's Ferry, the time has come for us to make his ass suck wind."

PART SIX

PART TWO

ONE

• • • Contrary to the general's orders that only a shallow line of breastworks be thrown up a quarter mile in front of our main fortifications to the south, Turnbull had caused his men to dig these forward ditches so deep that a man could stand almost erect without exposing himself to enemy bullets. Wiggins's brigade manned this outer work while the rest of the Confederates retired behind the even more elaborate main defenses to the rear.

"My God," Walther exclaimed to the general when he saw the intricate star forts erected on either side of the road. "I think your militia fellow may have outdid hisself."

"You may be right," the general replied. "I doubt that the defenses of our armies around Petersburg and Richmond would exceed these."

Turnbull was eager to show off the fortifications his militia had created to plug the two-mile gap between Stony Mountain and the Youghaloosa, but the general was too much concerned with the Federals to make a careful inspection.

He ordered Walther to draw his mounted infantry to the rear and rest both men and horses. "You have borne the burden long enough," he said. "Let our infantry and artillery take over while you prepare your men for our real work."

Turnbull had caused a large bombproof to be constructed to the rear of the two center star forts. There, under the protection of its log-and-earth roof, the general set up his headquarters.

Obviously the telegraph wires south of Yardley City had

been repaired, for a stack of messages awaited him from Governor Timmons. The general flipped through them and snorted to me, "Send him a reply acknowledging receipt of his messages. Say that my replies must wait until we have dealt with the imminent threat of attack by a large Federal force. Period. Who does the fool think he is to demand explanations of me?"

The Federal advance had been so deliberate, so ponderous that the general assumed his enemy would halt and regroup after seeming to have routed us at Fleming's Store that morning. He had meant to call a council of war in the late afternoon. But he had misjudged General McIntyre.

The respite lasted only until mid-afternoon when firing from Wiggins's fortified skirmish line broke out. I longed for another vantage point such as the belfry of Fleming's Store, but the best I could do was to run up to the rampart of one of the star forts and look north toward the smoke from Wiggins's muskets.

The firing grew in intensity. Spent Yankee minié balls started falling around the fort.

The general paced back and forth in the fort, muttering to Turnbull, "He must be just feeling us out. Surely he will delay his attack until morning. Surely his men must be weary."

The musketry slacked off briefly, and suddenly the Federal artillery opened with a fury on Wiggins's forward position. Shells burst all around the skirmish line. The bombardment started slowly and grew in intensity until it seemed that every one of McIntyre's twenty-four guns must be firing on Wiggins.

Our fourteen guns, under the command of militia Maj. Addison Bolick, lacking targets, remained silent. I took the opportunity to study the tall, raw-boned redhead as he paced outside the fort, obviously anxious to get into the action.

Remembering Colonel Turnbull's opposition to Bolick's being put in charge of all the artillery, I asked the militia commander why a man in his prime, with an obvious talent for artillery, was not in the regular Confederate army.

"He used to be an overseer on a big plantation," Turnbull said. "When the war broke out, the fellow was in the state penitentiary for murdering a slave. He claimed self-defense, but the jury didn't believe him."

"How did he get out of the penitentiary?"

"He served as an artillery sergeant in the war with Mexico. His friends persuaded the governor to parole him on the condition that he serve as commander of the militia artillery."

"That is why you advised the general against putting him in charge of all artillery?"

"Maybe I was wrong to do that. The crews of the two regular Confederate batteries seem to accept his authority, or maybe they are just scared of him. Anyway, he has them whipped into first-class shape and he has given me no trouble."

As the Federal bombardment heightened, Bolick became even more agitated. He entered the fort and saluted the general.

"Shall we join the fun, sir?"

"Not yet. Load with canister shot and wait until I tell you."

The Federal artillery halted and suddenly a storm of musketry sounded all across the skirmish front. Clouds of smoke arose from beyond Wiggins's line. A mighty chorus of Yankee "hurrahs" burst forth. Wiggins's men worked their muskets furiously for a few minutes, and then the general shouted, "Here they come."

Nervously, I raised my head above the rampart to watch Wiggins's men scampering from their forward breastworks back toward our main lines. A wave of blue uniforms surged up over the position, paused for a moment, and continued in pursuit of Wiggins's fleeing brigade.

The general put his fist to his forehead. "Dear God, don't let us start firing too soon."

Now the space between the forts and the skirmish line was clogged with men in blue. They made a splendid sight as they rushed forward with bayonets fixed, regimental flags flying, not taking the time to reload in their eagerness to overtake what they assumed to be a demoralized foe.

"Can we open up?" Bolick asked.

"Not until our infantry begins."

For once Bristoe did not jump the gun. Ensconced behind Turnbull's beautifully fashioned works, he held his fire until

Wiggins's brigade had reached safety and had time to reload. I could not believe the violence of our first volley. It sounded as though someone had slammed a giant door in an empty room.

Yankees were still streaming over the old skirmish line. But those in the front of the ragged advance stopped in their tracks, as though shocked at what was happening. Following their instructions, Bristoe's men leaped down from their firing steps to reload while the militiamen took their places and delivered a second volley. Then Wiggins's men jumped up to take their turn at the deadly work.

The general looked at Bolick and said, "Now."

"Fire!" the redheaded major roared.

There were three Napoleon cannon in the star fort. I thought my eardrums would burst at their blasts. The three Napoleons in the companion fort across the road boomed and shortly thereafter the other eight guns scattered along the line joined in.

Almost as quickly as they had advanced, the Yankees withdrew. Bolick's guns continued to spew canister balls until there were no more targets to be seen.

Turnbull's militiamen had cleared all underbrush in front of the main works. That bare ground now was littered with the fallen forms of Yankees.

As the smoke cleared, Turnbull's cadets let out a shrill Rebel Yell, which was taken up by the rest of the militia and finally the regulars.

McIntyre had hurled his two larger divisions into the attack, holding Kane's 3,000 troops and his colored brigade in reserve. The entire assault and its repulse had not lasted for fifteen minutes. With a loss of fewer than 100 men, we had inflicted over 500 casualties on the attackers.

Throughout the remainder of that day, we stood ready to turn back another assault, but the Yankees occupied themselves with bombarding our main positions, now that they knew where they lay. Bolick gave them back as good as he got, but as General Walther said, "This is mostly a fireworks show."

I had been shocked by the brutality of the encounter with the Yankee cavalry up at the camp grounds, but that was nothing compared with the agonizing cries for water that came from the fallen Yankees in front of our position as dusk came. Now I was seeing at first hand the horrors of war.

Under fire from Yankee sharpshooters, the general forbade anyone to assist the stricken Federals.

After night fell and it became evident that we could expect no more attacks that day, the general gave permission for volunteers to carry canteens of water to the wounded, but not to move them. Then he called a meeting in the command post.

He congratulated Turnbull on the excellence of his field works, Wiggins on the coolness of his men under fire, Bristoe on the accuracy of his musketry, Bolick on his skillful use of artillery, and Walther for covering the retreat from Fleming's Store.

After the general had instructed the others to post plenty of pickets through the night and to arouse their men before dawn, he and I ate our first hot supper since leaving the Yardley City hotel. Then we took off our boots and settled down for sleep.

Near midnight I was awakened by the voice of General Walther outside the redoubt, calling softly, "General Martin?"

"Yes."

"Would you step outside?"

Straining my ears, I heard Walther say in a moment, "This day did not go quite as we hoped, did it?"

"No. I was surprised that he followed up so quickly. I expected him to delay his attack until morning."

"And then he left off after just one try. I would have liked the chance to of done him more damage."

"Perhaps he means to make a fresh assault in the morning. That would best suit our purposes."

"Just so, General Martin. And I would like to give my men another day of rest before we pull out. . . ."

"Pull out?" The hair on my neck arose at this remark. I started to let them know that I was awake, but decided not to.

"Could you be ready to move out by day after tomorrow?"

"We can do it. Can Wiggins and Bristoe?"

"I should think so."

"And the artillery?"

"Are you certain we want to take all the guns with us?"

"If we don't, the Yankees will capture them. Miltia don't have sense enough to get their guns off. I will send Hooker out at first light to scout the road from Croxton's to Fleming's Store, in case McIntyre takes it in his head to move that way."

The men went on talking about how they meant to detach the brigades of Wiggins and Bristoe and follow Walther's horsemen off through Croxton's Crossroads and up into Tennessee, leaving the 1,500 men of the state militia to face McIntyre's entire corps alone. I gathered that they reasoned the militia would put up enough of a fight to delay the Federals for a while, after which the prospect of easy pickings to the south would deter the invaders from following Martin north.

At first I was appalled that these two men, one a Tennessean and the other a Philadelphian, were plotting to abandon the defense, indeed the defenders, of my native state to undertake an offensive. Yet I was so in awe of General Martin's alleged genius and so flattered by my role as his aide de camp that I told myself that surely he knew best and so tried to swallow my doubts.

After Walther left, I heard the general fumbling in his duffle bag for his pills. He was soon asleep, but I lay awake for the rest of the night, listening to his snores, the cries of the Yankee wounded, and to my own troubled thoughts.

The dawn attack that the general expected, indeed desired, did not come. Instead, at first light, a Yankee officer on horseback approached our lines carrying a large white flag. The general sent out a lieutenant who returned bearing a letter from General McIntyre.

"Read it," the general said to me.

"He asks for a truce until noon to remove his wounded. He says they have about a hundred of our wounded from the action at Fleming's Store and offers to return them to us."

"Write a note and tell him we agree to the truce but they can keep our wounded."

"Keep our wounded, sir?" I said. "He is offering to return them to our lines."

"Of course he is. Let his surgeons deal with them. It will save us much trouble."

My feelings must have shown in my face, for he smiled at me and said, "Really, Jackson, the Federals have good surgeons. I am happy for them to assume the care of our wounded."

Throughout the morning, Yankee litter-bearers labored away to remove their suffering comrades. Many had died during the night, of course. It was grisly work. Wiggins's men were used to such sights, but the militia was sobered by the spectacle, as was I.

By noon, the work was done. The Yankee artillery opened up again, in a desultory way. Bolick replied but after a few minutes, the general ordered him to stop wasting ammunition.

Throughout the day, my head spun with the knowledge that the general intended to abandon his defense of the state, leaving it at the mercy of a determined invader, to go chasing off on an invasion of his own. And I continued to be disturbed by the thoughts of abandoning our wounded men.

I slept better that night as did the general. Before dawn, we were awakened by a shell exploding overhead, then another and another. As the bombardment stepped up its intensity, the general drew on his boots and told me to "fetch General Walther."

It was an unnecessary command, for here came the Tennessean on foot, straight for the bombproof, ignoring the shells bursting around him.

I sat on a keg, with my hands over my ears as if trying to protect them from the concussion of the bursting shells. Actually, I held my hands loosely so as to hear their words.

"I am ready to saddle up and start moving."

"Then why don't you go ahead? I will start Bristoe and Wiggins after this racket dies down."

"Very well. I will move down to Milroy Station and then take the road to Croxton's Crossroads. We will wait for you there."

"We will do well to catch up with you by nightfall."

"Have you decided about the artillery?"

"I am going to have Bolick give them tit for tat for a while. He has more ammunition than he should take with him anyway. I will tell him to follow Bristoe when he pulls out."

"What will you tell Turnbull?"

"I will tell him we want to attempt a wide flanking movement and that he is to hold his positions as long as he can."

"That ought to do it. By the time McIntyre catches on, we will be on our way to Tennessee. Hot damn, I can't wait to reach Nashville ahead of Hood."

"Then go, and God bless you, General Walther."

The general, seeing the expression in my eyes, I suppose, put his hand on my shoulder and said, "You heard General Walther and me, didn't you?"

Not trusting my voice, I nodded.

"And you are upset?"

"To tell the truth, I am."

"We cannot cower in these trenches while the war is played out on other fronts. What will we profit the Confederacy if all we do is halt the vandalization of a few counties of one state?"

"But you mean to abandon the militia."

"Turnbull is a steady man. He may draw his men off in time for them to get away. All I need is a day or two. Now, it is up to you to decide whether you wish to accompany me or return to your home."

Often thereafter, I have wished I had taken my leave of the general at that point. My life would have taken a very different course had I done so. But my judgment was clouded by the excitement of the campaign and the prospects of serving as a latter-day Herodotus to the general and hopes of marrying his daughter. As I understand now, much of what passes for courage really is a dread of being considered lacking in that virtue, if virtue it is. If I were to leave now, I would appear to be little better than the deserters I had been arresting back in Yardley County. So I squelched my misgivings and muttered, "No, my place is with you."

"Thank you for not disappointing me. Who would have written my memoirs if you had decided otherwise?"

But the general was not able to draw his two regular brigades out of the lines that morning after all. The Federal bombardment continued for more than an hour. Then there suddenly appeared across our front a strong line of Yankee skirmishers. Their minié balls sang around our heads.

In one of the star forts, the general and I watched these developments with Colonel Turnbull. I could tell that the general was mightily annoyed by the demonstration, that he wanted to inform Turnbull about his "wide flanking movement," and be on his way to join Walther.

Any chance of his pulling out his two brigades right away faded when masses of Yankee troops rushed toward us and took cover behind the long mound of earth Turnbull's militia had thrown up in front of the ditch they had dug to cover the old skirmish line. They proceeded to pour a heavy musket fire at our main line. At such a distance and with the protection of the earthworks, their minié balls were not a great threat, but clearly the situation was not conducive to the general's plans.

Bristoe and Wiggins came to confer with him, to consider whether all this was a bluff or McIntyre was getting ready to launch a full-scale attack. As usual, Bristoe was for striking the first blow. Wiggins said that for his part he would welcome the opportunity to repulse such a Federal attack.

By mid-afternoon, it was clear that the Federal activity was a demonstration rather than the precursor of another general assault. By then it was too late for the general to join Walther at Croxton's Crossroads by nightfall.

The Federal artillery fell silent in the late afternoon, but that strong line of blue infantry kept up a harassing fire. The general called his lieutenants together and gave them their instructions. Bristoe nearly danced a jig. Wiggins rubbed his chin and shook his head. Turnbull turned pale and said, "You mean you want me to hold these works with just fifteen hundred men?"

"If we pull our two brigades out quietly this evening, they will not know it. They will assume our lines are too strong to be attacked. We can descend on them before they catch on."

Turnbull was not as naive as the General assumed. "I

never heard of such a wide flank movement," he said. "You'll have to march five miles south to Milroy Station, then about eighteen northeast to Croxton's Crossroads, and then it is a good ten or twelve miles west again to Fleming's Store. It will take you a day and a half to cover that much ground. We will be of no use to you."

"You'll be of enormous use, if you will hold this line. Come, Colonel Turnbull. Surely you will not disappoint me."

And then he gave his orders for first Bristoe and then Wiggins to withdraw their men from the works after dark and march them back to Milroy Station, pause there for a few hours of sleep, and then hurry up to join Walther at Croxton's Crossroads.

His plans provided for the militia cadets to build campfires every quarter of a mile along the road to Milroy Station as a guide to the troops. He dispatched his wagon trains early with instructions for hot food to be prepared for an early breakfast. He ordered that logs be protruded from the forts' embrasures as "Quaker guns" to hide the absence of artillery. And he instructed Turnbull to spread his adult militiamen out evenly five feet apart in the defenses, while holding back the cadets as a reserve. His plans indeed were meticulous. Again, I marvelled at what seemed to me at the time his great military skill and judgment.

TWO

• • • Bristoe's withdrawal began at 7 P.M. and was completed in little more than an hour. Wiggins's men had the task of carrying Bolick's guns from the star forts by hand, to avoid the telltale jangle of horses' harnesses. After the artillery was on the road, Wiggins's regiments formed up, and shortly after 10 P.M. the entire column was on its way. The general and I rode at the head of Wiggins's brigade, just behind the artillery. We were accompanied by several mounted militia couriers.

The fires lit by the cadets served as beacons in the night as the horses stumbled along the dark road back toward Milroy Station. At every fire, cadets standing guard officiously demanded the password, which was "North Star."

We were approaching the eighth of these campfires when we heard a commotion ahead. The general put his spurs to his horse and cantered ahead.

A cadet officer held the bridle of a scrawny horse while two of his "men" stood with muskets leveled at the rider. "What is going on?" the general demanded.

"We stopped this man and he don't know the password."

"I don't give a damn about passwords, you snot-nosed youngun. I tell you I have got to find General Martin. Now, turn loose of my horse and let me go."

"It is all right, young man," the general said. "I know this gentleman."

The general led Cyrus Hooker out of earshot of the cadets.

"Damn it to hell, General, I am glad I found you."

"What's wrong?"

"Just about everything. The Yankees are on the move."

"How? Where?"

"They pulled out two divisions early this morning and are moving them toward Croxton's Crossroads. I found out at noon and rode back to Croxton's. Ran into General Walther. He says he will try to hold them there but he needs your infantry as fast as you can march. He said to tell you the jig is up and you got to fight a battle out in the open whether you want to or not."

The general sat quietly on his horse, then asked in a surprisingly calm tone, "Which enemy divisions?"

"His two big ones."

"Then that was Kane's division making that demonstration?"

"That is my information."

"I was to rendezvous with General Walther tomorrow evening."

"He will have his hands full before then. I know a shortcut that could get you there by noon tomorrow. Just down the pike there is a sawmill road that don't show on the maps. Takes you through Mueller's Woods to the Croxton Crossroads–Milroy Station pike. It will cut six miles off your route. I just come that way."

"You are sure that only Kane's division remains below Fleming's Store?"

"I hid in the woods north of Stony Mountain and watched the others pass. Had a devil of a time working my way ahead of them so's I could ride on to Croxton's. I am sure, all right."

"So Jonathan Kane is sitting back there with three thousand troops. And we have nearly twice his strength. Here, show me the lay of the land on this map. Captain Mundy, hold your lantern."

At the conclusion of Hooker's lesson in local geography, the general hurled orders at his couriers. To one he said, "Gallop ahead and tell General Bristoe to halt his column and hurry back to join me here." To another, "Get Wiggins up here on the double." And to yet another, "Fetch me Major Bolick."

Wiggins joined us within a few minutes. The general explained the situation to him.

"We have the option of turning around and attacking Kane's division. We would have the numerical advantage there. If we were sure he had no artillery, that would be the best course."

"I don't like the idea," Wiggins said. "Even if our attack should succeed, it would cost us lives and time. McIntyre would get behind us and there'd be the devil to pay. I'd favor dropping back down to Milroy Station and entrenching."

"I did not ask your opinion, General Wiggins," the general said in an icy tone.

Hooker joined in with, "General Walther said he can't hold Croxton's Crossroads long without support."

"Damn Croxton's Crossroads. And God damn Jonathan Kane, deceiving us with his demonstration. I am a fool to let them get the jump on me."

Bolick had joined them by then. Bristoe soon galloped up on a horse whose heavy breathing sounded as if it were near collapse.

His tantrum over, the general said calmly, "Gentlemen, I had hoped to slip away from our enemy without bringing on a general engagement, but General McIntyre wants a fight and we must give it to him. Time is of the essence. Here is what we must do."

Again the orders flowed smoothly from his lips. Hooker would take two couriers with him and guide the leading regiment from Wiggins's brigade along the sawmill road through Mueller's Woods. The rearmost regiment of Bristoe's brigade would retrace its steps and follow the regiment from Wiggins's brigade. These two units were to reinforce Walther.

"How long will it take you to guide them to Croxton's?"

"We can reach there by noon. There is a large meadow a short way into the woods, an old sawmill clearing. We can rest there for three or four hours and get started before sunup."

"No more discussion then. Get moving."

He then instructed Bristoe and Wiggins to allow their other

men to fall out and sleep beside the road but to be ready to move at first light.

The ground was hard and the night air cold. I made Nellie lie down and, bundled in my great coat, huddled against her for warmth. I went to sleep assuming that the general intended to return to Milroy's Landing and join with the militia in an assault on Kane's division. Instead at the dawn of that cold, cloudy morning, he ordered the eight regiments remaining in his two brigades, just over 2,000 men, to move a few hundred yards off the road and to conceal themselves in the woods. The cadets were to throw up a breastwork of fence rails on either side of the road to the south.

Then he ordered Bolick to hitch up his horses and mules and move his artillery east to the sawmill clearing Hooker said lay in the middle of Mueller's Woods. After seeing these dispositions begun and holding a final conference with his two brigade commanders, he led me and his entourage of couriers through the western edge of Mueller's Woods.

"You know what I intend to do, Jackson?" he asked as we trotted our horses along the narrow logging road.

"I gather you don't mean to give battle at Croxton's as General Walther hopes."

"Correct. McIntyre is in for a surprise. If Walther and the two regiments I have sent him can hold the Federals up until tomorrow, that will give me time to destroy Jonathan Kane."

"I don't understand why you are sending off our artillery."

"I am not going to attack him head on. I mean to ambush him and wipe him out."

"How—" I began.

"You will see."

"If you fight here, what about your plans to take Nashville?"

He jerked the reins to halt his horse and leaned toward me so the couriers could not hear.

"If I can destroy Kane's division, the road to Franklin's Ferry will be unobstructed. It is a more direct route than the one we would have had to take from Croxton's Crossroads. Walther and our two infantry regiments can return to Milroy's Landing and follow us north as a rear guard. McIntyre will be left high and dry, minus one of his divisions. Come, enough talk. The time for action is at hand."

Hooker had told the general that the meadow in the midst of Mueller's Woods was large. The clearing stretched a good five-hundred yards wide and probably twice as long. A creek with steep banks meandered along the western edge of the meadow, that is, the side nearest Milroy's Landing. Several sawmill sheds with rotting roofs stood along the western bank of the creek. Piles of ancient sawdust rose above the expanse of broomstraw and little cedars.

Bolick had halted his gun crews and their teams in the shade of the trees fringing the meadow.

Without dismounting, the general told him what to do.

"Line up all fourteen of your guns parallel to the creek. Elevate their muzzles to the maximum. Do you know what a feu de joie is?"

Bolick looked puzzled. "Can't say that I do, sir."

"You load your guns with powder only. Prime them. Then at a signal, your first gun fires a salute, then the second, then the third and so on until your last gun fires. Meanwhile, your first gun crew is reloading. If you are fast enough, by the time the last gun has fired, your first will be loaded and ready again."

Bolick frowned. "That seems like a terrible waste of good gunpowder."

The general stared at him until he dropped his eyes. "If you do not want to obey my orders, I can find someone who will."

"I will do what you say, of course, sir."

The boom of that first cannon echoed through the woods, sending flocks of birds from their perches. Then the second, and on down the line. Soon a cloud of white smoke rose up against the low-lying clouds of nearly the same color. After several minutes of this, the general told a courier to "Go and inform General Wiggins that he may join in the demonstration now. Tell him to fire six volleys into the air and then to keep up a ragged musketry for half an hour."

As the courier galloped off, he turned his gaze back to the crews working away at firing their blank charges.

"You see what I am doing now, Jackson?"

"You want Kane to think there is a battle going on?"

"Exactly. And unless he has undergone a very distinct change in character, he will not be able to resist the temptation."

"To do what?"

"To attack our militia, thinking to get behind us. They will resist, of course, but they cannot hold him back for long, not without artillery or reinforcements. They will flee down the road toward Milroy Station. Kane will follow and, while he is strung out along the road, Bristoe and Wiggins will ambush him. It will be a massacre. If I know Jonathan Kane, even now he is starting to mass his men for their assault. Ah, Jackson, is not warfare a marvelous game of wits?"

Shortly we heard the crash of musketry to the west, six volleys, just as the general ordered, and then a rattle of continuing fire.

The general was right about his old West Point classmate. He could not resist the temptation. Not an hour had passed before we heard a heavier and more distant din of musketry, a sound that could only be caused by Kane's troops.

"I doubt very much that anyone at Milroy's Landing can hear us down here anymore," the general said, then shouted to Bolick to cease firing. With that, we rode back through the woods to where Bristoe and Wiggins waited just in sight of the road.

"General Martin," Bristoe said, "it sounds as if Kane is taking your bait."

"Good, good. Now General Wiggins, don't spring the trap until their vanguard has swept by you. Wait until they have passed General Bristoe's sector and their vanguard has encountered our line of cadets. Then you hit them hard. And when you hear the firing start, you hit them, General Bristoe. Keep your regiments around their colors. Once we have got them on the run, let's keep after them. Drive them toward the river. Don't give them a chance to stop and regroup. I have instructed the cadets to disarm prisoners and guard them. As soon as I am sure our plan is working, I will send couriers to inform General Walther to bring his mounted troops and our two infantry regiments back here to follow us north. Oh, and by the way, if you should bag Colonel Kane, don't interrogate him. Just bind and gag him and hold him until I can talk to him."

For two seemingly endless hours, we sat by that road, waiting for our prey to appear. During that time, musketry from up the road at Milroy's Landing sounded continuously, sometimes in volleys, and sometimes in ragged "at will" firing. But no frightened, fleeing militia appeared with masses of blue infantry on their heels, as the general expected. Nor did we hear the boom of Yankee artillery.

The general got off his horse and walked in circles, stopping now and then to cup his hand around his ear in the direction of the firing.

Bristoe offered to ride up to Milroy's Landing and notify the militia to quit their trenches and flee.

"That would be too obvious. Kane would recognize such a withdrawal as a trap. It is important that the militia put up a real scrap."

I had never observed the general taking one of the pills given him by the surgeon in daylight until that nerve-wracking wait there beside the road. In a few minutes his manner became less agitated, and he quietly asked me to ride up to Milroy's Landing and ascertain what was going on.

"If the militia breaks while you are in the vicinity, gallop back out of harm's way. In any event, avoid talking to Turnbull but do find out what is going on."

So, with my heart in my throat, I slapped Nellie on the rump and headed her north at a brisk trot. The nearer I drew to Milroy's Landing, the louder grew the sound of musket fire. The road was straight and fairly level until, just short of the Landing, it angled up a long slope toward the river. From the top of that slope, I could see puffs of white smoke rising from the defense works and even denser clouds from the lines of the enemy. To my left, down on the bank of the Youghaloosa, I saw a paddle wheel steamer docked at the landing.

I struck Nellie's flanks with the reins and galloped her

closer. Now spent minié balls were kicking up the dust around me. I bent low in the saddle and urged Nellie to press on.

At first I could not believe what I saw in the bivouac area beside the road. But there it was, a full-sized buggy with a pair of matched roan mules hitched beside a huge white canvas tent.

I halted and spoke to the Negro who sat in the shade cast by the buggy.

"What is General Postlethwaite's buggy doing here?"

"We brung it along on the boat," the Negro said.

"Where is General Postlethwaite?"

"He come along, too. Boat brought him and us and a passel of soldiers from Texas."

"Where did the Texans come from?"

The Negro laughed and said, "They come from Texas. Where you expect?"

"Don't you get impudent with me! I am Captain Mundy and General Martin has sent me to inquire."

The Negro stood up and said, "I knows who you is. Them Texans showed up at Yardley City and General Postlethwaite loaded them on the boat and here we is. We got here this morning."

What should I do? Race back to tell the general that Turnbull had been reinforced? Or find out the full story, despite my instructions to avoid talking to Turnbull? I decided on the latter course.

Leaving Nellie in the care of Postlethwaite's now-cooperative grooms, I walked toward the bombproof where the general and I had slept. Bullets were whining overhead. Our muskets were firing away in reply. And there in the doorway of the bombproof stood Adjutant General Postlethwaite, looking more than ever like a turkey with ruffled white feathers.

"Why, it is Captain Mundy," he said. "Here, Colonel Trasker, let me introduce General Martin's aide de camp."

The man in the faded gray uniform could not have weighed more than 120 pounds and he stood only a few inches over five feet. He was bald, but the lack of hair on the top of his head was more than compensated for by the luxuriance of his moustache and beard.

"Martin's aide? Hellfire, where is Martin himself? Where is his army? We got a chance to stomp the shit out of a whole division of Yankees and he sends a fellow with a club foot."

"The general sent me to ascertain the situation," I said, doing my best to conceal my indignation at the Texan's rudeness.

"Well, here is the situation. We got to Yardley City yesterday and General Postlethwaite had the gumption to commandeer a steamboat. Damned boat got stuck overnight on a mudbank. We reached here four hours ago and just in the knick of time, too."

"That is right," General Postlethwaite croaked. "Andrew Jackson himself could not have performed better. Shot the Yankees down same as we did the British at New Orleans."

Trasker leaned out of the bombproof, spat a great blob of tobacco juice, wiped his mouth and fixed his eye on me again.

"The Yankees hit them once, and they turned them back, with heavy losses. Then they come again with bayonets just as our boat was approaching. They overrun the fort at the left of the line, next to the river. My boys charged right off the boat and retook that fort, and a good hundred prisoners with it. Since then they been keeping up a harrassing fire."

"How many men did you bring?" I asked.

"My entire regiment. Three hundred and fifty of the meanest, toughest, fightingest roughnecks you ever saw. But let me tell you this, me and my boys have been in plenty of battles, but I got to hand it to these here militia. They have put up a good fight. Now when in the hell is your General Martin going to send us some support?"

I did not know how to answer beyond saying, "He has his hands full at present," and quickly adding, "We have heard no artillery fire from your front."

"They got no cannon," Colonel Trasker said. "Their prisoners say they sent off all their guns yesterday after their second division pulled out. What in the hell is your General

Martin up to anyway? If he was here, we could run right over this fellow Kane."

"Where is Colonel Turnbull?"

"The militia commander? Why, he is dead," Trasker said. "He was killed just before we got here. The militia was ready to break and run after he fell but they bucked up when my boys showed up and retook that fort."

"Who is in charge, then?"

"I am," General Postlethwaite said. "As Adjutant General of the militia for this state, I am in command here and I have appointed Colonel Trasker to serve as my second in command."

Shaken by both these pieces of news, before Trasker could pin me down as to the general's intentions, I walked out to the star fort beside the road. The militia captain in charge of the fort warned me to keep my head down, but I could not resist peering out through the embrasure now occupied by a log "Quaker gun." Again the forms of fallen Yankee soldiers littered the ground in front of our breastworks. I did not take the time to count them, but they lay almost as thickly as they had after McIntyre's attack by two divisions. And their moans and cries for water sounded just as piteous.

Assuring General Postlethwaite and Colonel Trasker that I would convey their request for reinforcements, I ran back to the bivouac, mounted Nellie, and set out at a gallop to deliver my report to the general.

Many fears and doubts ran through my mind on that fateful ride. Surely, now the general's dream of invading Tennessee was doomed. Indeed, with McIntyre moving 9,000 men around Stony Mountain we would be hard put to avoid being trapped against the Youghaloosa. It seemed to me that we would be better off if the general had done as Walther asked and hurried both brigades and the artillery up to Croxton's Crossroads. Now, I feared, it was too late to do anything but drop back and try to defend Milroy Station. Yet, the general had been right about Kane. He had mounted a very serious attack against the militia. And, except for the timely (or untimely) arrival of the Texans, the plan would have worked. The general would have driven Kane against

the river and compelled him to surrender, thereby opening
the way north into Tennessee.

I galloped Nellie all the way back to my starting point in
the woods just off the road. Cyrus Hooker was sitting on his
horse talking to the general. I could tell from the general's
expression that he was not hearing good news. I hated to tell
him mine.

THREE

• • • Seeing me approach, the general held up his hand for Hooker to stop talking and rode out to meet me. He listened closely, his eyes never leaving my face as I relayed my unwelcome information.

When I had finished, the general said, "What you have just told me, added to the report Mister Hooker has just delivered, is doubly disturbing, but it will do no good to rant and rave. Poor Turnbull. There was never a better man. And you say the militia was ready to break after he fell?"

"But then the Texans turned the tide."

"Remember that for future reference, Jackson. My plan was sound. It would have worked except for the interference of that wretched old Postlethwaite. Well, no use crying over spilt milk. Do you think they can continue to hold the line?"

"Kane lost a good many men but I still reckon he outnumbers us better than two to one. Anyway, Colonel Trasker is anxious for reinforcements."

"Then we will send up the cadets as a reserve. Let me attend to that and then I want you to accompany me to my rendezvous with General Walther."

"At Croxton's Crossroads?"

"No, he had to fall back from that place. He has sent Hooker to ask me to meet him at the intersection of the sawmill trace and the Croxton–Milroy Station road."

It took us more than an hour to ride into Mueller's Woods, across the sawmill meadow, and on through the heavier woods to the other side. There Walther was waiting beside a large oak.

The general rode up and saluted him. Walther did not return the salute or indulge in preliminary small talk.

"God damn it, General Martin, I don't like to criticize a superior officer, but it does seem to me that you let me down when you sent only two regiments to help me hold Croxton's. I was still outnumbered five or six to one."

"I apologize, but I saw an opportunity that I could not let pass."

As the general explained his plan to ambush Kane and how the arrival of the Texan regiment had caused the scheme to go awry, Walther's angry expression softened.

"And you say it almost worked? Well, you are soon going to have to do something about McIntyre. He got around both my flanks at Croxton's and come close to trapping me. I have fell back behind a creek just four miles up the road. It won't take them long to catch up and chase us out of there. I can't see any position strong enough to hold them this side of Milroy Station."

"I have been thinking over the situation on my ride here. Captain Mundy, bring out the map and let General Walther and me reason this thing through together."

After the war, I have read of how, at Chancellorsville, with a huge Federal army advancing on them, Robert E. Lee and Stonewall Jackson sat on a pair of cracker boxes and planned the counterattack that brought the South its most celebrated victory. There on the edge of Mueller's Woods, with two full Federal divisions fast approaching, Evan Martin and Monroe Walther knelt and with sticks drew out in the dirt diagrams of how they proposed to deal with their far more numerous enemy in a do-or-die counterstroke. The audacity of their scheme amazed me.

"So I am to draw the two infantry regiments you lent me back to just this side of Milroy Station," Walther said. "They will entrench a line about six hundred yards wide and hold it with my two guns. I will keep most of my men mounted behind that fortified line and ready to ride. The rest of my fellows will dismount and guard the flanks of our position."

"That is the idea," the general said. "And I will simply move our two brigades through the woods and line them up in four ranks out of sight. The plan is very much like the one I worked out to deal with Kane. It will be an ambush but this time your mounted infantry will circle around and strike them from the other side and our two regiments in front of Milroy Station will come from behind their breastworks and pile into the head of their column. We will use no artillery except for your two pieces. Indeed it would be impossible to deploy artillery in the woods. And they will have no opportunity to bring theirs into play. The trick will be to keep their attention fastened on Milroy Station, to make them think that we are prepared to fight to save it."

"I got just one thing to add, General Martin, and that is when we get them on the run, for God's sake let's keep after them. That damned fool Bragg let Rosecrans off the hook after Chickamauga. I'd hate for us to make the same mistake. It will take all your force."

At the time, I wondered whether the general was listening, for he seemed distracted as he said, "By all means. Quite right. Now let's go over our plans once more."

By late afternoon, both Wiggins's and Bristoe's brigades were encamped along the east bank of the creek in the sawmill meadow. The general would not allow any campfires, lest the smoke be seen by McIntyre's scouts. The sporadic musket fire he heard from the east, he took to be skirmishing between Walther and the Yankee cavalry. The general went over his plans several times with Bristoe and Wiggins. Bristoe was enthusiastic about the opportunity to attack and Wiggins, skeptical. "What happens if things don't go as you plan?" Wiggins asked.

"This time we cannot fail. We have our two infantry regiments back and General Walther's mounted infantry."

"Yes, and we will be tackling ten thousand Yankees instead of three thousand."

"You just follow your orders and I will take responsibility for the outcome," the general said. "Now let us to bed. Tomorrow we will write military history."

I was too keyed up by the day's events to be sleepy after our council of war. I was saddened by the death of Colonel Turnbull and chagrined that the general's plan to smash a Federal division had been undone by a twist of fate. And I was apprehensive about what the morrow would bring. With barely 4,000 men, including Walther's mounted infantry, the general planned to attack two full divisions and a cavalry brigade, some 10,000 troops. If the enemy were strung out along the road, in marching ranks as hoped, and if the general achieved total surprise, the plan had a fair chance of success. But if anything went wrong and the Yankees broke through and captured Milroy Station, we would be caught in a pocket between Kane's division at Milroy's Landing and the larger part of McIntyre's corps, with our backs to the river.

As we retired, the general commented, "When you told me what happened at Milroy's Landing, my first thought was that our situation had been rendered hopeless, that I had been done a grievous injury by the same man who injured me nearly twenty years ago and against whom I bear a deep grudge."

"General Kane?" I asked.

"Colonel Kane. He is merely a colonel. And when I am done with him, they will take away even that rank. No, Jackson, we have been handed, not a defeat, but a marvelous opportunity. Enough talking. This damp weather is causing me pain. I must sleep well on this of all nights. Ah, there are my pills. Good night, Jackson. Get your rest, for you will need it in the morning."

Unable to drop off to sleep quickly, I slipped from our tent and walked through the camp. The moonlight was just strong enough to enable me to avoid blundering into tents or stacked circles of muskets or stepping on the many soldiers who simply slept on the ground under blankets. Some of the men talked in low tones while others snored, broke wind or ground their teeth.

I wandered beyond the camp, toward the woods, wondering as I did just how I would conduct myself in a real battle.

"Halt! Who goes there?"

I could just make out the silhouette of a sentry.

"I am Captain Mundy, General Martin's aide de camp."

"Advance and be recognized. Oh, yes, you are the fellow with the club foot."

"That is a hell of a way to put it," I said. "Who are you to be making so bold with an officer?"

"My name is Homer Beecham. Private. I didn't mean no offense, Captain."

"It is all right, Private. I was just trying to catch a breath of fresh air."

"Well, sir, I am not supposed to let anybody pass beyond this point, no matter what his rank."

"This is far enough for me, anyway. Where are you from, Private?"

"From Georgia, up in the hill country near Rome."

"You are in General Wiggins's brigade then?"

"That is right, sir."

"Your brigade was engaged in trying to stop Sherman from taking Atlanta. You must have passed close to your own home."

"We did that. Camped about five miles from my house. In fact, me and two of the other fellows slipped off and paid our families a little visit. We did not have permission but we went anyway."

"Weren't you put on report as deserters?"

"No. They was so glad to see us when we showed up outside of Atlanta, they didn't ask no questions."

"How did you find your people?"

"Not too good. You must of heard the saying about how this is a rich man's war . . ."

"And a poor man's fight. Yes, I have heard that expression."

"There is a whole heap of truth in it. My pore old daddy is just about wore out trying to work our sixty acres with both his boys in the army and what little money he has not worth the paper it is printed on. You wouldn't know about that, would you? Your family is rich, ain't it?"

"What makes you say that, Private?"

"You ride a good horse. Your uniform looks new. You sleep in the same tent with General Martin. Now, don't tell me you ain't rich. Your family owns niggers, too don't they?"

"We had twenty slaves when the war began, but one has died and one ran away. But my family has suffered, too. My father also is 'just about worn out.' The war has been hard on everyone, rich or poor."

"It ain't quite the same, though, Captain. If we win, you get to keep your niggers. In fact they will be worth more than they was before the war, I reckon. Whereas, things will be the same as ever for poor crackers like me. Look a'here, Captain, you are a educated man, ain't you?"

"I attended our state university, yes."

"There ain't no schools where I live. I can't even write my name. Since you are the educated one, maybe you can tell me what you think this dadgummed war is all about, anyway."

"We are fighting for the independence of the South, the same as our ancestors fought to make the colonies free of British rule. We are fighting for states' rights . . ."

As I fumbled for further words, the sentry broke in with, "I don't mean to dispute the opinion of a educated man, but the way I see it, we are fighting to keep niggers in slavery."

"For slavery? You just said your family owns no slaves."

"No, but yours does and there is many right in our county that does. Now, as a white man, I don't aim ever to live in a country where niggers is free to come and go the same as me and members of my family. It is just that simple. I don't give a damn for states' rights and all that shit the politicians talk about. If we got to have niggers around us, they ought to be slaves. If I thought it was going to be any other way, I would take myself out to California where I hear there is few niggers now and never likely to be many."

I started to dispute the sentry's assertions, but decided instead to bid him good night and return to my tent.

Sad to say, even in 1901, there are many in my state and others of the South whose views on race relations are not that much different from those of that Georgia cracker's in 1864. Were that not the case, I would still be serving as a U.S. senator.

FOUR

• • • It was not yet full light when Bristoe and Wiggins quietly awakened their eight colonels, who in turn aroused their company commanders, who in turn awakened their lieutenants and sergeants and so on, down to the lowliest ragged and often barefoot private.

Wreathed in an early morning ground fog, the meadow on which this sleepy assortment of rude soldiery assembled sloped gently up from the creek east to the edge of Mueller's Woods. On this wide expanse of open ground, the two brigades lined up in four long ranks by regiments, as if on parade. Bristoe's four regiments were assigned to the right of the sawmill road, Wiggins's to the left. Each man had been ordered to prepare sixty rounds of ammunition and to keep his bayonet sheathed until the order to attack was given.

The general mounted his white horse and rode up and down the ranks. Then he assembled the eight regimental commanders on the sawmill road and gave them their final instructions.

"Our other two regiments are dug in across the road to Milroy Station just four miles from here, with General Walther's mounted infantry. We want to let the enemy column march right past these woods in pursuit of General Walther's skirmishers. You are to remain concealed until you hear Walther's two cannon begin to fire. That will be the signal for General Bristoe's front rank to fix bayonets and charge forth from the woods. Give them the Rebel Yell and open fire on them, at which point your second rank is to advance, cheering. They will come up with you and open fire. At that point, your third and fourth ranks will emerge and join you. Once the battle is fully joined, General Wiggins's front rank will charge forth and join the fray, striking the column directly in his front. And shortly thereafter, the larger portion of General Walther's men will circle to the east and fall upon them from the other side. We want to create panic in their ranks. Drive home your attack and you will break their column in two and trap the head between your brigade, General Bristoe, and our two regiments in front of Milroy Station. It is of the utmost importance, however, that we allow the front of the enemy column to clear the woods before we open our attack. I only hope that the fog is as thick on the other side of the woods as it is here. That will add to our enemy's confusion. Now gentlemen, I commend you to the Gods of War. Let our work begin."

During the review and the briefing of the colonels, Bolick's artillerymen lounged about their cannon as if the proceedings had nothing to do with them and, indeed, it was not part of the general's plan that they should. His instructions to them were to stand by their guns and keep their animals harnessed, ready to take the road promptly. Whereto, he did not specify.

The general also had ordered Major Ferebee and the other surgeons to set up their field hospital tents in the woods west of the creek and to stand ready to receive the wounded. "I do not expect heavy casualties, but it is best to be prepared."

The front regiments of first Bristoe's and then Wiggins's brigades moved forward and disappeared into the east woods, breaking ranks to pass around the trunks of the half-grown trees. They might have been ghosts, so quietly did they tread through the early morning mist.

The general sat on his horse watching as the second rank followed close behind the first. The two brigadier generals waited on horseback until he raised his hat, whereupon they led their third and fourth ranks into the ghostly woods.

The general turned to me and smiled. "Mark this scene well. Is it not a splendid spectacle? Now comes the waiting."

He had anticipated that it would be mid-morning before we would hear Walther's two cannon open up as the signal to launch the attack. Actually he never heard them fire at all. Spatters of musketry sounded from time to time during the next half an hour, sounds, we assumed, of skirmishing between Walther's men and the Yankee cavalry, but no artillery.

The general had dismounted to attend to a call of nature behind a clump of cedar bushes when suddenly an eruption of musket fire sounded to the east. I dismounted to help him button his trousers. By the time I had completed this embarrassing exercise, a Rebel Yell sounded, followed by a volley even larger than the first.

"Something is wrong," the general said. "The firing is too close. And we have not heard Walther's guns. Come, let us see what is happening."

He remounted his horse and cantered along the sawmill road into the east woods, followed by four couriers and one very frightened and dismayed aide de camp.

Often during the past thirty-seven years I have had a recurring nightmare in which a great battle is taking place in a tangled forest just ahead. Men are shouting in the distance. Bullets are singing overhead, bringing down showers of twigs and bark. Four men carrying a fifth on a litter appear on the road ahead. Out of the fog emerge other men with bleeding arms and shoulders. The farther I penetrate the woods, the louder grows the crash of muskets, thousands of them, banging away so fast that the din sounds like hail falling on a tin roof, only infinitely louder. The fog grows even more dense and the acrid smell indicates it is mixed with gunpowder smoke. Now the air becomes alive with bullets, buzzing like hordes of hornets. Any second one will strike me. And then I awake, often in a clammy sweat, with my heart beating hard and my breath coming in racking gasps.

What happened on that October morning in 1864 in the wilderness of second growth trees called Mueller's Woods was not so very different from my recurring nightmare. And there was no awakening from this nightmare once it had begun.

Long hours would pass before the general learned that McIntyre had not known of the presence of our two Confederate brigades in Mueller's Woods, that he had heard the mock firing of Bolick's cannon the day before and assumed that Kane's division was being attacked at Milroy's Landing.

Nor could the general have known that someone, probably a disaffected poor white of the area, had informed McIntyre of the shortcut through Mueller's Woods, causing the Ohioan to dispatch a brigade toward Milroy Station merely as a screen and to order his main column to move through the woods in the hope of getting behind and trapping our main Confederate force, only to blunder into those of our men concealed nearest the sawmill road.

And now a major battle developed in a way neither general had anticipated. It was to be what veterans call "a soldier's battle," one which, once joined, must be fought out on the ground, regiment by regiment, company by company, even man by man.

Neither the general nor I knew anything of this as we rode, now at a cautious walk, toward the maelstrom ahead.

The sawmill road was intended as the boundary between Bristoe's brigade on the right and Wiggins's on the left. This demarcation would have made no difference had the attack gone forward as planned. Like a rotten seam in a garment, however, it was the weakest point in our line now that we had been thrown on the defensive. And that was the point at which the head of the column of Yankees had been headed when they blundered into our troops.

Even with the hindsight of thirty-seven years, it is impossible for me to render a coherent, detailed account of what came to be called the battle of Milroy Station, although fought mainly in Mueller's Woods. The men of Bristoe's extreme right and center had no idea of what was happening to their comrades on the left. They could only hear the increasingly heavy firing from that sector. The same was true of the men on Wiggins's extreme left, only they could see a thick column of Yankees on the road in front of them. Neither General Wiggins nor General Bristoe knew what was going on any more than their soldiers. Bristoe could see no Yankees in his front. Wiggins saw plenty, but he had heard no boom of Walther's cannon and, steady, obedient soldier that he was, he delayed making his attack, which was just as well, as it turned out.

Meanwhile, the Yankees at the head of the column that was trying to penetrate Mueller's Woods were taking heavy fire from our men in position on either side of the sawmill road. Momentarily balked by this unexpected resistance, they contented themselves with blindly firing back at their unseen foes.

I do not know just where General McIntyre was situated during the battle of Mueller's Woods. I assumed it was very near the point where the general and Walther had conferred the day before. Nor have I ever discovered who sent orders down the road for the Yankee brigade closing in on Milroy Station to delay its advance, or who ordered the brigade just behind the vanguard approaching the juncture of the sawmill and the main road to wheel through the woods to try to get behind those "Rebels" firing furiously at the head of their column, or who, instead of withdrawing from the woods upon encountering this unexpected resistance, ordered a regiment of Negro soldiers to fix bayonets and clear a path along the sawmill road. It may have been no one person, but merely different officers reacting to some very confusing circumstances, each in his own way.

Thus developed the battle of Milroy Station. The Federal brigade ordered to wheel into the woods ran right into Wiggins's lurking men, but these steady Yankee veterans did not panic. Instead they held their ranks and returned our galling fire, volley for volley.

As we rode along that poor excuse for a road through Mueller's Woods, the general stood up in his stirrups trying to see. By now it was apparent that the fighting was taking place in the woods and not out on the main road as he had planned. He stopped his horse and slumped in the saddle, listening to the sounds of the growing battle. I had never seen such an expression of horror and disbelief. Something had gone wrong with his plans and there was no one for him to shout at or to question. For the moment, this man who loved power so much was powerless.

It was at that point when the first Yankee brigade encountered the bulk of Wiggins's men, for the firing spread to the north and increased to a new crescendo. Shortly after that, while the general was still trying to puzzle out this new circumstance, the musketry just ahead of us paused. I heard a roar which could only have come from Yankee throats and suddenly a mob of Confederate soldiers rushed along the sawmill road, panic in their faces.

The general drew his revolver and tried to stem this tide of fleeing men, but they ran right past him, back toward the meadow.

Waving a sword, a captain ran after the men, shouting for them to "Hold your ground, you yellow cowards!"

Seeing the general, he halted.

"They threw a whole army of niggers at us. We held them as long as we could but there's just too many of them. General Martin, you had better clear out or they will capture you."

The flow of routed soldiers halted briefly, as did the firing. Then a fresh volley crashed ahead of us and the air once more became alive with minié balls singing through the trees. The last—the bravest or the most stubborn or perhaps the stupidest—of the soldiers came running toward the general and me. One, a lanky sergeant, grabbed the reins of the general's horse and turned the animal's head toward the meadow.

"General Martin, you had better get your ass out of here," he said. And with that, he slapped the horse on the rump and continued his flight to the rear.

The horse seemed as anxious to quit the woods as the soldiers. The general was nearly thrown from the saddle by the animal's lurch, but he recovered his balance and snarled at one of the couriers, "Race back to the creek and tell Major Bolick to double load his guns with canister. Now, let's get out of here."

Wishing I had a faster steed, I leaned low in the saddle and thumped Nellie in the ribs with my heels. The general overtook the fleeing infantry at the edge of the meadow and shouted for them to reform their ranks on the opposite bank of the creek.

Had the battle occurred in open country where the soldiers could see what was happening, there would have been an uncontrollable panic throughout all of our ranks, for the enemy had broken the center of our line and there were no reserves to mend the break. But as it was, the bulk of Wiggins's men were occupied on the left with the hapless Yankee brigade who blundered into them and were holding their own, too. Except for those of his soldiers stationed along the sawmill road, Bristoe's men were still waiting in the woods, if not oblivious to, at least ignorant of what was going on.

I followed the general back across the meadow, through the still disorganized mob fleeing the woods, and across the creek. Bolick, normally so casual and lassitudinous in his movements, was raging at his artillerymen to load their pieces and roll them out toward the creek bank. He sited his six Napoleons a dozen yards apart in the center, with a battery of regular three-inch ordnance rifles drawn up on either side.

The Napoleon, although smooth-bored, was a favorite artillery piece of both armies. With a muzzle diameter of 4.62 inches, it took a larger charge and could be loaded faster than the rifled, smaller-bored ordnance gun. Made of bronze, it weighed half again as much as the iron-cast ordnance rifle and was less accurate, but for this situation, it was the ideal weapon. And Bolick, ruthless villain that he was, just may have been the ideal artilleryman, at least in those circumstances.

While Bolick and his artillerymen sweated away, the general shamed the refugees of the sawmill road encounter into reloading their muskets and forming a thin line of battle along the western edge of the meadow, just behind the cannon. The highest ranking officer among them was the captain we had met on the road. So the general took personal command.

The expression that I had witnessed in the woods had faded from his face. He rode back and forth, exhorting first Bolick and then the increasingly more confident infantrymen.

There was no time for throwing up breastworks or for further hortatory addresses, for out of the woods beyond the meadow there suddenly boiled a blue-uniformed torrent of black-faced soldiers. They paused for a moment, while an officer on a sorrel horse scanned the creek bank with his field glasses. He then raised his sword over his head and lowered the point toward our massed guns. And with that the Negro troops came howling across the meadow, over the mounds of sawdust and around old heaps of pine slabs. As they drew nearer, I made out that they were shouting "Ain't gwine take no quarter," but at the time attached no significance to their cries.

I looked along the scraggly line of Confederate infantry as they bit open the ends of their cartridges, rammed the charges down their musket barrels, stuck ramrods in the earth, cocked and capped their weapons and fixed their bayonets.

"Hold your fire until the cannon open up," the general shouted. "And make sure you don't shoot our artillerymen. If they get across the creek, go after them with the bayonet."

I marveled that our infantrymen did not again take to their heels, for the sight of so many soldiers trotting toward them, bayonets glinting in the faint sunlight, was awesome. So great was my fear, had I not valued my reputation, I would have led their flight myself.

"Are you ready, Major Bolick?" the general asked.

The redhead's face glistened with sweat as he replied, "We are ready. All guns are loaded and primed."

The artillerymen had drawn their limbers up about twenty yards behind the cannon and their caissons and horses back another thirty yards, in the edge of the woods with battery wagons and other impedimenta. At that point I would not have bet a depreciated Confederate bank note on their chances of surviving the tidal wave of shouting, blue-clad Negroes.

General Walther had expressed a low opinion of the value of artillery and for his type of fighting he was right. Soldiers dug in behind breastworks did not fear artillery, even bursting shells. But as a defensive weapon, firing canister at attacking infantry, artillery was another matter.

"Fire all your guns at once when I give the signal," the general shouted. "Then continue firing as fast as you can load."

Here let me point out that many Confederate soldiers felt a great hatred for their northern enemies, whom they considered invaders trying to despoil their land and force upon them a foreign way of life. But that hatred was felt even more intensely for Negro soldiers who donned the blue uniform. Sectional animosity mixed with racial antipathy to produce a seething rage, especially in those Confederates who, unlike me, had had little personal contact with slaves. I did not appreciate, much less sympathize with those feelings, but I did understand them.

For my part, having grown up with our family's slaves, I had developed a lasting affection for the black race, which partially explains why that awful day in October 1864 would be the longest and most terrible in my life.

FIVE

• • • I watched in fascinated terror as the black horde rushed across the meadow in a formless mass, as if drawn by a magnetic force toward our fourteen cannon sitting just behind the creek.

If they had held their fire until they reached the creek bank and then poured a volley into our ranks at that short range, the Negroes would have wiped out Bolick's artillerymen and a good part of our infantry in a twinkling. But instead they discharged their muskets on the run, in some cases in the air, as if to frighten our men away. Had they not paused near the edge of the creek, as if afraid of getting their shiny new brogans and fine wool uniforms wet, but had pressed through the water with their bayonets, they would have taken casualties, certainly, but enough survivors would have got among Bolick's crews to put his Napoleons out of business. But they did pause, to reload and to wait for the officer on the sorrel horse to catch up with them. And as they hesitated they taunted, "Ain't gwine take no quarter," meaning they meant to take no prisoners.

"You God damned niggers!" Bolick screamed and, without waiting for the general's order, jerked the lanyard of the first Napoleon. The cannon leapt backwards, spewing a great cloud of smoke clear across the creek, and in an instant the other five guns in the battery fired. Nellie, normally so placid, reared and shied from the noise, but before I could get control of her, the batteries of three-inch ordnance rifles joined in the carnage. An infantryman broke ranks to grab Nellie's bridle and calm her down. I dismounted and, with trembling knees, watched the rest of the action on foot.

All the cannon were firing canister, as the general ordered. At such a short range, this was like employing giant shotguns loaded with oversized buckshot. Upon leaving the cannon muzzles, the tin cylinders or canisters ruptured, spewing forth their deadly iron balls. Through the smoke I saw that swaths had been plowed through the mass of blue across the creek. Yet few of the black soldiers flinched. Many leapt into the water, so that when Bolick's guns fired their second blasts, the Negroes were protected by the creek banks. An intrepid few climbed up the bank and scrambled toward our cannon.

Bolick fired his revolver point blank at one Negro. Another was knocked down by a heavy rammer staff. One of the artillerymen took a bayonet in the thigh. Our infantry, having recovered their courage, charged forward and chased this vanguard of valiant blacks back into the creekbed. And again the cannon roared.

Now the Negroes on the opposite bank, no longer so thickly massed, fell back, loading and firing their muskets as they withdrew. The ground became littered with mangled forms. The victims cried out in pain. While Bolick's men reloaded, our infantry rushed forward and poured a volley into the Negroes. The officer on the sorrel horse clutched his stomach and slumped over his saddle's pommel, too stricken to stop the animal from bolting back across the meadow.

The now-leaderless black soldiers sullenly, slowly melted back from the creek bank but continued to return our fire. Several artillerymen were on the ground, their places taken by infantrymen.

I marvelled at the efficiency of Bolick's gun crews. No longer firing in unison, they moved like parts of a machine. With the others standing clear, one man would jerk the lanyard, the gun would roar and recoil several feet but, even before it stopped rolling, a crewman would run his long, sponge-tipped staff down the barrel, wait for another man to jam the fixed canister round in the muzzle, then would ram home the charge while the sergeant held his thumb over the vent and the lieutenant sighted the gun and helped others roll the carriage forward again.

Then, as the others stepped aside, the number three man thrust a pick into the vent to prick the cartridge. Another filled the vent with priming powder and cocked the firing device. All stood clear. Someone screamed "Fire!" and the complicated process began all over again. The farther away the Negroes withdrew, the less effective became the canister shot, however. Seeing this, the general ordered Bolick to "Switch to shells! Cut the fuses short."

"I am near out of cartridges," Bolick replied.

And in truth he was. He had a goodly supply of solid shot and shell but his demonstration of the previous day had used up much of his gunpowder.

That which remained was put to good use. The black soldiers had stood up courageously to canister fired at deadly close range, but as shells began to burst around them and over their heads, they took to their heels as rapidly as they had advanced.

"Cease fire!" the general shouted. "Infantry, follow me."

And off he took across the creek and over the bloody ground on the other side, his horse tossing his head and stepping around the forms of the fallen blacks. The infantry gave a mighty Rebel Yell and swept forward. Once they had cleared the creek and were running after the general, I mounted Nellie and followed.

In the creek a score of unwounded black soldiers cowered with their arms wrapped around their heads. I paused to look down at them from the opposite bank. Seeing my glance, Bolick said, "Don't worry about these niggers, Captain Mundy. I'll take care of them."

Nellie was reluctant to go forward because of the dead and wounded black soldiers on the opposite bank. I dismounted and led her over and around the mangled bodies. I had to steel myself not to stop and respond to the pleas for water and mercy.

I had gotten past the worst of the carnage and had remounted Nellie when someone called, "Massa Jackson! Massa Jackson! Please dear God, Massa Jackson!"

There, behind a sawdust pile, sat Ben, dressed in a new blue Yankee uniform, holding his leg just above its smashed kneecap.

"What the devil are you doing here?" I asked.

"Oh, Massa Jackson, help me. I am dying for water."

I dismounted and examined his knee. It was a bloody mess but he seemed in no danger of bleeding to death. The limb would have to be amputated, of course, but his life was in no immediate danger, or so I thought at the time.

With my pocketknife, I cut through the stout wool trousers leg and then washed the kneecap with water from my canteen.

"Please, can I have a drink?"

A dozen emotions ran through my heart as I watched him gulp the water: pity for his injury, anger for what I saw as his desertion of our family, and affection for the patience and kindness with which he had treated me when I was growing up.

When he had done drinking, I remained kneeling beside him.

"You have got some explaining to do, Ben," I said.

He began haltingly but soon his words began flowing faster and faster, interrupted only by an occasional groan at the pain.

It had taken him several weeks to make his way from Glenwood to a Federal cavalry camp in Tennessee. Mose somehow had got his hands on a printed pass form and had filled it in with the name of "Ben Mundy, blacksmith." Mose had instructed Ben on the story he should give any Confederate soldier or militiaman he should encounter on the road, namely that he had been sent to locate his master's son in a Federal hospital at Nashville. And Mose turned over to him all the coins he had amassed as tips during twenty years of working at the livery stable.

Gradually my indignation was overcome by my admiration for the audacity of what Ben had done. He said he would have been arrested several times except for that pass and the well-practiced story he learned from Mose, a story that was buttressed by his possession of so much money, which he claimed had been entrusted to him to purchase medicine and other necessities for the mythical wounded soldier son of his master.

A colonel of the Federal cavalry camp welcomed Ben and put him to work shoeing mounts.

As Ben told it, he might have continued working as a farrier and saving his money in this way until the end of the war had a newly recruited brigade of U.S. colored troops not been sent nearby to join General McIntyre's old division.

"I felt like if I did not join, I would regret it for the rest of my life. Maybe you would have to be black like me to understand that, too, Massa Jackson."

Tears were running down his face.

I had to chew my lips to keep from breaking down myself. I put my hand on his shoulder and asked about his experience in the Federal army.

Ben, like others in his unit, knew that the white soldiers doubted their courage and thought they would flee if put into a real battle.

As he was explaining this, one of the militia couriers came galloping back from the woods.

"General Martin sent me back here to see where you was. He says to fetch you back to him right away."

"Tell him I am coming," I said to the courier, then to Ben, "Why were you shouting that you would take no quarter?"

"Some Rebels, excuse me, I mean Confederates, in blue uniforms shot some of our pickets that was guarding our pontoon bridge up at this ferry landing. Shot 'em down in cold blood. They didn't take no quarter."

"Look, Ben, I have got to go. You stay here behind this sawdust pile. Keep my canteen. I will come back and see that a doctor looks after your knee."

With Ben's cries of gratitude in my ears, I galloped Nellie across the meadow and back into Mueller's Woods.

At the edge of the woods, I heard the sound of firing to my rear and thought for a moment that Yankees had got around our flanks. I looked back through my field glasses at the creek bank.

There were no Yankees in sight, only Bolick's artillery-men standing on the creek bank with revolvers in their hands and, to my horror, they were firing down into the water. It took a moment for the significance of the sight to sink in.

The general was sitting on his horse, far up the sawmill road in the woods, looking back at me. I galloped up to join him.

"Where the hell have you been?" he demanded.

"The artillerymen are shooting prisoners."

I told him what I had seen through my field glasses and implored him to go back and stop the slaughter.

The general looked at me incredulously. "In the midst of a battle you want me to go back to save the lives of a few Negroes?"

"May I ride back and tell them you order them to stop?"

"If they have begun the work it is better that they continue it. Now, come, let us follow the men."

"But it is monstrous what they are doing."

"You heard the Negroes shouting that they would take no quarter, did you not?"

"That was just an expression. Please, I will go and tell Major Bolick you say—"

"I do not wish the business to be ended. Either they should kill them all or none at all. Stop Bolick now and you would leave witnesses." He paused and seeing the sickened expression on my face, lashed out with, "Don't be a sentimental milksop, Mundy! This is war. One Bolick is worth a thousand Negroes. Never was artillery better handled. That man saved our army. This is an order. We will never again speak of this and you will advance with me. I have a battle to win."

The sawdust pile behind which Ben lay was far enough from the creek bank so that I did not fear for his safety. So, like the milksop the general had called me, I followed him back into the depths of Mueller's Woods.

I have wished a thousand times these past thirty-seven years that I had disobeyed the general's orders and taken whatever consequences that might have ensued. My conscience would have been far clearer had I done so. And the course of my life would have been far different.

SIX

● ● ● Yes, I have agonized through many a troubled night, wishing that I had defied the general's order and had galloped back to put a stop to the murder of those helpless black prisoners of war. But my shock at the shooting of the Negroes was mixed with my anxiety over the outcome of the battle, sounds of which still rang through the woods, for despite the general's brave words, the fighting was far from over. If the Negro soldiers had been reinforced, a second attack would have succeeded, for Bolick had run out of gunpowder and the Southern line of infantry was so thin.

In the end the general, or his soldiers, did win the battle of Milroy Station. It was not a crushing defeat for McIntyre but, against overwhelming odds, we did stop his advance and cause him to withdraw to Croxton's Crossroads. The battle did not follow the plan the general and Walther had concocted, but the results were nearly as good as they had hoped for, at least in the short run.

The surviving Negro troops fled clear through the woods and back to the Croxton–Milroy Station Road. They carried back hysterical reports of masses of artillery and huge reserves of infantry, thereby spreading panic among the already confused Yankee ranks.

Meanwhile, Wiggins's men continued their firefight in the woods to the left of the sawmill road. And shortly after the rout of the black troops, the brigade McIntyre had sent to feel out the defenses of Milroy Station withdrew and marched directly in front of Bristoe's brigade, still concealed in the woods to the right of the sawmill road.

I did not witness the attack Bristoe finally got to make, but from all reports—and especially from Bristoe's own—it was delivered flawlessly. I did hear the triumphant Rebel Yell as Bristoe's men drove home their charge and scattered the brigade before them.

The fighting continued hot and heavy for more than an hour. The head of the Yankee column withdrew gradually. I estimated that a good half of McIntyre's 10,000 troops were still lined up on the road leading from Croxton's and had not got involved in the battle at that point, but something had caused the Yankee general to lose his nerve. Neither the general nor I were to know the reason until the following day.

It had been threatening to rain all morning. Around noon, a downpour began and continued for more than an hour. When it stopped, we could see that McIntyre was in retreat.

The general was joined on the Croxton–Milroy Station Road by an exultant Bristoe. "General Martin, we drove them like a herd of cattle. They ran from us. It was wonderful."

Even Wiggins, coming from the woods to join them, was smiling. "Those fellows hung on like a case of the itch. We held our ground but we have taken a good many casualties."

Bristoe was all for regrouping his men and attacking McIntyre's rear guard. Wiggins favored getting his wounded out of the woods and giving his men a rest. Meanwhile fresh firing could be heard to the north, in the direction of Croxton's.

"I take that to be General Walther skirmishing with their rear guard," the general said.

I have often wondered what might have happened if the general had done as Bristoe advised, that is, leave a few men behind to carry the wounded from the woods and bury the dead, call up the two regiments from Milroy Station, and press north to overtake McIntyre and bring him to battle again while he was rattled. Subsequently we were to learn that the Federals had lost well over a thousand men that morning while our losses were only a few hundred. But McIntyre's corps, while shaken up and frustrated, had not been mortally wounded. He remained a dangerous adversary.

"Well, sir," Bristoe asked. "What are we to do?"

The general rubbed the stump of his right arm and frowned. "What's that?"

"We await your orders, sir. My men are ready to advance and join General Walther in pursuit of the enemy."

"McIntyre has much artillery."

"So do we."

"I fear we do not."

He told them about the stand in the meadow and the exhaustion of Bolick's ammunition.

Bristoe was crestfallen. Wiggins spoke up with, "I say let well enough alone then. We have whipped them. I say follow them at a safe distance and shoo them out of this area. I don't favor another battle, not when we lack gunpowder for our cannon."

Bristoe crossed his arms and shook his head. "I can't believe that we are to sit here and let them get off scot free."

The general straightened up and smiled.

"We are not going to just sit here. General Bristoe, have your men fall in and march them back to the sawmill clearing. General Wiggins, you fall in behind and follow."

"To the clearing?" Bristoe asked. "Why in heaven's name move in that direction, to the rear?"

"After you reach the clearing, take half an hour to rest and eat and then move on the double step up to Milroy's Landing. The landing is eight miles from here. Be there by half past five."

"What about my dead and wounded?" Wiggins asked.

"I will send Bolick's artillery crews out to carry your wounded back to the field hospital on the other side of the clearing. Let the dead bury their dead. No more talking. We must put the cap on this stellar victory. Come, let's get going."

Bristoe's brigade was well on its way to the clearing, and Wiggins's men were falling in on the sawmill road when up galloped the scout, Cyrus Hooker.

"General Walther has sent me to tell you he needs infantry support to keep the Yankees moving."

"Where is General Walther?"

"On the road about three miles from here. His boys are snapping at McIntyre's heels but he can't do them much damage without some help."

"It is too late. We are headed back toward Milroy's Landing. Tell General Walther that as soon as he is satisfied McIntyre is in full retreat I would like him to bring his entire force back through the woods and join me at the landing."

Hooker looked at the general with an air of disbelief.

"You mean you have whipped the enemy and have him on the run and you don't propose to follow up on your victory?"

The general's face clouded at the scout's impudence, but he kept his voice even as he replied.

"I would explain my intentions to General Walther in person if there were time but every minute is of the essence. You just tell him that we can achieve far greater results at Milroy's Landing than we can in harrassing McIntyre's main column. If McIntyre is withdrawing anyway, the last thing I want to do is to try to impede his progress."

"Monroe will not like this," Hooker said. "He believes that when you wound a bear you should move in and finish him off. He will not like this at all."

I had never witnessed an outburst of temper from the general such as that which followed.

"I have told you what message you are to relay to General Walther. If you were in uniform, I would place you under arrest for insubordination. Now, damn it, go and tell General Walther what I wish him to do!"

A man with lesser spunk than Hooker might have withered before this scathing rebuke. The scout's face darkened for an instant but he did not lower his eyes. Nor did he make a reply, although it seemed clear to me there was something else he wanted to say. Sullenly, almost leisurely, he turned his horse's head and set off at a trot to the north.

The general's hand was shaking as he fumbled in his coat pocket for his box of pills. Then he squared his shoulders and spurred his horse back through the woods toward the sawmill clearing.

To keep clear of the general until his mood improved, I rode well behind him. As we emerged from the woods, my eyes swept across the clearing. The once human blue-clad lumps lay still. I turned Nellie toward the pile of sawdust where I had left Ben.

He still lay there, on his back.

"How are you, Ben?"

For a moment, I thought he had gone to sleep or that he had fallen unconscious from the pain. His arms were flung out. And then I saw that his eyes were open, staring at the sky.

"Ben," I said. "Are you all right?"

I nudged the reluctant Nellie closer and saw at last the hole in the middle of Ben's forehead. My canteen lay beside him. I started to dismount, but did not trust my legs. The sky turned white. A wave of nausea rolled over me. I leaned over the saddle pommel and vomited on Nellie's mane. I could not bear to look down at Ben again.

Many is the night I have dreamed of that patient brown face turned skyward, the eyes staring toward heaven, with a round hole in the middle of the forehead. Many have been the waking hours in which I have reproached myself for not staying behind to protect him.

I turned Nellie's head and rode on toward the creek berating myself for having assumed that the artillerymen would shoot only the black soldiers cowering in the creekbed and for not thinking that they might extend their atrocities to include the murder of the wounded men beyond the creek.

At the sight of Bolick talking to the general, I had an impulse to ride up and shoot the artilleryman just where Ben had been shot, squarely between the eyes.

Instead, I approached the pair and said in a trembling voice, "General Martin, do you realize what this man has done?"

"If you are referring to Major Bolick, he has saved my army. I was in the process of congratulating him."

"He is a murderer," I said.

"What are you talking about?" Bolick said. "See here, this is uncalled for."

"He and his men killed those darkie soldiers in cold blood."

"Look a here, General," Bolick said. "Do I have to put up

with this kind of abuse? Them niggers refused to surrender."

"Captain Mundy!" The general's voice cracked like a whip. "I think you owe Major Bolick an apology."

"He does not deserve an apology. He deserves to be put on trial for the murder of prisoners of war."

The general turned to Bolick. "I will apologise for my aide, Major. Go about your business and we can discuss this matter later. Come, Mundy, follow me. That is an order! Disobey it and you will find yourself under arrest."

I was at the point of refusing when the general shrewdly added, "Yes, under arrest and placed in the custody of Major Bolick, I might add. Is that what you want?"

He set off at a brisk trot toward the main road between the station and the landing, with Bristoe's brigade in his wake. Outraged and resentful, I followed the line of march.

In a few minutes the general summoned me to ride up alongside and began speaking slowly and evenly as though his outburst had not occurred.

"This day has gone better than for a time I feared it would. Far, far better. Do you realize, Jackson, that we whipped a force of twice our size and did it at very small loss to ourselves? I am sorry to disappoint General Walther, but I fear that in the excitement of battle, he may have lost his perspective. When an enemy is doing what you wish him to already, in this case withdraw from your territory, it would be foolhardy to assail him afresh. Just you remember my reasoning when you record the doings of this day for posterity."

"I have noted all that happened today," I said with a sarcastic edge. "Everything. And I shall not forget one detail, I assure you."

The general looked at me, then smiled and turned his gaze back to the road before continuing.

"Yes, about all that happened, it should not be necessary to note my show of temper at Hooker. He did speak to me in a disrespectful way, did you not think?"

"There was something else he meant to say to you," I replied. "But you cut him off before he could say it. Just as I was trying—"

"Whatever it was, I merely want you to understand that I prefer no mention of the incident be made in my memoirs. Also, Jackson, that business about the Negroes was most regrettable. It should not have happened, but it did, and there is nothing more to be done. I have ordered Bolick to remain behind and strip the dead of their uniforms and bury the bodies deep in a common grave. I know you were shocked that I did not intervene or allow you to, but war is war. It would have been far more regrettable if I had neglected my responsibilities to our army. That might have cost us the victory and led to heavy loss of life among our soldiers."

I was tempted to point out that the general's presence had made little difference on the outcome of the battle after he had directed the last-ditch stand along the creek, but held my tongue and let him ramble on.

"So, in the larger scheme of things, what difference do the lives of a score or two of Africans make? And besides, Major Bolick assures me that those fellows in the creek refused to surrender."

I could remain silent no longer. "That is a goddamned lie. They were offering no resistance when I crossed the creek. And it was not just a score. There were many other wounded when I rode across the clearing, and they were all dead when we returned. One of them happened to be a slave from my father's plantation, our blacksmith in fact. He taught me to ride and fish. His wife is our family cook. I spoke to him when we advanced and promised to return to his aid."

"Really? How remarkable. Well, let's dwell no longer on that subject. We have more important things to concern us."

Again I started to reply, but the general looked me full in the eye and said, "I will regard it as a gross disobedience of orders, subject to severe discipline, if you mention this subject again."

He put his spurs to his horse and left me behind.

I halted Nellie and pondered what to do. It was too late to save Ben's life. If I were to leave now, I would be considered a deserter. Even if I escaped punishment, I would forever be held in contempt by my neighbors as a coward. And whatever hopes I had of winning Sarah Martin's hand would be destroyed. So, God forgive my failure of true courage once again, I kicked Nellie in the ribs and, feeling very sick at heart, followed General Martin; followed the man whom once I had thought could do no wrong, to perhaps the strangest part of all my story.

PART SEVEN

ONE

• • • The general had hoped to reach Milroy's Landing by 5:30. The first of Bristoe's regiments got there a half hour earlier.

We found old Postlethwaite sitting in a camp chair beside his buggy. His servants were serving him supper. Having regained his composure, at least outwardly, the general dismounted and greeted the old man with feigned enthusiasm.

"I want to offer you my heartfelt congratulations over your brilliant repulse of the enemy yesterday. Andrew Jackson himself would be proud of what you have done."

"We have been wondering where you were," Postlethwaite began.

"We have just smashed the other wing of the Federal army and have returned here to help you finish the job you so valiantly have begun. Now, where can I find the colonel of the Texans?"

"He is up at the bombproof. Here, I will take you to him."

"Please, please, don't interrupt your meal. If one of your boys will just look after my horse, I will go and pay my respects. Then I will return so that we can confer."

Before the old man could rise from his chair, the general was on his way toward the bombproof.

Remembering Colonel Trasker's rude criticism of the general when I came to ascertain why the militia had not given way, and with the volcanic encounter with Cyrus Hooker even fresher on my mind, I dreaded the meeting that was about to occur.

Trasker was sitting on a blanket in the bombproof playing chuck-a-luck with three fellow Texans. A whiskey jug sat beside him. The entrance to the bombproof was coated with tobacco juice.

"Which of you is Colonel Trasker?" the general asked.

"I am Colonel Trasker," the little man replied. "Who are you?"

"I am Major General Evan Martin."

Still sitting and holding his cards, Trasker said, "It is about time you got here. Where in the hell have you been?"

The general stared at the little man for a long while before replying, "If these other gentlemen would excuse us, I would like to speak to you in private."

At last rising, Trasker said, "Nothing wrong with that. Sam, Ralph, you fellows go check on things out on the firing line."

The general waited until they were gone and then said, "Now then, you asked where I had been. We have been engaged in heavy combat with two Federal divisions about seven miles from here. We have whipped the enemy and he is in retreat."

"Well I reckon that is all right—"

"Yes, it is all right. Now then, you answer me a question, Colonel Trasker. The War Department assured me that we would be met by two regiments of Texans at Yardley City two weeks ago. Did you receive those orders?"

"We got them, sure, but only one of our regiments was in shape to come."

"And you did come, but rather late, wouldn't you say?"

"I would say we got here at just the right time. Saved these poor militia from being wiped out."

"To use your expression, 'Where in the hell were you?'"

Trasker spat his tobacco quid into his hand and tossed it out the doorway. "Now, you look a here, General Martin, I am not used to being talked to like this. I would think you'd appreciate the fact that me and my boys retook a fort from the Yankees and prevented a rout amongst your militia."

"I would think that you would appreciate the fact that you are talking to a major general who is also your commanding officer. All it would take would be one more show of disrespect from you and I will put you under arrest and replace you as regimental commander."

Suddenly all the fight went out of the little man. "Now, there is no call for that, General Martin, sir. I reckon I mis-poke myself when you come in. Us Texans don't stand on ceremony, you know."

"Stand. You said 'stand.' If you are going to serve under me, you will stand when I approach you. It is common military courtesy. Now, then, you retook a fort?"

"We did that, and captured a hundred Yankees."

"Are you ready to fight again?"

"My boys are always ready for a fight."

"If you were backed up by two brigades of battle-tested regulars, as well as the militia, would you and your boys be willing to lead an assault on the enemy lines?"

Trasker stamped his foot and said, "My boys would follow me right into hell if I asked them to. When do we start? First thing in the morning?"

I could not believe the general's reply. "No. Within the hour. By the time night falls, I want to have whipped Kane to his knees. That would make this day complete."

From that point events moved so fast I could not compre-hend them. Allowing for their losses in repelling Kane's as-sault, there were about 1,500 militiamen and Texans already in the works. Bristoe's brigade would bring that strength up to about 3,000. The arrival of Wiggins's brigade would in-crease our strength to over 4,000; if Walther got there in time, that would add another 1,000 men. His heavy losses in his assault on the Milroy Landing defenses the day before left Kane with no more than 2,500 effectives, by my reck-oning.

Neither side would have any artillery. Ours was out of ammunition and, presumably, McIntyre's was all with him at Croxton's Crossroads.

The general sent a courier to summon Bristoe. As we waited, he talked to a now thoroughly overawed Colonel Trasker and the boy commander of the cadet regiment.

"With forty-five hundred men this day we have whipped an army of over ten thousand. 'We' includes General Walther's mounted infantry, of course. It is just as well that

we have no artillery. We would lose valuable time position-
ing our guns, and a bombardment would only alert Kane. He
will not be prepared for a surprise attack, would you think?"

"I reckon he figures our works are still occupied by nothing but the state militia and a bunch of ragged-assed Texans,
but we have taught him to respect us," Trasker said. "He
sure ain't bothered us much today, beyond taking potshots."

"And his forward line remains out there where Colonel
Turnbull dug those rifle pits for our skirmishers?"

"Near as we can tell, that is where they are."

"Good. Ah, here is General Bristoe. General, this is Colonel Trasker. We are planning our attack on Kane's division.
I must strike him before he is rejoined by McIntyre."

Bristoe's face went white when he realized that the general
expected his men, who had fought a brisk battle at noon and
then marched eight miles at a fast pace, to mount an attack
within a few minutes.

"But it will soon be dark."

"That is good. They will be eating their rations."

"My men are tired. They need time to rest."

"All that I ask is for them to go a few hundred yards more.
Colonel Trasker's valiant Texans will lead the charge. On
several occasions you have counseled me to attack. Here is
your opportunity to show what you and your men are made
of. Come, man, I am giving you a chance to make military
history."

"Very well, sir. Tell me what you want us to do."

As quickly as Bristoe's men arrived, they were sent regiment by regiment into the trenches on the right to crowd in
with the militia. Trasker concentrated his Texans in the center of the line. The plan called for Wiggins's men to bolster
the left of the line, but as the sun sank near the horizon, they
had not yet arrived.

By then Trasker had become fully caught up in the spirit
of the attack and was impatient to start. "In another half an
hour it will be too dark to begin."

"Very well, have your men load their muskets and fix their
bayonets. You do the same, General Bristoe. Colonel Trasker's men advance first, against the center. When they are

halfway over the intervening space, you launch your attack on the right, General Bristoe."

The commander of the cadet regiment was a broad-shouldered chap of seventeen. He interrupted to say, "General Martin, sir, we would like the honor of participating."

"Well said, young man. As soon as General Bristoe's men are across, then you lead your lads over, following behind Colonel Trasker's valiant Texans. And then I would like all of the rest of the militia to advance, on the left as well as the right."

"What about Wiggins?" Bristoe asked.

"He should be very near by now. Captain Mundy, please ride back and guide General Wiggins and his men up to their positions on the left. Tell him to feed his men into the battle regiment by regiment in support of the militia on the left as fast as they arrive. Hurry! The attack will begin in a quarter of an hour."

I ran as fast as my foot would allow back to where Nellie was tied up beside Postlethwaite's buggy. The old man tried to detain me as I mounted.

"General Martin said he was coming back to consult with me."

"Been delayed," I shouted, and lashed Nellie's flanks.

I found Wiggins only a quarter of a mile down the road, at the head of his lead regiment.

"Has the man lost his senses?" Wiggins said after I had told him what he was to do.

"He wants to take them by surprise, while they are eating supper—"

The long screech of a Rebel Yell pierced the chilly autumn twilight. It was followed by a sputter of musketry which was followed in turn by steady small arms fire.

"The attack has begun. You had better hurry."

Wiggins turned and shouted for his regimental commanders to come forward, then said to me, "I think the man is a damned fool, but it sounds like it is too late to stop him. Tell him we'll come as fast as we can."

A fresh Rebel Yell and a mighty outbreak of musketry rent the air as I galloped Nellie back toward Postlethwaite's camp. I tossed the reins to a servant. Strapping on his sword, Postlethwaite emerged from his tent.

"Captain Mundy, wait. I am coming, too."

I pretended not to hear as I hobbled toward the sounds of the full-scale battle that now raged.

The cadets were lined up shoulder to shoulder by companies in ten ranks. The general, oblivious to the hail of minié balls flying around him, stood at the rear of one of the star forts, completing an address to the boys.

". . . On this day you will attain immortality, young gentlemen. Present arms. Advance!"

The older, larger lads were in the front ranks. They went forward with a Rebel Yell, then the next rank and so on. Some of the boys in the rearmost rank looked as though they had not yet attained puberty. These babes in arms, some barely as tall as the Enfield rifled muskets they carried, stumbled forward, yelling their battle cries in soprano voices.

I told the general that Wiggins was on his way.

"He had better hurry, or he will miss out on the kill. Ah, Jackson, is not war splendid? I have lived all my life for this day. Ah, Jonathan Kane, I should hate to be in your shoes."

Directly ahead, in the center of the line, Trasker's Texans rushed up atop the mound of earth that marked the Yankee line and thrust down with their bayonets. Some disappeared on the other side and some fell back into the ditch. The cadets huddled behind, waiting for their chance to join in the fight. To the right, Bristoe's men were standing and firing away at point blank range.

At that point, the militia all along the line jumped over their parapets and went forward at a trot. The Yankee defenses to the left, toward the river, erupted in a wall of muzzle flashes. The militia fell in droves, but the survivors pressed on a few paces and halted when another volley struck them. Then they foolishly delayed their advance to fire a volley of their own. A great Yankee hurrah echoed all along that sector and, hit with yet another volley, the militiamen turned and fled back toward the safety of their defenses.

The general ground his teeth and swore. "Damn that Wiggins. Why can't he hurry?" Then he turned to a courier and said, "Run over and tell them reinforcements are on the way.

Tell them to advance again as soon as General Wiggins arrives."

He turned his gaze to the right. The militia in that sector had mixed in with Bristoe's struggling regulars so that it was impossible to see who was huddling in the ditch and who was scrambling up over the mound to get at the Yankees on the other side.

The struggle in the center of the line and to the right continued, with the cadets now joining in. The walking wounded were filtering back toward the old defenses. Each of the injured militiamen were being assisted by two or, in some cases, three concerned friends.

The general roared at these skulkers to stop playing the Good Samaritan and return to the battle. "Let them lie there if they can't come back on their own, you damned cowards. Return to your units."

It seemed an eternity before a fresh Rebel Yell sounded to the left, and there went Wiggins's brigade, not piecemeal by regiments as the general had ordered, but in one long rank, with regimental flags flying and bayonets poised. Wiggins had skillfully wheeled his brigade off the road and brought them up almost shoulder-to-shoulder to join the battle-shocked militiamen who huddled in the defenses. It was as neatly executed an attack as any delivered in the war, and it was made by a man the general had thought lacked élan. The Yankees opened up as soon as they began the charge but, unlike the militia and despite their losses, they did not pause to return the fire until they crossed the ditch and mounted the earthwork, at which point they fired down into the enemy and took possession of the defenses. Whereupon the militia advanced in their wake and followed them up and over the parapet.

Shortly thereafter, a cry of triumph sounded from the center and moments later, to the right, Bristoe's men surged out of their ditch and went over the top in their sector.

We had carried the Yankee works but the price in Southern lives had been high. Strewn over the same ground on which masses of blue-uniformed men twice had fallen dead and wounded, there now lay a litter of gray-and-butternut–clad forms.

General Postlethwaite chose that moment to appear. The general threw his arm about the old man's shoulders and danced him around in a circle.

"We have routed them, General Postlethwaite. Now we must clinch our victory."

He released the befuddled old man and whipped his revolver from its holder. "Come along, Jackson, let us see the denouement of this drama."

We ran across the intervening three hundred yards of cleared earth toward the center of what had been the Yankee line. All around lay fallen Confederate soldiers and militiamen. By now the sun was down and we could see but a short distance in the dying light.

The ground just in front of the Yankee line lay thick with wounded and dead Texans and cadets. The general took no notice of them in his eagerness to see what was happening beyond. He scrambled over the ditch and up to stand on the parapet. At his feet lay two or three scores of dead and wounded Yankees. Ahead, in the dusk to the right and left, the entire Southern force was feeling its way north in shadowy clumps. The firing had diminished now, and certainly, the general was justified in thinking that he had gained his much-desired victory over his old West Point classmate.

"I have ordered that we continue our advance until we have overrun their camps. Oh, if only we had another half an hour of daylight—"

Abruptly, without any warning, the terrain all across the front, about two hundred yards to the north, lit up with yellow and red darts of flame. The sound of more than two thousand Yankee muskets shattered the calm that had fallen briefly over the darkening battlefield. Again, the Rebel Yell sounded, to be answered by hoarse hurrahs. For the next fifteen minutes the firing continued at a mad rate.

Several times I urged the general to come down from his exposed position atop the parapet but he acted as though he could not hear.

"What can be happening?" he asked. "They seem to be making a fresh stand."

He soon got his answer. Out of the dark, our soldiers began walking back toward us. Unwounded men they were, still carrying their muskets.

The general screamed at them to stop, to turn around and return to the battle but, not knowing him in the dark, they ignored him. At last Trasker appeared being half carried by two of the officers with whom he had earlier been playing cards.

"What is the meaning of this withdrawal?" the general demanded.

"They outfoxed us," Trasker said. "We should of waited until morning. They all run back to a line of rifle pits back there. They have put abatis all along the front. We couldn't see where we were going. My poor fellows. Half of them have been hit."

"You turn around and lead your men back or I will find someone who will."

"You are going to have to find someone anyway. I have took a ball in my belly."

Leaving the survivors of the attack huddled in their ditch, the general and I withdrew to the bombproof, where we were soon joined by Bristoe and Wiggins. From them we learned what had happened.

Before he pulled out his two divisions to try to get around our flank, McIntyre apparently had created an extensive set of defense works for the very use to which Kane had put them, that was, as a refuge in case of an attack by a more numerous foe. He had combed the countryside for saplings and tree branches to be turned into sharpened stakes and fashioned into abatis. And he had created fields of fire into which our men, thinking they had the enemy on the run, had blundered.

The general listened to their reports in glum silence. No one was sure what their casualties had been. The Texans thought they had lost half of their men. Bristoe reckoned that only two thirds of his remained alive and unscathed in the old skirmish line ditch. Wiggins counted his losses at perhaps 25 percent. The militia had no idea of its casualties.

The general sat on a keg and listened to the dismal reports of his lieutenants. His shoulders sagged and his face looked

as though he had aged ten years in that one day. From time
to time he massaged his arm stump and made a face.

All the while that this conference was going on, litter-
bearers bringing in the wounded streamed past the bombproof back to the field hospital Major Ferebee had set up to
the rear. The moans and curses of the stricken men at times
made it difficult to hear what was being said.

At last Bristoe and Wiggins fell silent and waited for the
general to speak.

He stood up and squared his shoulders, then said in a quiet
voice, "Gentlemen, I salute you on your success thus far in
this battle. The great state of Texas can be proud of what its
sons did here today when they broke the center of the enemy's line. And General Bristoe, your men demonstrated the
kind of stubborn courage that makes an army indomitable.
Our militia had already shown its pluck on the defense and
now we know they can fight equally well on the offense.
And I speak in particular of the brave young cadets. I shall
carry to my grave the image of those valiant young men
springing forth to support the Texans. And finally my old
war horse General Wiggins, I was impatient when you did
not appear as promptly as I had wished but then when I saw
that line of infantry charging so cooly, so magnificently, I
was overcome with admiration both for their disciplined
courage and for the consummate skill of their commander.
Yes, gentlemen, I salute you all. The first phase of this battle
has gone well. Tomorrow will bring the completion of our
victory."

Wiggins and Bristoe looked at each other. This time it was
Wiggins who spoke first.

"General Martin, I would have to say that this battle is
over. I don't see what more we can accomplish. My men are
just plain fought out."

"I hate to admit it," Bristoe said, "but General Wiggins is
right. Kane is too well dug in for us to get him out, not with
frontal assaults."

The general continued as though he had not heard them.
"Always, in every great battle, there comes a point where
the outcome turns on which side slackens its effort and which
presses on. Military history is replete with examples of vic-

tories which were won by fresh effort in the face of discouraging reports."

Wiggins interrupted. "Meaning no disrespect, General Martin, I think if you had been out there after we overran their first line, you would understand why we had better let them well enough alone. Kane's lines are just too strong to break with the manpower we have available."

The general continued, "Yes, fresh efforts will bring fresh results. Since the dawn of this long, long day we have whipped the larger part of the enemy host and sent it reeling in ignominious retreat. We have doubled back and driven the smaller part of our foes from one line of defenses—"

"And we have lost a lot of men, too many men for my stomach," Bristoe said.

"—from one line of defenses, and in the morning we will demolish the remnants of his forces."

"You really want us to renew the attack?" Wiggins asked.

"At dawn every man and boy in our command will go forward in one grand rush. My only mistake this evening was in not waiting until General Wiggins was on the scene. I will not make that mistake again. And by morning we will have General Walther and his mounted infantry."

"Mounted infantry will be useless in an assault against well prepared breastworks and rifle pits," Bristoe grumbled.

"General Walther and his mounted infantry will ride forward after we have flushed the enemy from their works and they will chase down and harass the fleeing remnants. And then he will have the honor of leading our triumphant little army northward into Tennessee."

"General Martin," Wiggins said. "Please, listen to reason. You don't understand what you are asking us to do."

"I am asking that you do your duty, that you live up to the oath you took when you accepted your commission. We will attack in the morning at first light. Anyone who declines to join in the attack should declare himself now and I will strip him of his command and rank and send him out of our lines in disgrace as a coward and a slacker."

Wiggins exchanged a glance with Bristoe, and said, "May I make one request of you, General Martin?"

"What request is that?"

"Please, do not send those cadets into battle again. Some of those boys are babies. They are the seed corn of the South. They must be kept back for the future of our people."

"He is right," Bristoe said. "Hold back the cadets. Enough have fallen already."

"I will not use the cadets unless absolutely necessary. That is understood. Mass all your men in the old skirmish line, you on the right, General Bristoe, and you on the left, General Wiggins. You will assume command of the militiamen in your respective sectors. And once again our brave Texans will occupy the center of our line. At dawn, you will hear the bugle call to charge and this time you will press forward just as General Wiggins did this evening. Well, it is growing late. To your posts, gentlemen."

Bristoe spoke again. "General Martin, we are clearing our wounded from the ground over which we made our first attack. What about all our poor fellows who are lying out there beyond?"

"They will have to lie there for a while longer. We can pick them up in the morning after we have finished off the enemy. Besides, our surgeons have their hands full as it is."

"By morning a good many of the wounded will be dead," Bristoe said.

"In that case we will have to bury them. Now, good night gentlemen. This council of war is adjourned."

The general left the bombproof to attend to a call of nature. I sat in a state of shock at his ruthlessness. I did not know the full extent of our casualties any more than anyone else, but it was plain that we had suffered very heavy losses. And now the general was prepared to risk even more lives, and for what? To avenge himself on a longtime personal enemy? To follow his will-of-the-wisp dream of invading Yankee-held territory, with the fought-out remnants of two brigades and fourteen pieces of artillery which now lacked proper ammunition?

My mind still reeled from the knowledge of the slaughter of the Negro prisoners, yes, and at the General's callous disregard of the atrocity. But was he not showing equal callousness in leaving his own wounded soldiers to lie unattended out there in the cold dark? Did this vainglorious man really care one whit about the South and its people of either race? Was he concerned about anything other than his own lust for military glory?

As I pondered these questions, my eye fell on the jug Trasker had left in the bombproof. As suddenly as though someone had lit a candle in a dark cave, I knew what should be done. Without a thought for the personal consequences of my impulsive act, I picked up the jug. It was perhaps a quarter full. The general had taken off his coat before going outside. I fumbled in the pockets until I found the box of pills. Apparently he had obtained a fresh supply from Major Ferebee, for the box was nearly full.

I spilled six pills into my hand, and replaced the box in the coat pocket. Then, looking out to make sure the general was not approaching, I poured the opium pellets into the whiskey and shook the jug vigorously.

The general returned soon thereafter and sat down on his cot to remove his boots.

"This has been a long day and a hard one, too, Jackson," he said. "But it has been exhilarating as well. And tomorrow will be more so. When you write your history of this battle, do not overlook the fact that I resolved to continue our attack when those of weaker hearts and smaller minds counseled me to cease. Ah, this arm gives me such pain."

He took his box of pills from his coat and frowned when he saw how few there were. Then he drew out two.

"Sir," I said, "you seem very tired."

"And with good reason, would you not say?"

"Yes. Anyway, I notice Colonel Trasker left his whiskey jug behind. Thought you might like a dram to ease you off to sleep."

For a moment, I feared that he would refuse.

"Yes, that might be helpful. . . ."

"Here is your cup. Shall I pour?"

"Easy there, Jackson, not too much. Will you join me?"

"I drink only wine, sir."

"Suit yourself," and with that he raised the cup to his lips and drained it.

"Vile stuff," he said, making a face.

"Would you like more?"

"No, no. I must have a clear head in the morning. Make sure I am awake well before dawn, in case I do not arise first. There, there . . ."

He lay down and drew a blanket over himself. "Put out the lantern, will you, Jackson? God, I am so very weary."

TWO

• • • Within seconds after I extinguished the lantern, the general was snoring. I poured the remainder of the whiskey on the ground and stretched out on the floor of the bombproof. But sleep was out of the question, so furiously was my mind working.

Thus I was wide awake when a voice called, "General Martin. Are you there?"

"He is asleep," I said softly. "Who is it?"

"This is Monroe Walther and you can just wake his royal highness up. Him and me has got some talking to do."

I prayed that the general would not awaken. My prayers were answered. The snores continued.

"Do you hear me? Wake the son-of-a-bitch up."

I scrambled to my feet and got to the door of the bombproof in time to block Walther's entrance.

"General Walther, I want to confer with you."

"I don't want to confer with no little lap dog. I want to talk to the master himself, Almighty Evan Martin—"

"This is serious, General Walther. We must talk."

I stepped outside the bombproof and seized the horseman's elbow. Walther shook off the grasp, but did stop to hear what I had to say.

"Make it short and to the point. I got a bone to pick with Major General High-and-Mighty Martin."

"We have had a terrible battle this evening," I began.

"I can tell that. I just come by the surgeon's tents. Looks

like them butchers will be hacking away until sunup. What happened to cause all them casualties?"

Going back to the first of the day's events, I related everything that happened right up to the conference shortly before, everything, that is, except Bolick's slaughter of the Negro prisoners. I was still too shocked to talk about that.

"You have been at his side all day?"

"Practically."

"Then you heard what he said to my friend Cyrus Hooker."

"I did hear it. If Mr. Hooker was upset, I can understand why, but the general was in a tense situation and Mr. Hooker did talk back to him."

"I don't give a good country shit about who talked back to who. I had McIntyre on the run and Martin let me down."

"He was afraid of bringing them to battle again. Like I said, we used up the last of our artillery's gunpowder in repulsing the attack by the colored troops. Without artillery, he thought the odds would be against us."

"That damned fool," Walther said. "McIntyre didn't have no artillery either. That's how come he retreated. Cyrus would of told Martin if the man had let him finish what he was to say."

"What do you mean?"

"When I seen how thick the Yankees was massed along the road past the woods I wasn't about to attack there as we had planned. So we rode on across the country to the north, out of sight of the road, and struck their wagon train. It was pure luck they had no cavalry escort. The mule drivers took to the woods. We overturned their wagons and cut their teams loose and drove them off. Then we rode back south and overtook their train of artillery. We shot half of their crews and the rest skedaddled, so my boys chopped up the spokes of their gun carriages and spiked their cannon. If we had not of done that, McIntyre would never of turned back."

"We assumed he had withdrawn because we handled the head of his column so roughly," I said.

"That ain't the story we got from prisoners. One of them told me McIntyre near went to pieces when he heard he had lost his artillery and a good part of his wagon train. Be that as it may, I still want to talk to Martin right now."

"That is impossible," I said. And then I told him why.

"You mean to tell me you have drugged the man's whiskey?"

"I could see no other way to prevent him from causing the pointless slaughter of hundreds more of my fellow Southerners."

"If one of my chaps was to do that to me, I would have him shot. No, I would shoot him myself. Do Bristoe and Wiggins know what you have did?"

"No one knows but you."

"Son of a bitch, Mundy. I figured you for a little spoiled rich boy playing soldier. You got more grit than I give you credit for, but you have took a hell of a big risk. Martin could be right, you know. One big rush at dawn might do the trick. Did you think about that?"

"There wasn't time to think about anything. All I know is that General Martin has some sort of obsession about humiliating his old classmate and invading Tennessee and he doesn't care what price we have to pay to achieve his desires."

"What do you mean, obsession?"

I explained what I knew at that time of the General's antipathy for Jonathan Kane, then added, "and I fear that the pills Major Ferebee has given him have warped his judgment. He has been taking more of them than he should."

"How old are you, Mundy?"

"Twenty-three."

"That's mighty young to be taking it upon yourself to disable your commanding officer and mess up his plans. Whose side are you on, the North or the South?"

"I am a true born Southerner and I realize that General Martin does not give a hang about the South. I also realize that if he is incapacitated, that you would be on the scene to take charge, since you are senior to both Wiggins and Bristoe. And you have the common sense to know whether we should continue the attack in the morning or leave it alone."

"So, you are trying to involve me in your shenanigans?"

"I trust your judgment. I no longer trust General Martin's judgment or his motives."

"We'll leave it at that. I am going to see my fellows bedded down for what is left of this night. I will meet you at first light. Maybe we should have a little talk with Wiggins and Bristoe before we disturb General Martin's slumber."

After Walther had left and I had lain down again, the enormity of what I had done finally sank in. What if the general were right, what if I had robbed him of a great victory, thereby causing our horrible losses to have been in vain? Had I done a courageous or a foolhardy thing?

I was still awake when the first light appeared. The general slept on, as deeply as ever. I looked down into his face and wondered how I could have been so taken in by the man's charm. "General Martin," I said tentatively. "It is time to get up."

As I hoped, the general slept on. So, I put on my coat and walked out to the star fort beside the road. Wiggins and Bristoe were already leaning against the rampart, watching as their men began stirring in the old skirmish line breastwork across the way.

"Where is General Martin?" Bristoe asked.

"He will be along in a little while."

"He wanted to start the attack at dawn."

"I don't think he meant right at the crack of dawn."

"Well, it is all right with me if he wants to wait till Christmas," Wiggins said. "What do you think, Bristoe?"

"I have been thinking, and maybe Martin is right. It would be a shame to stop if one more push would do the job."

Wiggins shook his head, then looked at me and said, "Captain Mundy, I want to ask a favor of you."

"Certainly, General Wiggins."

"I want you to hold my watch and this picture of my wife and daughter. And here is a letter for my wife, as well. Just in case, you know."

I took the items.

"I wonder what happened to Walther," Bristoe said.

I bit my tongue to keep from telling of the arrival of the mounted infantry. Wiggins and Bristoe left to go and see to the preparation of their troops for the attack. The seventeen-year-old commander of the cadets came and joined me in the fort.

"You are Captain Mundy, aren't you?" the boy said.

I acknowledged that this was so.

"And I hear tell that you have served in the Confederate War Department in Richmond and have been over in London with General Martin. I'd give anything to do something like that. General Martin is a wonderful man, don't you think? We are lucky to have him on our side. That is the kind of soldier I want to be. When the war started I was just thirteen and I was afraid it would all be over before I got old enough."

"How many of your boys got killed last night?" I asked.

"I don't know for a fact. A lot of them just didn't come back. I reckon it was only a dozen or so that we lost."

"I would have thought it would be a lot more than that. I saw you help break the first Yankee line."

"Yes, but after that, when it started to get dark, Colonel Trasker made us turn around and go back. He wouldn't let us follow them when they made the next attack. But we are ready this morning. I wouldn't miss this for anything."

I did not have the heart to dash his enthusiasm by telling him there very likely would be no attack and that, even if there were, he and his cadets were not supposed to take part.

By now the rim of the sun had cleared the horizon. Wiggins and Bristoe returned to the fort.

"My men are ready and so are the militia," Bristoe said.

"So are mine," Wiggins said. "As ready as they'll ever be."

The major who had replaced Trasker as commander of the Texans appeared.

"Where is General Martin?" he asked.

"He is still fiddling around back in his nice warm bombproof," Bristoe replied.

"Well, I got trouble."

"We all have trouble, or soon will," Wiggins said.

"I mean our fellows don't want to lead the charge this morning. They say they led off last night and that it is someone else's turn."

"There is no problem with that," Bristoe said. "General Martin has decreed that everyone will go forward at once. All except for the cadets. He will hold them back."

"What did you say, sir?" the boy commander asked.

Bristoe explained what he meant. The boy's face crumpled and for a moment I thought he would cry. "That is not fair. We have as much right as the next ones. Where is General Martin? He can't do this to us."

And before I knew what was happening he was running across the killing ground back toward the old lines. I called after him to stop, but he only ran faster.

THREE

● ● ● A good ten or fifteen minutes passed before I saw the general riding toward us with the cadet commander leading his horse.

His coat was buttoned the wrong way. His hair and beard were streaming water. Apparently he had soaked his head in a bucket to get himself awake; the steam coming from his nostrils made it appear that he was breathing fire.

And so, he was, in a metaphorical sense. He made straight for me and demanded in a slurred, angry voice, "What are you doing out here? Why did you not awaken me at dawn as I ordered?"

I hate lying and despise liars, but in this case I could not tell the truth, and so said with a shaking voice, "Why, sir, I did speak to you and you answered. I came out to tell Generals Wiggins and Bristoe that you were awake."

He looked at me with a fierce gaze. "You should have stayed until I was dressed. Look there, the sun is well up."

"Maybe you want to postpone the attack," Wiggins said.

"Never! Are your men ready as I instructed?"

"Mine are," Bristoe said.

"And so are mine," Wiggins said with an air of resignation.

"Where are our brave Texans? They must be given the honor of leading the advance."

The Texan major said, "Our fellows have asked me to say that they would just as soon you gave somebody else the chance to distinguish themselves. They don't want to hog all the glory."

The general looked at the Texan with contempt. "Colonel Trasker said his men would follow him to hell."

"He ain't here. And the boys ain't all that fond of me."

"Sir," the cadet commander said. "The cadets of the Francis Marion Military Academy request that they be given the privilege of leading this attack."

"My brave, brave young man," the general said.

Wiggins walked closer to the general's horse and said, "General Martin, last night at our council of war, we asked you to hold the cadets out of the battle today and you said you would."

"No, General Wiggins. You and General Bristoe requested that I do so but I made you no promises. I will not deny this young hero's request. Line up your cadets and prepare to advance."

Back on the rampart of the star fort beside the road, General Walther was waving his arms to attract our attention. I pointed him out to the general.

"You tell General Walther that I want him to saddle up his horses and prepare to follow us. Do you think you can carry out that one order at least, Captain Mundy?"

"He is mounting his horse. I think he wants to talk to you."

"It is too late to spend time conferring. Bugler, sound the call to charge."

And with that he put the spurs to his horse. Up the bank the steed climbed and forward rushed the two hundred cadets, screaming their adolescent Rebel Yells. Wiggins's men, or most of them, scrambled out of their ditch and swept forward, following their regimental flags. The militiamen moved with less alacrity. In their ranks there was much stopping to tie shoe strings and to pick up dropped equipment. In fact more than a few never left their trench at all. To the right, Bristoe's brigade now went forward and, again, only part of their assigned militiamen joined them.

General Walther, breathing hard and sweating, galloped up beside me. The general's horse was going at a trot, just fast enough so that he did not leave behind the cadets.

"General Martin wants you to saddle your horses and pre-

pare to follow him as soon as he takes the enemy's works,"
I said.

"General Martin is out of his mind if he thinks I am going
to join in this foolishness . . . Oh, my God, he is leading an
infantry charge against fieldworks on horseback. And a white
horse at that. What a damned fool."

I braced myself for the Yankees' first volley and prayed
that the cadets might be spared.

The ground over which the Confederate infantry moved in
a mile-long line was dotted with the forms of soldiers who
had fallen the night before. And the closer the line swept
toward the abatis in front of the Yankee works the thicker
lay the clumps of the dead.

Here and there along the enemy works, puffs of smoke
arose.

"They must be holding their heavy fire until we get tangled
up in the abatis," Walther said.

The forward rank surged up to the rows of sharpened
stakes and piles of felled bushes. The soldiers lifted the ob-
stacles out of the way. Again puffs of smoke arose sporad-
ically from the Yankee works, but still they held their "heavy
fire."

Then, to my amazement, the entire Confederate line joined
in a Rebel Yell, and, with the general still astride his horse,
they rushed right up the slope and began planting their regimental flags atop the parapets until all ten flew there.

"I will be God damned," Walther said. "They have took
the works. Here, Mundy, climb up behind me and let's see
what is going on."

I clung desperately to Walther's broad back, trying to keep
my seat on the horse.

"How in the hell did he manage to wake up?"

I told him about the cadet commander.

"And does he know what you did?"

"I think he may suspect. He is very angry at me."

At the edge of the earthworks, Walther stopped and let me
slide down from his horse. I climbed up to the top. Except
for one lone soldier sitting down and holding his ankle, there
was not a Yankee in sight.

The general was standing up in his stirrups, gazing to the

north through his field glasses. All around him militiamen were cheering. The cadets were tossing their kepis in the air and slapping each other on the back. Bristoe's and Wiggins's men were searching around the enemy works for plunder.

Pointing to the lone Yankee prisoner, Walther commanded, "Bring that fellow over here."

He was a tubby little Irishman, very near to crying from the pain of his presumed wound. Walther did not find it necessary to threaten him with his revolver to get him to talk.

"Colonel Kane pulled out last night, about an hour after yer attack. He left our regiment behind to keep campfires going and to sharpshoot at yer. Everybody ran when ye reached our abatis. Just me luck to turn me ankle, and not one of me friends would stop to help."

"Where is your division headed?"

"Sure and ye wouldn't expect a poor private to know that, would ye?"

Seeing Walther and me, the general rode over.

"General Walther, I am glad you have at last arrived."

"Yes, General Martin, I have arrived."

"Captain Mundy told you what I wish you to do?"

"He said you requested me to follow up your attack and harass the survivors."

"I am glad that he could remember to do that. And where are your men and horses?"

"They are back in camp eating breakfast."

The general seemed bewildered for a moment, then frowned and said, "I would like my orders to be carried out with more alacrity, sir. Our victory will not be complete until we have run Kane's division to earth and destroyed it."

"What victory are you talking about?"

"The one we have just achieved by taking these field-works."

"General Martin, meaning no disrepect, I was just talking to this prisoner. He says Kane pulled his division out before midnight and left just one regiment behind to fool you. These works was not defended. By now Kane is a good ten miles or more from here—"

"Wherever he is, I want you to run him down and keep

him engaged until the rest of our army can close in on him."

"General Martin, sir, let me suggest that we withdraw to your command post and confer together with General Bristoe and General Wiggins about this here situation."

"Don't be ridiculous. We must advance, not withdraw."

"Well, then, maybe it would save time if we met in that little gin house down the road there toward Fleming's Store. You will want to hear my report on yesterday. And we ought to figure what our remaining strength is, don't you think?"

"Very well, but let's not drag out this talking. We must strike again while the iron is hot."

The tin-roofed gin house had served Kane as his divisonal headquarters. Some of Bristoe's men were busy ransacking the place when the General and Walther rode up, followed by Bristoe and Wiggins, and of course, a very apprehensive Captain Jackson Mundy. The looters scattered like chickens from a hen house at the approach of a fox.

The four generals dismounted and went in. As I stepped on the porch, a private said, "You are General Martin's servant, ain't you?"

"I am his aide de camp," I replied.

"Whatever you call yourself, we found this here nailed to the door here."

He handed me a manila envelope which seemed to contain a small package. And on the front of the envelope was written:

TO MAJOR GENERAL "ABLE" MARTIN, FOR HIS EYES ONLY

I slipped the envelope in my pocket and thanked the soldier.

Inside, Walther was telling an impatient General Martin of the remarkable success he had achieved the day before in disrupting McIntyre's wagon train and disabling his artillery.

"That is how come I sent Cyrus Hooker to get you to come up and take after McIntyre. I have to admit, General Martin, I did not appreciate the way you treated my scout."

"General Walther, the personal feelings of one spy do not figure large in my scale of what is important. What matters now is that we do not lose the fruits of our victory."

"Maybe it don't matter what you said to Cyrus, but if you had heard him out he was supposed to tell you what we done.

My fellows put more than twenty Yankee guns out of action. And we overturned half of their wagons. How come you think McIntyre turned around and started retreating?"

I saw that the general was having a hard time controlling his temper. His hand trembled and his face twitched.

"Congratulations are in order for you and your mounted infantry," he replied, paused and continued with a tinge of sarcasm, "as they are for Major Bolick for his superb repulse of the Negro troops, and for General Wiggins for steadfastly standing his ground in the woods, and for General Bristoe for his timely attack on his front. There was glory enough in yesterday's exploits to satisfy us all. But this is no time to rest on our laurels. Are you prepared to advance, find what is left of Kane's division and engage them until Generals Bristoe and Wiggins, with the militia, come up and finish the job?"

"No," Walther said. "I am not prepared to do that."

The general's jaw dropped open. Wiggins raised his eyebrows. Bristoe looked at the floor in embarrassment.

"Let me make sure of what you are saying," the general said. "Do you mean to declare, in the presence of witnesses, that you refuse to carry out the order of your commanding officer? Think carefully before you reply, General Walther."

The general had picked the wrong man to try to overawe.

"Maybe you would like to excuse these here other gentlemen so we can talk in private," Walther said.

"No, I want them to remain. The issue is joined and we might as well settle it here and now. Do you refuse to obey my order?"

"Maybe we ought to get something clear, General Martin. My instructions from the War Department was to cooperate with you in the defense of this state. My command is independent. I recruited my men and paid for their weapons and equipment out of my own pocket. I have been cooperating with you because I know an army can't have two bosses. So why don't you get off your high horse and face what kind of mess we have got ourselves in here, instead of talking some more of your horse shit?"

The general's face went white. He flexed his fingers. His face twisted as he leaned against a crude table and shook his head. "I cannot believe what I have just heard. General Wiggins, General Bristoe . . ."

Wiggins cleared his throat and raised his eyes to meet the general's.

"I don't know anything about who General Walther is answerable to. All I know is the condition of my brigade. I brought a thousand six hundred men into this state three weeks ago. I don't think I have half of them left and they are played out, tired to the bone, and without proper rations for two days. I can't march my men another step until they have been fed and rested."

Bristoe joined in, saying, "I think that a roll call would show that my strength is under a thousand. And I brought a good thousand nine hundred with me to Yardley City. And the militia has taken some pretty heavy casualties, too."

"I don't give a damn about the militia," the general said. "I care about completing the task we set out to do."

Wiggins continued. "So we have at most about eighteen hundred regulars. Now, I have never refused to obey an order, General Martin, but last night when you threatened to strip anyone of his rank if he did not go along with your plan to attack this morning, I gave serious thought to handing you my resignation on the spot. I am proud of what me a̲ my men have done. And I was impressed by the way yo̲ handled this campaign right up to when Captain Mundy me̲ me out on the road and told me to join an attack in fifteen minutes with night coming on. Up to that point, we had done a good day's work. Then you threw it all away in a single hour or so.

"General Martin, I love my soldiers. I love the South and I love its people. My soldiers are not a bunch of checkers that you sacrifice to win a game. They are real men and they have wives and mothers and brothers and sisters at home praying for their safety. The South has been bled white by fools who order charges against well-prepared defenses on the off chance they might succeed. I thought Hood was the biggest damned fool in the Confederacy, but I think I may have been wrong about that. I think you might be the best candidate for that distinction. So, what I am saying in a nutshell is that if you order me to lead my brigade forward in its present condition, then I am going to have to resign my commission as a brigadier general in the Confederate army and go back to Georgia and pray that this foolish war ends with as little more bloodshed as possible."

The general looked at me and said, "Captain Mundy, you have heard what these men have said. You will be my witness at their court-martial proceedings."

I took a deep breath and choked out "I have heard them," paused and added, "and, with all respect, it appears to me that they are right. It would be a mistake to move forward."

"Et tu, Brute," the general murmured with a look of hatred.

There was a long silence which Bristoe, for once, had the grace not to break. I began to feel embarrassed for the general's sake. Clearly he was stunned. The color of his face turned from white to scarlet. His hand fidgeted and his mouth turned downward.

Walther had been listening to Wiggins with his arms crossed. He uncrossed them and said, "There is nothing more for me to say. I reckon I had better be getting back to my fellows. They will want to hear of this great victory that has took place here."

I have often pondered on the effect of Walther's sarcastic remark. It very nearly cost him his life. And it did alter the course of mine.

"God damned you, sir," the general cried, and drew his revolver from its holster.

Walther stopped in the doorway and turned to face him.

For a second I thought Walther was about to draw his own weapon. Bristoe shrank back from their line of fire. Wiggins said, "Wait, General Martin . . ."

Walther looked at the general and laughed. "You been playing general and now you are playing the roughneck. You don't scare me." And, with that, he turned and walked onto the porch.

The general cocked his revolver and with a cry of rage, almost like the growl of a wounded bear, started after Walther. Without thinking, I flung himself against him and seized his arm. The room seemed to explode with the noise of the revolver's discharge. My foot, my deformed foot, felt as though an enormous horse had stepped on it. But I still clung to the general's arm until Wiggins wrenched the weapon away.

Walther, his own gun now in his hand, returned to the room. The general, sweating and trembling, backed away from him. I fell to the floor, moaning from the pain in my shattered foot.

Walther closed the door and said very calmly, "General Martin, don't you think it would be a good idea if you was to hand over command of this army to me until you can pull yourself together and rest for a few days?"

"Yes, General," Wiggins said. "That would seem to be a commonsense step."

Bristoe, who was examining my foot, said, "I agree. And I think we ought to get Captain Mundy back to the surgeons."

Walther said, "If you two gentlemen would attend to Captain Mundy, I would like to remain here with General Martin and see if we can work out a reasonable solution to this here situation."

FOUR

• • • Wiggins and Bristoe carried me out of the gin house and summoned a squad of soldiers.

"Captain Mundy's revolver went off accidentally," Bristoe explained. "Don't stand around gawking. Help us get him back to the surgeons."

The soldiers carried me back to Kane's breastworks and lifted me over the parapet. I gritted my teeth to keep from crying out at the pain.

At first I thought I was hallucinating but sure enough, on the road near the line of abatis Kane had thrown up in front of his works, there sat Adjutant General Postlethwaite in his buggy, and with him was Governor Timmons. And around this pair jostled a crowd of militia men, mostly cadets, boasting of the great victory they thought they had won.

The governor and Postlethwaite graciously vacated the buggy so that it could convey me back to the field hospital. My teeth chattered with pain as the buggy bumped up and over the mound of earth that marked the old skirmish line and then across a bridge of heavy boards that had been placed over the main defense trench as a special accommodation for the governor.

Major Ferebee was asleep in a camp chair outside his tent. His sleeves were rolled up past his elbows, and his arms still bore traces of blood. His assistants were loading a wheelbarrow with severed arms and legs, evidence of a long night of surgery.

One of the Negro drivers said, "The governor hisself sent this here man back. He got shot in the foot."

Ferebee sat up and rubbed his eyes. "Good Lord, it's Mundy. I never heard of an aide de camp being wounded in battle."

"There is a first time for every thing, Major," I replied.

Inside his tent, the doctor offered me a dose of laudanum, but, remembering the general's addiction, I refused. I almost relented as the surgeon was cutting my special boot from the mangled foot, however.

"The foot will have to come off," Ferebee said as he donned his blood-caked apron. "Do you mind?"

"I am glad to get rid of the thing," I replied. "It has been an impediment to me all my life."

"Well, it is a blessing you didn't get shot in your good foot. Yes, and it is a blessing, too, that I have a little chloroform left. Sure you don't want some laudanum first?"

"I am positive."

"Then let's get this over with. I guess there will be other casualties coming in, even though I heard very little firing."

"Beyond a Yankee prisoner with a sprained ankle and me, I don't think you will have much fresh work," I said. "It wasn't much of a fight. The defenses were only lightly defended and the enemy ran away at our approach. However . . ."

Before I could tell him about the wounded still lying on the field from the night attack, the surgeon had put a rag over my nose and mouth and had picked up a bottle.

"Just breathe in the fumes deep and slow and start counting from one to ten."

The last number I remembered saying was seven.

The first person I saw after I came out from under the chloroform was Monroe Walther.

"Where are you?" he repeated my mumbled question. "You are in Doctor Ferebee's butcher shop, where else? How are you feeling, Mundy?"

"Nauseated," I said. "And my foot hurts like pure hell. I thought they were going to take it off."

"They did. It always happens that way. Arms and legs still

hurt even after they are hacked off. It will go away in time."

"Where is the general?"

"He is with Governor Timmons and old Postlethwaite, celebrating our so-called victory."

"How did you . . ." I fumbled for the right words.

"How did we settle our dispute? Like two good Christian gentlemen. My boys is going to scout out the Yankees. Once we are sure McIntyre don't take it into his head to move south again, we will march everybody back to Yardley City for a parade and speeches to celebrate. I will take my fellows and join Hood to march into Tennessee with him. The War Department will have to decide where to send the infantry."

"What did you actually say to the general?"

"Don't ever repeat this to a soul, Mundy, but I was prepared to give his ass a good whipping but then I seen the man had gone crazy as a bed bug. I thought, 'Now, Monroe, do you want the reputation of beating up one-armed lunatics?' so I just smiled and said, 'General Martin, you have been under a lot of pressure these past few days and you have not had much chance to rest. I would like to help you by letting you shift some of your duties over to me.' And you know what, Mundy? The man broke down and cried like a baby. Then he took one of them opium pills and pulled hisself together. Then Wiggins come back and said the governor and old Postlethwaite was there. So I told him to bring them over to congratulate General Martin on his success."

"Wasn't there a showdown between the governor and the general, about the militia and all?"

"No, them cadet boys had told them we had won the battle, so they was more interested in hearing about that than in rehashing an old quarrel. Also, them two has never visited a field after a hard battle. The governor liked to of turned green at the sight of so many dead men. But that Martin, he is something else again, I tell you."

"What do you mean?"

"He wiped off his tears and walked out to meet the governor and proceeded to hand him the biggest load of horse shit I ever heard. He even bragged on Postlethwaite for holding back Kane with the help of the Texas outfit. The governor swallowed the story hook, line and sinker. I thought

Wiggins would explode. Even that horse's ass Bristoe looked like he would throw up."

"Where is the general?"

"He is on his way with the governor to make an official report to the state legislature in special session. And he has left me in command of what he still has the gall to call 'my splendid little army.' I swear, Mundy, the man is as full of shit as a Christmas turkey. I feel like a fool not to have knowed him for what he is from the outset."

"He is a brave man," I said weakly. "You should have seen him when he rallied our artillery in the sawmill meadow and then led the counterattack in person."

"I seen him leading that so-called attack this morning, on horseback. You can call that brave, if you want, but I call it plain foolhardy. We are lucky Kane did not stay behind and fight. He could have did us a lot more damage. No, Martin is a pure fool. Or maybe it is just all them pills he has been taking."

He paused and then said something which I cherish to this day. Taking my hand in his great paw, he said, "Mundy, I have seen lots of brave things done in this war but what you did was plumb heroic. It ain't something we can talk about, but you have won my admiration. Now, you get well and take care of yourself. Don't get yourself involved with no more damn fools like Evan Martin."

Major Ferebee came by and decreed that I looked too weak to talk anymore. Walther left me with tears in my eyes. I pulled the blanket over my head and wept for the first time since I was a little boy, not so much from the pain as from emotional exhaustion and a sense of a loss. I had admired, even loved, the general, and I had discovered the man had not only feet of clay, but a stony heart and a deranged mind as well. Evan Martin, the real man, had survived the battle of Milroy Station, but his image as my hero had been slain as surely as the poor fallen soldiers they had started burying out there on that bloody ground, and I grieved for the loss of my ideal. And yet, there still remained my nagging love for Sarah Martin. I continued to hope that somehow we could be reunited.

Three days later they took me back to Milroy Station in

an ambulance and put me on the train with several hundred other wounded men to be hauled down to Yardley City. There the hotel had been turned into a hospital. They put me in the same room that I had occupied at the beginning of the campaign. Only now I shared it with five other wounded officers.

From all over the state, people came up to Yardley City by train as well in as buggies and wagons and on horseback to seek out their fallen loved ones.

After all the returns were in, it was discovered that the price of driving Kane from his forward position back to his main defenses ran to about 1,600 men. Added to the 500 casualties suffered in the fight at Mueller's Woods, that brought the total of Confederate dead, wounded and missing for the day to about 2,100, including Captain Jackson Mundy.

Yes, the record of my war service at the state capital indicates that I was wounded in the foot at Milroy Station. Even my own family does not know the real story. Major Ferebee thought it odd that the bullet had entered the foot at the top, but he did not remember one wound from another after he had completed his grisly work. And I was to learn later that Bristoe, Wiggins and Walther had taken a solemn Masonic oath never to reveal what occurred in that little gin house near Milroy's Landing.

Father and old Slocum, our slave foreman, rode over to Yardley City from Glenwood to seek me out. Father wanted to take me straight home with him but the surgeons thought I should not be moved for a few more days. Father, who had been reading accounts of the battle in the newspapers, was full of questions about what had happened.

"It was a great victory, was it not?"

"We won, but the cost was pretty high."

"Yes, but you probably saved Glenwood from destruction."

"I would hope so."

"And General Martin is an able general, is he not?"

"Did you say 'able,' Father?"

"Yes, able. The *Leader* compared his victory to that of Lee and Jackson at Chancellorsville."

" 'Able?' Yes, Able Martin. Father, would you look in my coat hanging on that peg and see if there is an envelope in it?"

He kept talking as he fumbled in my coat pocket. "The Confederacy needs a new crop of generals like Martin. Jackson, Stuart and Albert S. Johnston are all dead. And have you heard the news from Tennessee? Yes, there is an envelope."

"May I have it? What news?"

I took the envelope and looked at the note on the front:

TO MAJOR GENERAL "ABLE" MARTIN, FOR HIS EYES ONLY

"The reports are that Sherman has had to send a big batch of his army back to protect his base at Nashville. He is afraid of General Hood, and I say with good reason."

I did my best to pay polite attention as Father rambled on about how it was too bad the Yankees had seen fit to re-elect Abraham Lincoln and that the Northern populace would pay a big price for its shortsightedness. . . .

"Father, if you don't mind, I am feeling very tired."

"Very well, Jackson. I will say goodbye to you now. I will come back next Sunday with the buggy to take you home. Your mother and sisters can't wait to get you back in their care again. And Lucinda in particular asked me to tell you that she is praying for you. Just think, you will be home for Christmas. While you are recuperating here, I want you to give some serious thought to the possibility of merging our plantation with that of Cousin Horace."

After Father had gone, I turned the envelope over and saw that it was not sealed. I opened the flap, and a deck of cards fell out. There was a note in the envelope. As the envelope was not sealed, I read the note.

Dear Abe,

I would like to stick around and give you another fight but my orders are to rejoin our main body. If you had been more patient, you could have saved yourself all those casualties. I was going to pull out in the morning anyway. You are mighty profligate with Southern blood, Abe. Would you have been equally so if the Federal government had taken you rather than the Johnny Rebs? If so, I am glad you ended up on the other side.

The cards are a gift from me. These are unmarked. Thought I would give you the pleasure of marking them. Your old roommate,

  "Cain"

I put the cards and the note back in the envelope, and closed the flap.

When Major Ferebee came around on his next visit, I told him about the envelope, and, without mentioning the message, asked how it might be sent to the general. "That is simple enough. He is back in Yardley City now for the final review of the troops and the militia tomorrow. He is to make a speech. I'd be glad to give the packet to the pretentious son-of-a-bitch."

"Just tell him that I am here and that he can pick it up if he wants to."

"As you wish. Now let's see how that stump is healing."

FIVE

• • • By the next day, I was the only patient left in the room. One of my roommates had died and the relatives of the others had taken them away. Still confused and disconsolate, I lay there, reliving the horrible experiences of recent days and dreading the boredom that would be my lot back at Glenwood, and at times even regretting my role in thwarting the will of the general, yes, and missing his company, too. Then I would remember Ben lying on his back with a bullet hole in his forehead and reflect on how I could have prevented at least that one murder if only I had been more resolute.

I mourned the death, also, of my dream of returning to England and there attaining literary fame as a biographer and journalist. Oddly, however, I clung to my dream of becoming the husband of Sarah Martin.

Outside the hotel, I could hear the creak of wagon wheels and noise of the crowds that had come in for the review of the troops before they were dispersed. A military band tooted out a thin rendition of "Dixie."

Boots tramped down the hallway outside. A nurse said that the soldiers were lined up in front of the hotel to hear speeches delivered from the second floor porch, and she saw no reason not to leave my door open so that I could listen.

The governor spoke first. He congratulated the soldiers for "helping the militia repel the invasion of our state." He praised the militia for "springing to the defense of their homes and hearths" and exhorted all present to cherish their freedom from centralized authority whether in Washington or Richmond. Then he introduced Adjutant General Postlethwaite.

They let the old man ramble on for a quarter hour. He likened the battle of Milroy Station to New Orleans, naturally. And he compared the Texas regiment to Jean Lafitte's pirates, who bolstered the Americans against the British. He started in to sing the praises of General Martin, but the governor—who I supposed had grown as sick as everyone else of the old man by then—got the floor away from him by saying, "General Postlethwaite, if I may be so bold, General Martin is here to speak for himself, and since we are holding a train for him . . ."

I sat up in bed and cupped my hand behind my ear so as not to miss a word.

It was not a long speech but it was eloquent, delivered in more of an English than a Philadelphia accent, and it was about as false and self-serving a statement as ever I had heard.

"I was born in Philadelphia, as many of you know, but my grandfather came from Virginia and I spent many of my formative years in the South and, later, many adult years in England," he began. "I enjoyed a prosperous and satisfying life in England but when I heard that the Southern states had broken away from northern tyranny and that Lincoln proposed to raise troops against what he called 'the Rebellion,' I made a decision which I have never for one moment regretted. Yes, I gave up my lucrative position, said a sad farewell to my family and . . ."

He proceeded to outline his version of the campaign. He praised Bolick's artillerymen for preventing a breakthrough of his lines, but did not specify the race of the troops who were repulsed or, naturally, mention the slaughter of the prisoners. Nor did he mention the fact that Walther's men had destroyed McIntyre's wagons and artillery. Nor did he mention his aborted ruse to lure Kane into attacking the militia. He also failed to mention that he waited a good many months after the Southern victory at Manassas Station to tear himself from his family. And he said never a word about his dashed hopes of leading an invasion into Tennessee in a search for military glory.

But he waxed eloquent in describing his twilight assault on Kane's division, making it sound as though he had driven the Yankees completely off the field that night.

When he finished there was only polite applause from his war-weary audience.

Soon Martin himself put his head in the door to my room.

His face was haggard. His uniform hung loosely. His eyes looked cloudy.

"So, Captain Mundy. You have a message of some sort for me, I understand."

"Yes, sir."

I handed him the envelope.

"How did you come by this?"

After I told him the circumstances, he said, "You were rather dilatory about getting this to me."

"The soldier handed it to me just as I stepped on the porch of the gin house. When I went in you were talking with General Wiggins and of course after that . . ."

"Of course. Well then, it is too bad about the regrettable accident, but you must admit that you brought it on yourself."

"If that is how you wish to view the matter, I will not disagree. I was wondering, though. My father will be carrying me back to our plantation on Sunday. I am at loose ends here. I feel well enough to prepare your official report on our campaign before I leave, if you would like me to."

"No!" his voice cracked like a whip. "You will not write my report for me. I shall perform that duty for myself, thank you all the same. And what's more, I shall take it up to Richmond myself and submit it to President Davis himself, so that he will hear firsthand of what we achieved in this crucial battle. Consider yourself relieved of all miltary duties. And, as for my memoirs, I will write them for myself. If I require assistance I will seek it from someone with a stronger sense of loyalty than yourself."

"You accuse me of disloyalty?"

"The scales have been removed from my eyes where you

are concerned, Mundy. I see now that you conspired with Walther and the others to rob me of the credit for winning a great victory. Oh yes, I have learned that, although Walther's brigade arrived not long after I retired, you deliberately failed to awaken me."

"You said you wanted very much to sleep. Besides, what difference did it make?"

"I could have had Walther's men saddled up and ready to follow after we took those final works."

"Kane had already withdrawn most of his troops. He left behind only one regiment—"

"And Walther could have captured that regiment at least. No, don't try to defend yourself. You came very close to costing me my reputation, but, thank the Almighty, others of more consequence than you and your co-conspirators recognize the magnitude of what I have accomplished these past few weeks. Let me tell you this, Mundy, your betrayal will cost you dearly. You have lost your opportunity to achieve distinction as Boswell to my Johnson. And you have lost a higher prize. My wife intercepted a letter you wrote to our daughter from Wilmington. She wrote to me that you seemed to presume that you might someday win her hand in marriage. Miriam was horrified at your presumption, but I was not. No, I was so taken in by your show of innocence and loyalty that I considered you a sort of son already. As your father-in-law, I could have opened doors for you in this country and England. Anyway, that is water over the dam. I will bid you adieu and leave you to live out your drab little life in obscurity."

As he talked he had laid Kane's envelope on my bed.

I picked it up and said, "Don't forget your message. Shall I open it for you?"

Without waiting for his answer, I opened the flap and handed the envelope to him.

His face turned dark red. He spilled the deck of cards on the foot of the bed and reread the message.

"Does anyone else know about this?"

"Major Ferebee knows I had a message for you, but nothing more. And I think the soldier who gave it to me was illiterate."

"I would appreciate it then, if no further mention of this were made."

"And how about the murder of the colored prisoners? I suppose you wish nothing said of that either."

"I don't know what you are talking about. I saw no one murdered—"

"General Martin?"

A young woman dressed in black stood in the doorway.

"I am General Martin, yes."

"And I am Martha Jane Pettis from Cool Springs. I heard your speech out there and I just wanted to meet you in person."

She was a brunette of just below average height with a creamy complexion accentuated by apple-red cheeks.

The general bowed and said, "I am pleased to meet you, Miss Pettis. I would stay and converse but, as you heard the governor say, they are holding a train for me."

"I had a brother in the cadet corps with you up at Milroy's Landing."

"Did you indeed? Well those lads distinguished themselves. You can be very proud of your brother." He bowed again and put on his hat.

"I was proud of my brother. So were my daddy and my mother and my three little sisters. He was my only brother. He was killed at Milroy's Landing. He was only fifteen years old."

"I am sorry he died. You can take special pride in his heroism."

"No, General Martin, my brother did not just die. He was killed. That is why I wanted to meet you in person."

"I am honored that you should seek me out. If only I had more time—"

"Yes, I wanted to meet the person who killed my little brother Richard. . . ."

Her voice broke and she put her face in her hands.

"That seems a harsh thing to say. The enemy killed your brother, not I. Now, I really must go. I am expected in Richmond."

She brushed the tears from her cheeks and said, "The legislature gave you a special vote of thanks. The governor has eulogized you. You were willing to hang about listening to their fulsome praise. You surely can spare me a moment so that I can tell you to your face that I regard you as a butcher, to send boys not old enough to shave into battle."

"War is a cruel business, Miss Pettis. And now, if you would be so kind as to step aside, I can no longer delay my departure."

"Before you go, General," I interjected, "I would like you to hear what I have to say to Miss Pettis."

"Really, Mundy, I haven't time for this."

"It will take only a moment. Miss Pettis, my name is Jackson Mundy, and, until a few minutes ago, I was General Martin's aide de camp. You have called him a butcher and have accused him of killing your young brother."

"And I suppose you are going to defend him," she said with flashing eyes.

"No, you are wrong. I am not going to defend him. I think you are right. He is a butcher and he surely did cause the needless death of your brother and hundreds of others."

My last image of Evan Martin was of his expression of amazement and rage. Then he turned and shoved the young woman from his path and rushed out of the room.

SIX

• • • With a few cruel words, Evan Martin dashed my hopes of marrying his lovely daughter Sarah. My prospects for achieving literary fame were as dead as the Negro soldiers in Mueller's Woods. Yet, despite my disillusionment with the man, I continued to think of him with a measure of gratitude.

He opened the door for me to become a journalist and showed me a way of life I never would have discovered on my own. Inadvertently, he caused me to shed my club foot so that after the war I appeared no less normal than many other maimed Southern veterans.

And from him I learned about the true nature of courage in all its various facets. I was enormously flattered when Monroe Walther praised my grit in thwarting General Martin's plans to launch yet another attack on Kane's division. Walther's brand of courage was nothing like mine. He simply forged ahead without fear, meeting danger head on and overcoming it. Evan Martin possessed courage to a remarkable degree but it was motivated by an overweening desire for personal glory. He lusted after military recognition so ardently that his fear was overcome.

From my experiences in the battle of Milroy Station and its aftermath, I learned the value of moral courage, the willingness to risk position and reputation, to sacrifice personal desires, on ethical grounds. It is a trait that has got me into considerable difficulties at times, but I am glad that I developed it.

I am grateful also to Evan Martin for providing me with the occasion to meet Martha Jane Pettis and win her admiration for my courage in speaking out to him. If I had not spoken up as I did, I doubt she would have taken further notice of me.

As it was, she remained after the general left and talked to me for more than an hour. She returned every day for the rest of the week to bring me delicacies from her father's plantation and to talk and talk. Martha Jane, I discovered, is one of your natural born talkers. Her artless chatter took my mind off the pain of my amputation and my feelings of guilt and loss. To this day, I find it hard to remain cheerless in her company.

The day after my final encounter with the general, I was awakened from a nap by a rough hand on my shoulder. I opened my eyes to look into the face of Addison Bolick, the artillery man. And, standing beside Bolick was a paunchy fellow whom I recognized as Bolick's second in command.

"Captain Mundy, Captain Dilson and me are about to put our guns on the train and haul them and our men back down to the capital and we thought we just ought to have a word with you before we depart."

I felt uneasy at the way the two men stood so close to my bed. I kept my voice low and gruff to hide my nervousness as I replied, "I don't have anything to say to you, Bolick."

"We just wanted to clear up what seems to be a misunderstanding about them nigger soldiers."

"I understand only too clearly. You slaughtered them."

Bolick shook his head and grinned at his companion. "I wish you would listen to that, Captain Dilson. The poor young fellow's mind is playing tricks on him. He must have forgot."

I raised myself on my elbows and spluttered, "What is your game, Bolick?"

The redhead's face hardened. "I have not forgot what you said to me in front of General Martin. At first I couldn't understand why you would say such bad things, but me and Captain Dilson have figured it out."

"Get out of my room," I said.

"No, you had better hear us out. Don't you think he should, Captain Dilson?"

"If he knows what is good for him, I reckon he should."

"Then say what you have to say and get out."

"Captain Dilson and me, we was so struck dumb by the accusations you made toward me and our men that we compared notes to try to figure out why you would say such things. Right, Captain Dilson?"

"That is right, Major Bolick. We had better refresh his memory. Shall I do it?"

"No, I will do it. You remember how them niggers came at us shouting that they wasn't going to take no quarter?"

"That did not give you the right—"

"Hear me out. Then, after we repulsed their attack and saved our army, the general led the counterattack, leaving all them niggers in his rear with no one to guard them."

"To become your victims," I said bitterly. "One of them was the blacksmith on my family's plantation."

"I will get to him in a minute. After a bit, you got on your horse and started to follow the general. You remember that, don't you?"

"I wish you would get to the point and leave," I said.

"There is no call for you to go insulting me, now Captain Mundy. Remember that I outrank you."

"Then why don't you put me on report and ask for a court-martial against me?"

"I am thinking of your reputation. Anyway, you stopped and saw that gang of niggers down in the creekbed. You remember that, don't you?"

"Bolick, if you are trying to justify what you did—"

"It is Major Bolick. Anyhow, you stopped and looked down and then, well, Captain Dilson, repeat what it was you heard Captain Mundy say to me."

"Captain Mundy, he pointed to the nigger soldiers and told Major Bolick that he should take care as they was still armed."

"That is not true," I said. "They had thrown down their weapons."

"I am just telling you what you said."

"And what he is prepared to swear to under oath, if necessary," Bolick said. "Go ahead, Captain Dilson. Finish your testimony."

"And then Captain Mundy said that the general asked him to tell us to take extra precautions with them, that he could not risk leaving a batch of armed enemy soldiers in his rear with no infantry to guard them."

"I never said any such thing," I spluttered.

"But you did. You said that at the slightest show of resistance you felt General Martin would expect us to take the necessary steps. Those were your very words. Naturally, we thought you was repeating the general's instructions."

"I have never heard such a monstrous lie in all my life."

"Go ahead, Captain Dilson. Tell what happened after that."

"Then Captain Mundy rode his horse across the creek and got off and walked several hundred feet until he came to a pile of slabs. I saw him pull out his revolver and shoot one of the wounded niggers."

"That is right," Bolick said. "Now, tell the rest."

"And then he seemed to get carried away. He walked around shooting other wounded colored soldiers until he run out of bullets. Then he got on his horse and rode toward the woods."

"Exactly," Bolick said. "And later we figured out that he was so enraged to find one of his own slaves in a Yankee uniform that he lost control of himself. Which we took to be our signal to proceed with subduing the niggers in the creekbed."

"Only they refused to throw down their muskets and come up on the creek bank with their hands over their heads—"

"Major Ferebee!" I shouted. "Major Ferebee! Come here, please. I need your help."

Bolick laid his hand on the stump of my leg, gently at first, and said in a low voice, "We could provide other witnesses if necessary, you know."

"Major Ferebee!" I shouted again.

Bolick seized the stump of my leg and squeezed it hard. I cried out from the pain. The room went white. The last thing I could remember before fainting was the redhead's face looking down at me with a smirk.

When I regained consciousness, Bolick and Dilson were gone and the surgeon was leaning over me trying to staunch the hemorrhaging of the stump of my leg.

I was drenched with sweat. "Keep them away from me. Don't let them in here again."

"Who, Major Bolick? He said he wanted to pay his respects before they leave. What happened? Did he say something to upset you?"

I started to explain but felt too weak to make the effort. But I gained the surgeon's permission to lock my door at night. And I kept my revolver under my pillow until the following Sunday when my parents were to come to take me home.

Martha Jane was visiting me when they arrived. Mother thought the girl was a mite forward and opinionated but liked her well enough to invite her to bring her mother and visit at Glenwood, which they did the following Easter. In fact they were visiting when the news came of Lee's surrender, marking the long overdue end of the war.

She has made me a better wife than I deserved. Unfortunately she has a jealous streak, so I have never told her about my infatuation for Sarah Martin in England. Although I cherished my memory of Sarah, I realized that ours had been a sort of puppy love fantasy whereas my relationship with Martha Jane has been 100 percent real. And I liked Martha Jane's mother as much as I disliked Sarah's.

I liked her father, too. A big, hearty gentleman, Colonel Pettis served with Lee in Virginia. He came home and, after a year of trying to grow cotton with ex-slaves as hired hands, sold his plantation to a carpetbagger from Massachusetts and used the proceeds to get into the railroad and insurance business. He also bought the *Yardley County Leader* and hired me, as a sort of wedding gift, to edit it. Then, when he died, the paper was left to Martha Jane and me as part of our inheritance.

The battle of Milroy Station was overshadowed by other military events in those fading hours of the Confederacy's brief day among the nations of this earth. After subjecting his dwindling army to a bloodbath at Franklin, Tennessee, Hood sat outside Nashville, daring General Thomas's larger

Federal army to come out and fight. Thomas did and scattered Hood's army like chaff before a whirlwind. Good old steady Wiggins was killed in that battle and Bristoe was wounded and died a few years later of consumption.

Meanwhile, Sherman completed his march to the sea, leaving a swath of destruction across Georgia, and then turned north to wreak even worse vengeance on South Carolina.

Father never admitted that the South was beaten. He just stopped talking about the war at all. For that matter, I did little talking about it myself in general and nothing at all about certain things, such as Bolick's slaughter of the colored troops. Despite Bolick's effort to intimidate me, I returned to Glenwood intending to write a report of the incident and carry it up to Richmond for submission to the Confederate War Department, but by the time the war ended, I had not sufficiently recovered to do this. After that, fearing the consequences if the massacre were to be revealed to the Federal army of occupation, I kept my guilty silence. Nor did I speak about spiking the general's whiskey with opium or how I came to be shot in my deformed foot.

After Martha Jane and I were married, Ben's wife, Mattie, became our family cook. She never gave up hope that Ben would reappear someday. I trust God will forgive me, if I was wrong to keep the knowledge of his fate from her as long as I did.

I pray His forgiveness, too, for my failure to interrupt the slaughter of those brave colored soldiers while there was still time to save some of their lives, including Ben's.

So, that is pretty much my story of what I did and did not do during the great War Between the States. As for what happened after the war . . .

SEVEN

• • • To this day the slaughter of the Negro soldiers has never come to light. A big fuss was made about the alleged massacre by Nathan Bedford Forrest's men at Fort Pillow. And I think they hanged some Confederates for killing wounded colored prisoners at Saltville, Virginia, late in the war. But the Mueller's Woods massacre remains buried along with its victims there in the mass grave Bolick's men dug at General Martin's direction.

I would have spoken out after the war, but dreaded having to take part in an inquiry that would only have brought more grief for my native section, already occupied by Federal troops and under military law. It was cowardly of me, perhaps, but I just wanted to let sleeping dogs lie.

I did make inquiries at the state capital as to what happened to Bolick, casting about for some sort of personal retribution I might take against him. The records show that he and all his men deserted from the militia early in '65. I would guess that, like so many Confederate deserters, they took off for the West. I don't really know, but from the court records I did find out a curious thing about the murder charges on which he was convicted before the war.

One of the Negro teamsters on his plantation caught him in carnal embrace with his wife and attacked him with an axe. Bolick shot the husband "in self-defense." I hope that Satan employs a few Negro guards in Hades and that Addison Bolick will be assigned to their care when his time comes, if it has not already come.

My reputation as a so-called war hero began soon after my showdown with the Klan; that is, about 1870. I was sitting in my office one morning when I heard this big voice boom from our waiting room. "Is this here the office of Captain Jackson Mundy?"

There stood a strapping gray-haired gentleman wearing a fine dark worsted suit. He wore a diamond stick pin in his tie and carried a gold-headed cane. You would have thought him the most cultivated man you ever saw. I said, "This is indeed Jackson Mundy, sir. This wouldn't be Brigadier General Monroe Walther, would it?"

"By God, Mundy, I should've known I couldn't fool you."

"You have shaved off your beard but I would have known you even in the dark," I said.

Walther stayed for more than an hour, bringing me up to date about himself. He had returned to Tennessee and taken up the breeding and selling of mules again, with Cyrus Hooker as a junior partner. Then he had branched out and bought a farm in Kentucky and started raising race horses.

"Not meaning to brag, Mundy," he said, "but I was a rich man before the war. And you want to know something? I am a hell of a lot richer now that we have got all that slavery business out of the way."

He laughed so loudly that my fellows came out of the print shop to see who was making all the noise. When I introduced him, they all wanted to hang around and hear him tell stories of the exploits of his famed mounted infantry.

After a while, he sort of ran down and said something I wished he had not. He said, "Well, boys, it has been a pleasure talking to you. I did a lot of fighting in the war. Me and my fellows killed more than our share of Yankees, I reckon. I seen a lot of brave deeds done during my four years in the saddle, but none braver than what your own boss done at Milroy's Landing."

"We can't get Captain Mundy to talk about the war," my head printer said. "What did he do?"

With a grin and a wink at me, Walther said, "He saved my life, that is what he done. He took a bullet that was meant for yours truly. Your boss has true courage."

It was a long time after that before my employees stopped pestering me to tell them the story. But they did not stop telling others of Walther's remarks, and with each retelling, the tale of my alleged heroism grew.

Out on the sidewalk, General Walther invited me to accompany him up to Milroy Station. "I want to hire me a horse and ride over the country and figure out what happened exactly where. The war has been over for five long years, and I have told so many damned lies about what I did that now I can't remember what really did happen. Why don't you come along and we can reminisce?"

"I wish I could, General Walther, but this is a busy week for us."

"That is a shame. I heard tell that the artillery killed a passel of nigger soldiers at one point. But I seen none of them laying dead, nor among the prisoners. Would you know anything about that?"

I started to tell him the story but decided against it. "I am afraid I can't help you, General."

The next year I read that he had suffered a fatal stroke in Kentucky while watching a horse race. It was his stripe of bold leadership that made the South so hard for the North to conquer. What a man was Monroe Walther.

As a tenth wedding anniversary present, I took Martha Jane up to New York City. That was when I got myself fitted for my false foot made of cork and was able to discard my crutches. What I have never told anyone, not even Martha Jane, is that on impulse one day, while she was shopping, I looked in the city directory under the Ks, and sure enough there was listed JONATHAN KANE, ESQ., ATTORNEY AT LAW.

I took a hack down to Wall Street and introduced myself to the clerk at his law firm.

"What did you wish to see Mr. Kane about?"

"Tell him that I was aide de camp to Major General Evan Martin during the War Between the States."

A few minutes later I was being ushered into an oak-panelled office big enough to hold our entire *Leader* plant. A slender fellow with thin sandy hair and a devilish gleam in his eye came out from behind his desk to shake my hand.

"So you served with Abe Martin in the Rebel Army?" he said after seating me in a leather chair. "How did that come about?"

I told the story as succinctly as I could.

"And you went over to England with him?"

"Indeed I did. I lived in the same house with his family."

He wanted to know all about that experience and then switched over to the subject of the Milroy Station campaign. I told him about how we fired off artillery blanks and discharged muskets to make him think a battle was going on so he would attack our militia and we could ambush him.

"Is that what all that fuss was about? Well, by Jove I fell for it, I must admit. Isn't that just like Abe, to pull a trick like that? But tell me, Captain Mundy, whatever possessed him to attack me in the dark? That gave me a wonderful chance to turn the tables on him. I was all set to withdraw the next morning anyway. If he had delayed his attack until dawn, he would have caught us breaking camp and undoubtedly could have wiped out my division. Not that I am complaining, but why was he so eager to attack?"

"He seemed to bear you a special animosity. He never said why, but it was like an obsession for him to whip you."

"He did have his reasons not to love me, Captain Mundy."

And then the truth came out. As classmates at West Point, Martin and Kane had studied and drilled and played games together all year. And their favorite game was poker.

"Abe was one of the most successful poker players I ever came up against," Kane said. "He raked in a lot of money that year. My mother was a widow and I didn't have much to gamble but I kept trying to beat him. He left me penniless and a good many others, too. We lived by the honor code at West Point, as they still do. We finished our first year and took our exams. Abe was not a brilliant student. History and English were his best subjects. Mathematics and engineering were mine, so we helped each other in our studies.

"At the end of the year, he left a day or so before me to go back to Mobile. I was rooting around in our room and I found two decks of Abe's cards in his study desk. The fellow next door came in to say good-bye and he picked up the cards and examined the backs. He noticed tiny little marks on the backs of the face cards. We looked at the other deck and they had been marked in the same way.

"Now, Abe was my best friend and maybe I would have just kept my mouth shut, but the other fellow was all for living up to the honor code. So we took the cards to the superintendent. And, to make a long story short, he wrote to Abe that he would be suspended unless he wanted to return and face a hearing."

"He made it sound like he left West Point to go and help organize a company to fight in Mexico," I said.

"He did help organize a company, but only after he learned he could not return to the Point without a trial. He wrote me a silly letter charging me with betraying him, and saying I would regret my charges when he returned as a great military hero. I never answered him. Then back around the end of 1861 I got an inquiry from the U.S. War Department in Washington saying that an Evan Martin had arrived from England and was offering his services to the Federal government."

I nearly fell off my chair at this intelligence.

"You seem surprised," Kane said. "But, of course, he would not have told you that. Anyway, a friend in the War Department remembered I was in the same class and sent me a telegram asking what I knew about Evan Martin. What could I do but tell them the truth? My friend wrote me later that further investigation brought out the fact that Abe had resigned as captain of the company he helped raise and never went to Mexico at all. I assumed he feared a scandal over the marked cards."

"He told me he resigned to marry his wife and return to England with her," I said.

"Abe had a very active imagination. It was hard to tell when he was telling the truth and when he was blowing smoke."

"So, he applied first for a commission in the Yankee army."

"In the Federal army," Kane said a with a smile. "But I would say that for his purposes, he did a lot better by hooking up with the Rebels."

"The Confederates," I responded.

Kane laughed at that. "So at last we have got at the truth. What else can I tell you about Abe?"

"I am curious about the nickname by which you call him."

"The fellows at the Point called us Cain and Able, that is C-A-I-N, as in the Bible. I don't remember who started that, but it stuck. With Kane as my last name, Cain is understandable. Able got started because Abe made the mistake of saying that he was able to do anything he set his mind to."

"I wondered about your use of the name on the message you left on the door of your headquarters at Milroy's Landing."

He looked puzzled for a moment and then laughed. "I had forgot about that. He got my message then?"

"Yes, and he was furious when he saw it."

"I could not resist guying him. Abe wasn't such a bad chap, I suppose, but he had an exalted notion of himself and he wasn't entirely scrupulous in his methods of going after his goals. He thought he could talk his way out of any situation. I wonder how he is getting on. He is back in London, I suppose."

"I would think so. We do not correspond."

"So, what brings you to New York then?"

I told him about my false foot and that I had lost the original at Milroy's Landing.

"I suppose one of my boys shot you. I am sorry about that."

"They also killed my wife's baby brother."

"I am sorry about that, too."

I figured I had taken up enough of his time and, frankly, I was afraid the subject of the black soldiers might come up, so I arose and said, "Neither my wound nor the boy's death was the fault of your men. Evan Martin was the real culprit."

"If you say so, Captain Mundy. Now look here, you drop in to see me the next time you are in New York. My wife will be interested to hear about your visit. She was the daughter of a professor at the Point. Abe was in love with her. All the boys were, but Abe in particular. But I took her away from them all. Do you suppose that is the real reason Abe hated me so? Well, that is another story. Here, I will see you to the door."

When I read in the New Orleans paper about General Martin's death in England, back in '89, I left the office and went home so my employees would not see me shed tears. Martha Jane did not make things any easier by calling me a fool for grieving over the death of a man who had treated me so shabbily and who "killed my baby brother." She did not understand my mixed feelings for Evan Martin.

How could I explain to her that I had been a backward club-footed lad when I met him, and he had lifted me out of my ingrown, countrified existence to show me a larger world and a more capable me? Had he not ordered that foolhardy night attack, or had he permitted me to go back and stop Bolick from killing those colored prisoners, or had Postlethwaite not brought up that regiment of Texans, or had McIntyre delayed his enveloping maneuver for another day or had I not given the General that drugged whiskey, how different his life and mine and scores of others might have been.

Conceivably all of our lives might have been worse, of course. Once the loom of time has woven its fabric, all we can do is study the design of the cloth. God himself, in all his awesome power, cannot unravel and reweave it into a new pattern. But we can learn from our acts and their consequences. In my case I learned the value of trusting my instincts for recognizing the right thing to do in a crisis and then having the moral courage to do it, letting the chips fall where they would.

Often during the past thirty-odd years, I have pondered on just what the War Between the States was all about. We liked to say it was for states' rights. Lincoln started out saying he was fighting to preserve the Union and didn't much care one way or the other about slavery as long as it wasn't expanded into the territories. Then, when he took his oath of office to begin his second term, when the Confederacy was on its deathbed anyway, he asserted that, no, it had been slavery all along.

Our Southern politicians almost to a man were owners of slaves who, like my own father, had an unjustified fear that the election of Abraham Lincoln in 1860 would mean the inevitable loss of their human property. They could not, or would not, see that slavery was bound to die at some point, with or without Lincoln. It is a shame that so many men perished along with that abominable institution. I often heard the remark that it was "a rich man's war and a poor man's fight." I was engaged both in the war and the fight, and for the good of the nation and, ultimately, for the South itself, it is well that we failed.

So, that is my story about Major General Evan Martin and our relationship, and about the battles of Fleming's Store, Milroy's Landing and Mueller's Woods, known collectively, and in my view erroneously, as the battle of Milroy Station. That is my story of the heartless murder of the Negro soldiers by the militia's artillerymen, General Martin's failure to punish or even to rebuke the murderers, and my own guilty silence about the atrocity. I apologize to my readers of the next century for my delay in getting to the outcome of the proposition Marc Hanna put to me, but what I have written is necessary prologue to an account of how and why I reached my decision in the matter.

EIGHT

• • • In 1894, with Evan Martin dead and largely forgotten and the massacre of the Negro soldiers still unrevealed, I was persuaded by my lifelong friend, Dr. Charles Fitzpatrick, to allow him to lobby our state legislature to send me to Washington as a junior senator. I assumed that after thirty years, the possibility that the Mueller's Woods massacre would come to light was remote indeed.

The looming 1896 campaign for the presidency of the United States was an entirely different matter. The glare of national publicity would be merciless compared to that of a contest settled quickly by a state legislature's Democratic caucus. If even a hint of the Mueller's Woods Massacre, and my part in it, were to come out in the Northern press, it would cause a ruinous scandal for McKinley and me. And although the largest of several serious considerations to be weighed, yet it was only one vexing aspect.

Early the morning after Hanna's proposition, after a near sleepless night, leaving Martha Jane still sleeping, I crept out of bed, drew on my dressing gown and went downstairs to my study. As was my habit when struggling with a decision, I made two columns on a sheet of paper, one for reasons why I should do something and one for why I should not. By the time Martha Jane and Aunt Mattie had arisen, both columns were full. As I put away my pen and paper, my mind was far from made up, however. Throughout that long Saturday and the following night, I continued to stew.

On Sunday morning again I arose and, after reviewing my

notes and adding to them, I set them aside to eat breakfast. In church later that morning I prayed silently but ardently for divine guidance in reaching my decision.

By Monday morning, things were getting sorted out in my mind and heart, or so I thought. It may have been the fires of ambition that lay banked in my bosom; it may have been the delight with which I felt Martha Jane would welcome the prospects of being the wife of a vice president; it may even have been the feeling that a McKinley-Mundy ticket really could be the solution for a nation so sorely divided between debtor and creditor; between the poor and hopeless and the rich and greedy; between North and South. At any rate early on the Monday morning of my deadline for responding to Hanna's offer, again I had arisen early. In fact I had set aside my list of pros and cons, along with my reservations, and been about to begin writing a note of acceptance.

Before I had dipped pen in ink, however, Mattie—on her way to the kitchen—interrupted me to say, "Mr. Jackson, how come you to be getting up so early every morning and working so hard? You gonna ruin your eyesight if you ain't careful."

"Actually, Aunt Mattie," I replied, "what I have been doing has helped me see things more clearly."

"What you talking about?"

"I was speaking metaphorically."

"Listen to you, using big words like that when I knowed you before you could talk or walk."

"I wasn't able to sleep, Aunt Mattie. So I thought I would get a little work done."

"I didn't sleep very good neither. I keep dreaming about Ben. You ever think about Ben, Mr. Jackson?"

"Yes, Aunt Mattie, I suppose I do."

"Seem like he come to me every night lately. Make me wonder whether he still be alive. What do you think, Mr. Jackson?"

"Why, Aunt Mattie, how would I know that?"

"Running off the way he done. Leaving me without a word. That wasn't like Ben. It was a long time ago, I know, but it still hurts. I still aches to know what become of him."

As she started to leave, I said, "Aunt Mattie, I never asked you this before. Why do you think Ben ran away?"

She shook her head. "Mr. Jackson, I used to think maybe he was running away from me, because he didn't even tell me good-bye. Made me think he didn't really love me. But you want to know the truth?"

"Yes, Aunt Mattie. Let's hear the truth."

"He just wanted to be free, that's all. Everybody wants to be free, don't you think, Mr. Jackson?"

"I reckon you are right."

"You want me to tell you something else?"

"I wouldn't know how to stop you."

"White folks could have saved themselves a whole lot of grief and pain if they had of understood that without the war. I ain't trying to make you mad because I know how you suffered in that ole war, but you tell me now if I am lying. White folks and black folks went through a whole lot of misery, and it didn't have to be that way. It didn't have to be that way at all. Now, you brought the subject up, remember, so just let me tell you again, all Ben wanted was to be free. I just hopes he found his freedom."

I barely touched my breakfast that morning. After swallowing the rest of my coffee, I took a hack down to the Willard Hotel and went directly up to Hanna's apartment.

A napkin in his hand, the great conniver answered the door himself. Wearing carpet slippers and a dressing gown, his hair still uncombed and his face not yet shaved, he looked even more unkempt than he had at our previous meeting.

Obviously surprised at my early morning visit, he invited me into his sitting room. Seeing the room service tray on a small table, I apologized for interrupting his breakfast.

He shrugged and asked if I would not join him in a cup of coffee. I declined, not wishing to drag out my mission, but I did accept his offer to take a seat.

"You have had time to think about my proposition, I assume," he said before I could marshal my speech.

"Perhaps too much time."

"Then I assume that you will accept."

"No, Mr. Hanna, I cannot."

For once he lost his customary air of sly self-confidence. "Why ever not?"

"My reasons are complex and not easily explained. It boils down to this. I am a loyal Democrat. To do what you ask would be to spit in the face of my party. It would make me a pariah in the eyes of my own people. You cited the example of Lincoln's choosing Andrew Johnson, a Southern Unionist, as his running mate in 1864. Not only was Johnson a failure as president, he was regarded as a Judas by the rank and file citizens of his own native South. There is more. My differences with McKinley on the tariff question are too pronounced for me to pretend that this would not be an issue. I cannot stifle my principles on that question. I admit that your idea is flattering, even tempting. But, no, I cannot do it."

All the while that I was delivering these remarks, there ran through my mind the images of that dreadful scene in Mueller's Woods when I found Ben staring up at the sky with a bullet hole between his eyes. It was a scene that had plagued me ever since my conversation with Mattie that morning. But I ended my explanation without uttering the real reason for my decision. That was a feeling of guilt, of unworthiness for my long ago lapse of courage.

For once, Hanna was slow to reply. He just sat there, holding his coffee cup, those shrewd brown eyes studying my face. Then he set down his cup and said, "And that is your final answer?"

"It is the only answer I can make."

"I think you are committing a great error. You could become a national figure rather than merely a junior senator."

"I am not without ambition, but I also value my integrity."

"If that is your final decision, I can only say that I hope you will not regret it. Now then . . ." Here he paused to stand and hold out his hand. "Speaking of integrity," he continued, "you and I pledged to each other that we would never reveal these discussions."

Still grasping my hand, he was ushering me toward the door before I could frame my reply.

"It is not necessary to remind me. I will honor my pledge."

The history books tell the rest of the story. Thanks largely to Hanna's efforts, two-thirds of the Republican delegates who arrived in St. Louis on June 16 were already committed to voting for McKinley as their party's nominee. And whom did he choose as his running mate but a political crony, one Garrett A. Hobart, a state senator from New Jersey.

In the election that fall, McKinley got 271 electoral college votes to William Jennings Bryan's 176. Of the popular vote, he got 7,102,000 to Bryan's 6,492,000.

I wondered at the time what the outcome would have been had I accepted Hanna's offer. Would the presence on the ticket of a reconstucted Southern senator allegedly wounded in the service of the Confederacy really have made any difference? Would the ugly secret of the Mueller's Woods Massacre really have come to light?

I confess that it hacked me a bit to see McKinley give an unprecendented degree of authority to Hobart, more than any vice president in history, I believe. Some even called the New Jerseyite "the assistant president." But then, near the end of 1899, Hobart died and McKinley finished out the remaining year of his first term without a vice president.

As his running mate in 1900, McKinley chose the self-aggrandizing Theodore Roosevelt, the so-called hero of San Juan Hill in the Spanish War, as his running mate and proceeded to beat Bryan even more handsomely than in 1896 both in the electoral college and popular votes.

I, alas, got turned out of my senatorial office that same year. Some laid my loss of favor with the legislature to my unyielding stand against the free coinage of silver, but in truth it was because of murmurs among the legislators that "Mundy is a nigger lover."

This despicable whispering campaign did not arise because of my well-known opposition to the Ku Klux Klan or my support for improved education of our black citizens. It arose because in 1897, following McKinley's inauguration, I persuaded our new president to sign a most unusual private Civil War pension bill on my behalf.

Actually, he signed the bill on behalf of one Mattie Mundy, a Negro woman who was certified as the widow of Ben Mundy, a U.S. Colored Troops recruit whom records listed as "missing in action and presumed dead" in October of 1864.

I had said nothing to her or Martha Jane about gaining a copy of Ben's service records from the War Department or about my drafting a private pension bill and ushering it through the Senate, or about my letter to President McKinley seeking his approval.

I waited until all the red tape had been attended to and then laid the papers out on the kitchen counter for Mattie to see.

A puzzled look came over her kindly brown face.

"You gonna have to read that to me, Mr. Jackson."

It took several minutes before the import of the documents sank in for her.

"You mean Ben ran away to join the Yankee army?"

"That is exactly what he did."

"And they think he is dead?"

"I am afraid so."

"And they wants me to be paid a pension as his widow?"

"Indeed they do. President McKinley himself has signed the papers. The government will pay you twenty dollars per month for the rest of your life."

To her credit, Mattie was overwhelmed by the knowledge of how Ben had ended his life and not by the prospect of a pension.

She sat down on a kitchen stool and put her hands over her face to staunch the tears running down her cheeks. "Thank you Jesus," she moaned. "Thank you for letting me know what my man did. He was a soldier. That's how come he left me."

Martha Jane came into the kitchen to see what the commotion was all about. She put her arm around Mattie and comforted her.

As for myself, I pleaded ignorance of any further details of Ben's death. To this day I have not confessed to Mattie or anyone else that I saw and spoke to him in his final hour, indeed that had I acted with dispatch I could have saved his life.

Later, after Mattie had decided to take her pension and move back to Yardley County and there buy herself a cottage in which to finish out her days, Martha Jane tried to pin me down as to my motives for seeking the pension.

"That was a noble thing to do. But I have often wondered at your timing. Why did you wait so long to investigate?"

"Something Aunt Mattie said made me think of the possibility. She told me she thought Ben wanted everybody to be free. Call it a hunch if you will. So I went to the War Department and there his record was: Ben Mundy, a blacksmith from Yardley County, recruited as a volunteer in the Colored Volunteers in August, 1864, listed as missing in action and presumed dead."

"So no one knows where he is buried?"

"It would appear so."

"Has it occurred to you that if you had let sleeping dogs lie, we would not have lost a trusted servant?"

"I never gave that a thought, Martha Jane. It made Aunt Mattie happy to learn what happened to her husband, with or without the pension. I certainly do not regret what I did."

"I hope you never do."

To this day, I am not sorry for gaining that pension for Mattie but I do wish that I had sworn her to keep her mouth shut about the matter when she returned to Yardley County. She would tell her colored neighbors of what Senator Mundy had done for her and those neighbors would tell others.

None of this got into the newspapers but word did reach the ears of some silverite legislators and they seized the opportunity to influence enough of their black-hating colleagues to thwart my efforts to gain a second term in the Senate. Their stated reason was that I had "lost touch with the people," that in the words of William Jennings Bryan, I wanted to crucify the little farmers and artisans of our state "on a cross of gold," etc.

So, as I write these final words, had I it to do over again, would I have sought that pension for Mattie? If I had not done so, Martha Jane and I would still be living and serving in Washington. No matter. I am glad I did what I did.

And if I had it to do over again, would I accept Marc Hanna's offer to run for the vice presidency in 1896? That question cannot be so easily answered. McKinley might have disagreed with Hanna and chosen Hobart anyway. Or he might have decided that he did not need me as his running mate in 1900.

As Shakespeare in his *Julius Caesar* has Brutus say, "There is a tide in the affairs of men/Which, taken at the flood, leads on to fortune/ Omitted, all the voyage of their life is bound in shallows and in miseries."

This was bold talk for one of the murderers of Julius Caesar. It was not long after that, having been vanquished by Mark Antony's army of revenge, he—Brutus—committed suicide by falling upon his own sword.

Evan Martin also was a great one for taking affairs at the flood—and look where it got him and hundreds of other better men than him at Milroy Station.

Some might say to me today, if they knew my full story, "Why, Mundy, if you had played your cards right, you would be president of the United States right now. You and your wife would be living in the White House. You would go down in the history books as the nation's twenty-sixth president."

As I complete my story I can say without reservation that I have no regrets for my decision in 1896. And most assuredly my life has not been bound in shallows and miseries since I spurned Hanna's audacious offer; nor since I sought that pension for Mattie. I have led a full and useful life, one not devoid of disappointments, but in the main satisfactory. Having learned the value of moral courage, I am at peace with myself and my conscience.

My gravestone will read simply "Andrew Jackson Mundy, U.S. Senator 1894–1900, editor-publisher of the *Yardley County Leader*." Who needs epitaph more than that?

6360
11727